The Irregular at Magic High School

21

Tsutomu Sato

Illustration **Kana Ishida**
Illustration assistants
Jimmy Stone,
Yasuko Suenaga
Design **BEE-PEE**

The Thirteen Apostles and Their Strategic-Class Magic

The Thirteen Apostles is the name of a group of formally recognized strategic-class magicians.

Strategic-class magic is defined as a type of magic that can eliminate a city of more than fifty thousand people or destroy an entire fleet of ships with a single spell.

○ Angie Sirius

Commander of the USNA's magician unit, the Stars, which reports directly to the USNA Joint Chiefs of Staff. She is the youngest magician to join the Thirteen Apostles. Her real name is Angelina Kudou Shields.

Uses the strategic-class magic spell Heavy Metal Burst.
This typed magic radiates plasma in all directions from the point of activation and is one of the most powerful spells wielded by the Thirteen Apostles. It can be fired as a concentrated beam by using the magic weapon Brionac.

○ Igor Andreivich Bezobrazov

Leading authority on magic research at the New Soviet Union Science Academy. Although he is officially a scientist, his eloquence is said to be on par with the Minister of Defense's.

Uses the strategic-class magic spell Tuman Bomba.
This is the only one of the ten types of strategic-class magic used by the Thirteen Apostles with an effect and appearance that remain undisclosed.

○ Miguel Diez

A soldier in the Brazilian military. While he is the most famous strategic-class magician among the Thirteen Apostles, his family information is kept strictly confidential.

Uses the strategic-class magic spell Synchroliner Fusion.
Hydrogen plasma clouds collide over a target, triggering a nuclear fusion reaction. The resulting heat and shock waves destroy the target area. Since the Brazilian military actively uses this spell in demonstrations, its properties are some of the most well known among strategic-class spells.

○ William MacLeod

A British professor and prodigy who has earned several teaching accolades from universities abroad. He is also highly influential in the realms of strategic magic promotion and engineered magician construction.

Uses the strategic-class magic spell Ozone Circle.
This spell quickly produces a large amount of thick ozone gas to create a fast-acting poison that paralyzes one's opponent. It is relatively easy to cast from a distance, making it a highly adaptable spell. According to one of MacLeod's lectures, there are magicians other than himself who, although they are not quite as powerful, can cast Ozone Circle. Jasmine Williams, a girl Tatsuya fought in Okinawa, is one of these magicians.

○ Karla Schmidt

A professor who works at a lab at Berlin University in the German federation. Unlike other strategic-class magicians, she keeps her distance from the military.
Although her name is listed as one of the Thirteen Apostles due to the German federation's wishes, Karla is searching for a path where magic is used for peace.

Uses the strategic-class magic spell Ozone Circle.
While MacLeod created this spell, it has become widely known thanks to a pact by the former European Union that made the spell public.

The five magicians above, plus eight others, are known as the Thirteen Apostles.

Igor Andreivich Bezobrazov

A New Soviet Union strategic-class magician and one of the Thirteen Apostles.

Shiina Mitsuya

Daughter of the Mitsuya family, one of the Ten Master Clans. Enrolls in First High in the spring as the top student. Always wears custom earmuffs due to her keen sense of hearing (said to be a result of magical perception).

"Huh...?"

"By the way, Shiina, is the boy trying to access this room with perception-type magic your brother?"

"Are you a new student? Come with me. We need to talk."

Tatsuya Shiba
Class 3-E. Miyuki's older brother. Approaches everything in a detached manner, except his role as Miyuki's Guardian.

Miyuki Shiba
Class 3-A. Tatsuya's younger sister. An honors student and a member of the student council. Specializes in freezing magic. Dotes on her older brother, perhaps a little too much.

your childhood friend?"

"Great Asian Alliance, perhaps?"

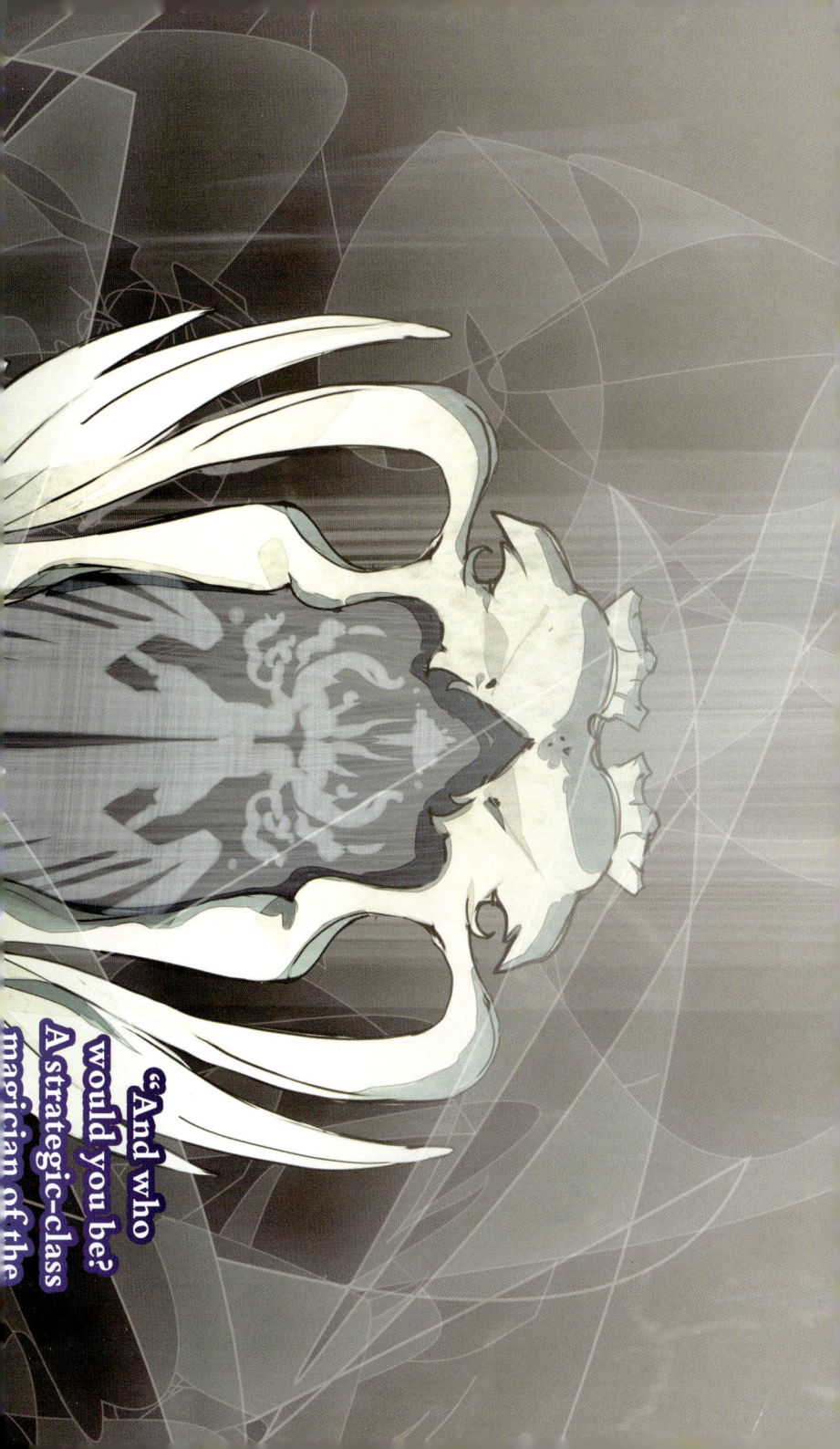

"And who would you be? A strategic-class magician of the

Saburou Yaguruma

With a birthday only two days apart from Shina's, Saburou and Shina have been childhood friends since birth. He is Shina's self-proclaimed bodyguard and very attached to her.

"—What?!"

The Irregular at MagicHigh School

UPHEAVAL PROLOGUE ARC I

21

Tsutomu Sato

Illustration Kana Ishida

YEN ON
NEW YORK

THE IRREGULAR AT MAGIC HIGH SCHOOL
TSUTOMU SATO

Translation by Kenia A. Hara
Cover art by Kana Ishida

MAHOUKA KOUKOU NO RETTOUSEI Vol. 21
©Tsutomu Sato 2017
Edited by Dengeki Bunko
First published in Japan in 2017 by KADOKAWA CORPORATION, Tokyo.
English translation rights arranged with KADOKAWA CORPORATION, Tokyo, through Tuttle-Mori Agency, Inc., Tokyo.

English translation © 2024 by Yen Press, LLC

Yen On
150 West 30th Street, 19th Floor
New York, NY 10001

Visit us at yenpress.com
facebook.com/yenpress
twitter.com/yenpress
yenpress.tumblr.com
instagram.com/yenpress

First Yen On Edition: January 2024
Edited by Yen On Editorial: Ivan Liang
Designed by Yen Press Design: Wendy Chan

Yen On is an imprint of Yen Press, LLC.
The Yen On name and logo are trademarks of Yen Press, LLC.

Library of Congress Cataloging-in-Publication Data
Names: Sato, Tsutomu. | Ishida, Kana, illustrator.
Title: The irregular at Magic High School / Tsutomu Sato ; Illustrations by Kana Ishida.
Other titles: Mahōka kōkō no rettosei. English
Description: First Yen On edition. | New York, NY : Yen On, 2016–
Identifiers: LCCN 2015042401 | ISBN 9780316348805 (v 1 : pbk.) | ISBN 9780316390293 (v. 2 : pbk.) |
    ISBN 9780316390309 (v. 3 : pbk.) | ISBN 9780316390316 (v. 4 : pbk.) |
    ISBN 9780316390323 (v. 5 : pbk.) | ISBN 9780316390330 (v. 6 : pbk.) |
    ISBN 9781975300074 (v. 7 : pbk.) | ISBN 9781975327125 (v. 8 : pbk.) |
    ISBN 9781975327149 (v. 9 : pbk.) | ISBN 9781975327163 (v. 10 : pbk.) |
    ISBN 9781975327187 (v. 11 : pbk.) | ISBN 9781975327200 (v. 12 : pbk.) |
    ISBN 9781975332327 (v. 13 : pbk.) | ISBN 9781975332471 (v. 14 : pbk.) |
    ISBN 9781975332495 (v. 15 : pbk.) | ISBN 9781975332518 (v. 16 : pbk.) |
    ISBN 9781975332532 (v. 17 : pbk.) | ISBN 9781975332556 (v. 18 : pbk.) |
    ISBN 9781975343835 (v. 19 : pbk.) | ISBN 9781975345167 (v. 20 : pbk.) |
    ISBN 9781975345181 (v. 21 : pbk.)
Subjects: CYAC: Brothers and sisters—Fiction. | Magic—Fiction. | High schools—Fiction. |
    Schools—Fiction. | Japan—Fiction. | Science fiction.
Classification: LCC PZ7.1.S265 Ir 2016 | DDC [Fic]—dc23
LC record available at http://lccn.loc.gov/2015042401

ISBNs: 978-1-9753-4518-1 (paperback)
        978-1-9753-4519-8 (ebook)

10 9 8 7 6 5 4 3 2 1

LSC-C

Printed in the United States of America

The Irregular at Magic High School

UPHEAVAL PROLOGUE ARC I

An irregular older brother with a certain flaw.
An honor roll younger sister who is perfectly flawless.

When the two siblings enrolled in Magic High School,
a dramatic life unfolded—

Character

Tatsuya Shiba

Class 3-E. Advanced to the newly established magic engineering course. Approaches everything in a detached manner. His sister Miyuki's Guardian.

Miyuki Shiba

Class 3-A. Tatsuya's younger sister; enrolled as the top student last year. Specializes in freezing magic. Dotes on her older brother.

Leonhard Saijou

Class 3-F. Tatsuya's friend. Course 2 student. Specializes in hardening magic. Has a cheerful personality.

Erika Chiba

Class 3-F. Tatsuya's friend. Course 2 student. A charming troublemaker.

Mizuki Shibata

Class 3-E. In Tatsuya's class again this year. Has pushion-radiation sensitivity. Serious and a bit of an airhead.

Mikihiko Yoshida

Class 3-B. This year he became a Course 1 student. From a famous family that uses ancient magic. Has known Erika since they were children.

Honoka Mitsui

Class 3-A. Miyuki's classmate. Specializes in light-wave vibration magic. Impulsive when emotional.

Shizuku Kitayama

Class 3-A. Miyuki's classmate. Specializes in vibration and acceleration magic. Doesn't show emotional ups and downs very much.

Subaru Satomi

Class 3-D. Frequently mistaken for a pretty boy. Cheerful and easy to get along with.

Eimi "Amelia Goldie" Akechi

Class 3-B. A quarter Japanese. Almost everyone calls her "Amy." Daughter of the prominent Goldie family.

Akaha Sakurakouji

Class 3-B. Friends with Subaru and Amy. Wears gothic lolita clothes and loves theme parks.

Shun Morisaki

Class 3-A. Miyuki's classmate. Specializes in CAD quick-draw. Takes great pride in being a Course 1 student.

Hagane Tomitsuka

Class 3-E. A magic martial arts user with the nickname "Range Zero."

Mayumi Saegusa

An alum and former student council president. Has advanced to the Magic University. Has a devilish personality.

Azusa Nakajou

An alum. Student council president after Mayumi stepped down. Shy and has trouble expressing herself.

Suzune Ichihara

An alum and former student council treasurer. Calm, collected, and book smart.

Hanzou Gyoubu-Shoujou Hattori

An alum. Former student council vice president. Head of the club committee after Katsuto stepped down.

Mari Watanabe

An alum and former chairwoman of the disciplinary committee. Mayumi's good friend. Good all-around and likes a sporting fight.

Katsuto Juumonji

An alum and former head of the club committee. Has advanced to Magic University. "A boulder-like person," according to Tatsuya.

Koutarou Tatsumi

An alum and former member of the disciplinary committee. Has a heroic and dynamic personality.

Isao Sekimoto

An alum and former member of the disciplinary committee. Lost the Thesis Competition. Committed acts of espionage.

Midori Sawaki

An alum. Former member of the disciplinary committee. Has a complex about his girlish name.

Takeaki Kirihara

An alum. Member of the *kenjutsu* club. Junior High Kanto Kenjutsu Tournament champion.

Kei Isori

An alum. Former student council treasurer. Excels in magical theory. Engaged to Kanon.

Sayaka Mibu

An alum. Member of the kendo club. Placed second in the nation at the girl's junior high kendo tournament.

Kanon Chiyoda

An alum. Former chairwoman of the disciplinary committee. As confrontational as her predecessor, Mari.

Kasumi Saegusa

A junior. Mayumi's younger sister and Izumi's older twin sister. Cheerful and bright personality.

Takuma Shippou

A junior. Eldest son of the Shippou, one of the Eighteen, families with excellent magicians.

Izumi Saegusa

A junior. Mayumi's younger sister and Kasumi's younger twin sister. Meek and gentle personality.

Minami Sakurai

A junior. Presents herself as Tatsuya and Miyuki's cousin. A Guardian candidate for Miyuki.

Kento Sumisu

A junior. A Caucasian boy whose parents are naturalized Japanese citizens from the USNA.

Koharu Hirakawa

An alum and engineer during the Nine School Competition last year. Withdrew from the Thesis Competition.

Chiaki Hirakawa

A senior. Holds enmity toward Tatsuya.

Shiina Mitsuya

A new student enrolled at First High this year. Always wears custom earmuffs due to her keen sense of hearing.

Saburou Yaguruma

Shiina's childhood friend and self-proclaimed bodyguard.

Haruka Ono

A general counselor of First High. Tends to get bullied but has another side to her personality.

Yakumo Kokonoe

A user of an ancient magic called *ninjutsu*. Tatsuya's martial arts master.

Satomi Asuka

First High nurse. Gentle, calm, and warm. Smile popular among male students.

Kazuo Tsuzura

First High teacher. Main field is magic geometry. Manager of the Thesis Competition team.

Jennifer Smith

A Caucasian naturalized as a Japanese citizen. Instructor for Tatsuya's class and for magic engineering classes.

Tomoko Chikura

An alum. Competitor in the women's solo Shields Down, an event at the Nines.

Tsugumi Igarashi

An alum. Former biathlon club president.

Yousuke Igarashi

A senior. Tsugumi's younger brother. Has a somewhat reserved personality.

Kerry Minakami

An alum. Male representative for the main Monolith Code even at the Nines.

Kumiko Kunisaki

An alum. Eimi's teammate in the Rower and Gunner event at the Nine School Competition. Frank personality.

Masaki Ichijou

A senior at Third High. Direct heir to the Ichijou family, one of the Ten Master Clans.

Gouki Ichijou

Masaki's father. Current head of the Ichijou, one of the Ten Master Clans.

Shinkurou Kichijouji

A senior at Third High. Also known as Cardinal George.

Midori Ichijou

Masaki's mother. Warm and good at cooking.

Akane Ichijou

Eldest daughter of the Ichijou. Masaki's younger sister. A junior in middle school. Likes Shinkurou.

Ushio Kitayama

Shizuku's father. Big shot in the business world. His business name is Ushio Kitagata.

Ruri Ichijou

Second daughter of the Ichijou. Masaki's younger sister. Stable and does things her own way.

Benio Kitayama

Shizuku's mother. An A-rank magician who was once renowned for her vibration magic.

Wataru Kitayama

Shizuku's younger brother. Just started middle school. Dearly loves his older sister. Aims to be a magic engineer.

Harumi Naruse

Shizuku's older cousin. Student at National Magic University Fourth Affiliated High School.

Pixie

A home helper robot belonging to Magic High School. Official name 3H (Humanoid Home Helper: a human-shaped chore-assisting robot) Type P94.

Ushiyama

Manager of Four Leaves. Technology's CAD R & D Section 3. A person in whom Tatsuya places his trust.

Toshikazu Chiba

Erika Chiba's eldest brother. Has a career in the Ministry of Police. A playboy at first glance.

Ernst Rosen

A prominent CAD manufacturer. President of Rosen Magicraft's Japanese branch.

Naotsugu Chiba

Erika Chiba's second-eldest brother. Mari's lover. Possesses full mastery of the Chiba (thousand blades) style of kenjutsu. Nicknamed "Kirin Child of the Chiba."

Retsu Kudou

Renowned as the strongest magician in the world. Given the honorary title of Sage.

Inagaki

An inspector with the Ministry of Police. Toshikazu Chiba's subordinate.

Makoto Kudou

Son of Retsu Kudou, elder of Japan's magic world, and current head of the Kudou family.

Anna Rosen Katori

Erika's mother. Half Japanese and half German, was the mistress of Erika's father, the current leader of the Chiba.

Minoru Kudou

Makoto's son. Junior at National Magic University Second Affiliated High School, but hardly attends due to frequent illness. Also Kyouko Fujibayashi's younger brother by a different father.

Mamoru Kuki

One of the Eighteen Support Clans. Follows the Kudou family. Calls Retsu Kudou "Sensei" out of respect.

Maki Sawamura

A female actress who has been nominated for best leading female actress by distinguished movie awards. Acknowledged not only for her beauty but also her acting skills.

Harunobu Kazama

Commanding officer of the 101st Brigade's Independent Magic Battalion. Ranked lieutenant colonel.

Gongjin Zhou

A handsome young man who brought Lu and Chen to Yokohama. A mysterious figure who hangs around Chinatown.

Shigeru Sanada

Executive officer of the 101st Brigade's Independent Magic Battalion. Ranked major.

Kyouko Fujibayashi

Female officer serving as Kazama's aide. Ranked first lieutenant.

Xiangshan Chen

Leader of the Great Asian Alliance Army's Special Covert Forces. Has a heartless personality.

Hiromi Saeki

Commander of the Japan Ground Defense Force's 101st Brigade. Ranked major general. Superior officer to Harunobu Kazama, commanding officer of the Independent Magic Battalion. Due to her appearance, she is also known as the Silver Fox.

Ganghu Lu

The ace magician of the Great Asian Alliance Army's Special Covert Forces. Also known as the "Man-Eating Tiger."

Muraji Yanagi

Executive officer of the 101st Brigade's Independent Magic Battalion. Ranked major.

Rin

A girl Morisaki saved. Her full name is Meiling Sun. The new leader of the Hong Kong–based international crime syndicate No-Head Dragon.

Kousuke Yamanaka

Executive officer of the 101st Brigade's Independent Magic Battalion. Physician ranked major. First-rate healing magician.

Sakai

Belongs to the Japan Ground Defense Force's general headquarters. Ranked colonel. Seen as staunchly anti–Great Asian Alliance.

Miya Shiba

Tatsuya and Miyuki's actual mother. Deceased. The only magician skilled in mental construction interference magic.

Honami Sakurai

Miya's Guardian. Deceased. Part of the first generation of the Sakura series, engineered magicians with strengthened magical capacity through genetic modification.

Sayuri Shiba

Tatsuya and Miyuki's stepmother. Dislikes them.

Yuuka Tsukuba

A candidate to become the next leader of the Yotsuba clan. Twenty-two years old. Former vice president of First High's student council. Currently a senior attending the Magic University. Strong in mental interference magic.

Yoshimi

A Yotsuba magician related to the Kuroba. A psychometrist specializing in reading the psionic traces left behind in psionic information bodies. Very secretive.

Maya Yotsuba

Tatsuya and Miyuki's aunt. Miya's younger twin sister. The current head of the Yotsuba.

Hayama

An elderly butler employed by Maya.

Katsushige Shibata

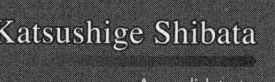

A candidate to become the next leader of the Yotsuba clan. Employed by the Ministry of Defense. An alum of Fifth High. Specializes in convergence magic.

Kotona Tsutsumi

One of Katsushige Shibata's Guardians. A second-generation Bard series engineered magician. Specializes in sound-based magic.

Kanata Tsutsumi

One of Katsushige Shibata's Guardians. A second-generation Bard series engineered magician. Like his older sister, Kotona, he specializes in sound-based magic.

Angelina Kudou Shields

Commander of the USNA's magician unit, the Stars. Ranked major. Nickname is Lina. Also one of the strategic-class magicians called the Thirteen Apostles.

Virginia Balance

The USNA Joint Chiefs of Staff Information Bureau Internal Inspection Office's first deputy commissioner. Ranked colonel. Went to Japan in order to support Lina.

Silvia Mercury First

A planet-class magician in the USNA's magician unit, the Stars. Ranked warrant officer. Her nickname is Silvie, and Mercury First is her code name. During a mission in Japan, she served as Major Sirius's aide.

Benjamin Canopus

Number two in the USNA's magician unit, the Stars. Ranked major. Takes command when Major Sirius is absent.

Mikaela Hongou

An agent sent into Japan by the USNA (although she actually works as a magic scientist for the Department of Defense). Nicknamed Mia.

Claire

Hunter Q—a female soldier in the magician unit Stardust for those who don't make it as Stars. Q refers to the 17th pursuit unit.

Alfred Fomalhaut

A first-degree star magician in the USNA's magician unit, the Stars. Rank is first lieutenant. Nicknamed Freddie. Currently AWOL.

Rachel

Hunter R—a female soldier in the magician unit Stardust for those who don't make it as Stars. R refers to the 18th pursuit unit.

Charles Sullivan

A satellite-class magician in the USNA's magician unit, the Stars. Called by the code name Deimos Second. Currently AWOL.

Kanda

A young politician affiliated with the Civil Rights Party. Supporter of civil rights in opposition to the military. Also anti-magician.

Raymond S. Clark

A student at the high school in Berkeley, USNA, where Shizuku studies abroad. A Caucasian boy who wastes no time making advances on Shizuku. Is secretly one of the Seven Sages.

Kouzuke

A young Tokyo-based politician in the ruling party. Known as a legislator with favorable views toward magicians.

Igor Andreivich Bezobrazov

A strategic-class magician of the New Soviet Union and a leading figure at the Science Academy.

William MacLeod

A British strategic-class magician. A prodigy who has earned several teaching accolades from universities abroad.

Karla Schmidt

A German strategic-class magician and academic who is conducting research at Berlin University.

Gu Jie

One of the Seven Sages. Also known as Gide Hague. A survivor of a Dahanese military's mage unit.

Joe Du

A mysterious man aiding Gu Jie's escape from Japan. Skilled enough at his job to consistently evade the Ten Master Clans magicians hunting them.

Kazukiyo Oumi

Known as the Dollmaker, he is a magic researcher who specializes in necromancy and a practitioner of ancient magic. Rumored to use forbidden magic to reanimate corpses.

Bradley Chan

A deserter from the Great Asian Alliance military. Ranked first lieutenant.

Daniel Liu

Like Chan, a deserter from the Great Asian Alliance military. Also one of the architects of the sabotage operation in Okinawa.

Joseph Higaki

A military magician who fought the Great Asian Alliance alongside Tatsuya during the previous invasion of Okinawa. One of the Leftover Blood—descendants of orphaned children of the American soldiers who'd been stationed in Okinawa.

Mitsugu Kuroba

Miya Shiba and Maya Yotsuba's cousin. Father of Ayako and Fumiya.

Ayako Kuroba

Tatsuya and Miyuki's second cousin. Has a younger twin brother named Fumiya. Student at Fourth High.

Fumiya Kuroba

A candidate for next head of the Yotsuba. Tatsuya and Miyuki's second cousin. Has an older twin sister named Ayako. Student at Fourth High.

James Jackson

A tourist visiting Okinawa from Australia. Actually a——

Jasmine Jackson

James's daughter. She is only twelve but acts mature for her age.

Mai Futatsugi

Head of the Futatsugi, one of the Ten Master Clans. Resides in Ashiya, Hyogo Prefecture. Publicly she is the majority shareholder in a variety of industrial chemical- and food-processing companies. Responsible for the Hanshin and Chugoku regions.

Kouichi Saegusa

Mayumi's father and current leader of the Saegusa. Also an ultra-top-class magician.

Saburou Nakura

A powerful magician employed by the Saegusa family. Deceased. Mainly served as Mayumi's personal bodyguard.

Gen Mitsuya

Head of the Mitsuya, one of the Ten Master Clans. Resides in Atsugi, Kanagawa Prefecture. While it isn't exactly public knowledge, he works as an international small arms broker. Manages Lab Three, which is still operational to this day.

Isami Itsuwa

Head of the Itsuwa, one of the Ten Master Clans. Resides in Uwajima, Ehime Prefecture. Publicly the executive and owner of a marine-shipping company. Responsible for the Tokai, Gifu, and Nagano regions.

Atsuko Mutsuzuka

Head of the Mutsuzuka, one of the Ten Master Clans. Resides in Sendai, Miyagi Prefecture. Publicly the owner of a geothermal energy exploration company. Responsible for the Tohoku region.

Raizou Yatsushiro

Head of the Yatsushiro, one of the Ten Master Clans. Resides in Fukuoka Prefecture. Publicly a university lecturer and majority shareholder in several telecommunications companies. Responsible for all of the Kyushu region, except Okinawa.

Kazuki Juumonji

Former head of the Juumonji, one of the Ten Master Clans. Resides in Tokyo. Publicly the owner of a civil engineering and construction company that primarily serves the armed forces. Shares responsibility for the Kanto region, including Izu, with the Saegusa family.

Aoba Toudou

Referred to by Yakumo as His Excellency, Priest Seiha. An old man with the shaved head of a priest; his origin and past are unknown. Per Yakumo, he appears to be a sponsor of the Yotsuba family.

Tsukasa Tooyama

A Tooyama magician and a member of the Eighteen Support Clans, which aid the Ten Master Clans and exist to protect the functions of the state rather than the people.

Glossary

Course 1 student emblem

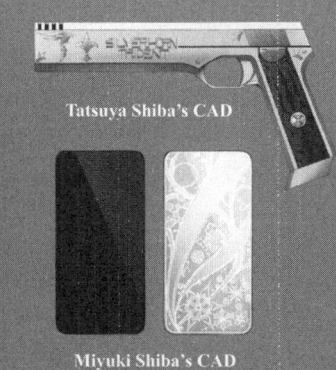

Tatsuya Shiba's CAD

Miyuki Shiba's CAD

Magic High School

Nickname for the high schools affiliated with the National Magic University. There are nine schools throughout the nation. First High to Third High adopt a system that splits its two hundred incoming freshmen into Course 1 and Course 2 students.

Blooms, Weeds

Slang terms used at First High to express the gap between Course 1 and Course 2 students. Course 1 student uniforms sport an eight-petaled emblem on the left breast, while Course 2 student uniforms do not.

CAD (Casting Assistant Device)

A device that simplifies magic casting. Magical programming is recorded within. There are many types and forms, some specialized and others multipurpose.

Four Leaves Technology (FLT)

A domestic CAD manufacturer. Originally more famous for magical-product engineering than for developing finished products, the development of the Silver model has made them much more widely known as a maker of CADs.

Taurus Silver

A genius engineer said to have advanced specialized CAD software by a decade in just a single year.

Eidos (individual information bodies)

Originally a term from Greek philosophy. In modern magic, *eidos* refers to the information bodies that accompany events. They form a so-called record of those events existing in the world, and can be considered the footprints of an object's state of being in the universe, be that active or passive. The definition of *magic* in its modern form is that of a technology that alters events by altering the information bodies composing them.

Idea (information body dimension)

Originally a term from Greek philosophy, pronounced "ee-dee-ah." In modern magic, *Idea* refers to the *platform* upon which eidos, or information bodies, are recorded. The primary function of magic is to yield a magic program (a spell sequence) on this *Idea* medium and overwrite the eidos recorded there.

Activation sequence

The blueprints of magic—and the programming that constructs it. Activation sequences are stored in a compressed format in CADs. The magician sends a psionic wave into the CAD, which then expands the data and uses it to convert the activation sequence into a signal. This signal returns to the magician with the unpacked magic program.

Psions (thought particles)

Massless particles belonging to the dimension of spirit phenomena. These information particles record awareness and thought results. Eidos are considered the theoretical basis for modern magic, while activation sequences and magic programs are the technology forming its practical basis. All of these are bodies of information made up of psions.

Pushions (spirit particles)

Massless particles belonging to the dimension of spirit phenomena. Their existence has been confirmed, but their true form and function have yet to be elucidated. In general, magicians are only able to sense energized pushions. The technical term for them is *psycheons*.

Magician

An abbreviation of *magic technician*. *Magic technician* is the term for those with the skills to use magic at a practical level.

Magic program

An information body used to temporarily alter information attached to events. Constructed from psions possessed by the magician. Sometimes shortened to *magigram*.

Magic-calculation region

A mental region that constructs magic programs. The essential core of the talent of magic. Exists within the magician's unconscious regions, and though he or she can normally consciously use the magic-calculation region, they cannot perceive the processing happening within. The magic-calculation region may be called a black box, even for the magician performing the task.

Magic program output process

❶ Transmit an activation sequence to a CAD. This is called "reading in an activation sequence."

❷ Add variables to the activation sequence and send them to the magic-calculation region.

❸ Construct a magic program from the activation sequence and its variables.

❹ Send the constructed magic program along the "route"—between the lowest part of the conscious mind and highest part of the unconscious mind—then send it out the "gate" between conscious and unconscious, to output it onto the Idea.

❺ The magic program outputted onto the Idea interferes with the eidos at designated coordinates and overwrites them.

With a single-type, single-process spell, this five-stage process can be completed in under half a second. This is the bar for practical-level use with magicians.

Magic evaluation standards

The speed with which one constructs psionic information bodies is one's magical throughput, or processing speed. The scale and scope of the information bodies one can construct is one's magical capacity. The strength with which one can overwrite eidos with magic programs is one's influence. These three together are referred to as a person's magical power.

Cardinal Code hypothesis

A school of thought claiming the existence of a total of sixteen foundational plus and minus magic programs within the eight types of magic—acceleration, weighting, movement, vibration, convergence, dispersion, absorption, and emission.

Typed magic

Any magic belonging to the four families and eight types.

Exotyped magic

A term for spells that control mental phenomena rather than physical ones. Encompasses many fields, from divine magic and spirit magic—which employs spiritual presences—to mind reading, astral form separation, and consciousness control.

Ten Master Clans

The most powerful magician organization in Japan. The ten families are chosen every four years from among the following twenty-eight families: Ichijou, Ichinokura, Isshiki, Futatsugi, Nikaidou, Nihei, Mitsuya, Mikazuki, Yotsuba, Itsuwa, Gotou, Itsumi, Mutsuzuka, Rokkaku, Rokugou, Roppongi, Saegusa, Shippou, Tanabata, Nanase, Yatsushiro, Hassaku, Hachiman, Kudou, Kuki, Kuzumi, Juumonji, and Tooyama.

Numbers

Just like the Ten Master Clans contain a number from one to ten in their surname, well-known families in the Hundred Families use numbers eleven or greater, such as Chiyoda (thousand), Isori (fifty), and Chiba (thousand). The value isn't an indicator of strength, but the fact that it is present in the surname is one measure to broadly judge the capacity of a magic family by their bloodline.

Non-numbers

Also called Extra Numbers, or simply Extras. Magician families who have been stripped of their number. Back in the day when magicians were used as weapons and experimental subjects, success cases were given numbers, while failures—those who did not produce sufficient results—were not.

Various Spells

• Cocytus

Exotyped magic that freezes the mind. A frozen mind cannot order the flesh to die, so anyone subject to this spell enters a state of mental and physical stasis.

• Rumbling

An old spell that vibrates the ground as a medium for a spirit, an independent information body.

• Program Dispersion

A spell that dismantles a magic program, the main component of a spell, into a group of psionic particles with no meaningful structure. Since magic programs affect the information bodies associated with events, it is necessary for the information structure to be exposed, leaving no way to prevent interference against the magic program itself.

• Program Demolition

A typeless spell that rams a mass of compressed psionic particles directly into an object without going through the Idea, causing it to explode and blow away the psionic information bodies recorded in magic, such as activation sequences and magic programs. It may be called magic, but because it is a psionic bullet without any structure as a magic program for altering events, it isn't affected by Information Boost or Area Interference. The pressure of the bullet itself will also repel any Cast Jamming effects. Because it has zero physical effect, no obstacle can block it.

• Mine Origin

A spell that imparts strong vibrations to anything with a connotation of "ground"—such as dirt, boulders, sand, or concrete—regardless of its composition.

• Fissure

A spell that uses spirits, independent information bodies, as a medium to push a line into the ground, creating the appearance of a fissure opening in the earth.

• Dry Blizzard

A spell that gathers carbon dioxide from the air, creates dry-ice particles, then converts the extra heat energy from the freezing process to kinetic energy to launch the dry-ice particles at a high speed.

• Slithering Thunders

In addition to condensing the water vapor from Dry Blizzard's dry-ice evaporation and creating a highly conductive mist with the evaporated carbon dioxide in it, this spell creates static electricity with vibration-type magic and emission-type magic. A combination spell, it also fires an electric attack at an enemy using the carbon gas-filled mist and water droplets as a conductor.

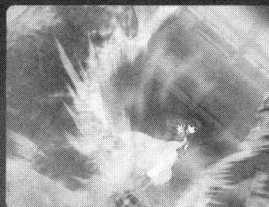

• Niflheim

A vibration- and deceleration-type area-of-effect spell. It chills a large volume of air, then moves it to freeze a wide range. In blunt terms, it creates a superlarge refrigerator. The white mist that appears upon activation is the particles of frozen ice and dry ice, but at higher levels, a mist of frozen liquid nitrogen occurs.

• Burst

A dispersion-type spell that vaporizes the liquid inside a target object. When used on a creature, the spell will vaporize bodily fluids and cause the body to rupture. When used on a machine powered by internal combustion, the spell vaporizes the fuel and makes it explode. Fuel cells see the same result, and even if no burnable fuel is on board, there is no machine that does not contain some liquid, such as battery fluid, hydraulic fluid, coolant, or lubricant; once Burst activates, virtually any machine will be destroyed.

• Disheveled Hair

An old spell that, instead of specifying a direction and changing the wind's direction to that, uses air current control to bring about the vague result of "tangling" it, causing currents along the ground that entangle an opponent's feet in the grass. Only usable on plains with grass of a certain height.

Magic Swords

Aside from fighting techniques that use magic itself as a weapon, another method of magical combat involves techniques for using magic to strengthen and control weapons. The majority of these spells combine magic with projectile weapons such as guns and bows, but the art of the sword, known as *kenjutsu*, has developed in Japan as well as a way to link magic with sword techniques. This has led to magic technicians formulating personal-use magic techniques known as magic swords, which can be said to be both modern magic and old magic.

1. High-Frequency Blade

A spell that locally liquefies a solid body and cleaves it by causing a blade to vibrate at a high speed, then propagate the vibration that exceeds the molecular cohesive force of matter it comes in contact with. Used as a set with a spell to prevent the blade from breaking.

2. Pressure Cut

A spell that generates left-right perpendicular repulsive force relative to the angle of a slashing blade edge, causing the blade to force apart any object it touches and thereby cleave it. The size of the repulsive field is less than a millimeter, but it has the strength to interfere with light, so when seen from the front, the blade edge becomes a black line.

3. *Douji-Giri* (Simultaneous Cut)

An old-magic spell passed down as a secret sword art of the Genji. It is a magic sword technique wherein the user remotely manipulates two blades through a third in their hands in order to have the swords surround an opponent and slash simultaneously. *Douji* is the Japanese pronunciation for both "simultaneous" and "child," so this ambiguity was used to keep the inherited nature of the technique a secret.

4. Zantetsu (Iron Cleaver)

A secret sword art of the Chiba clan. Rather than defining a katana as a hulk of steel and iron, this movement spell defines it as a single concept, then the spell moves the katana along a slashing path set by the magic program. The result is that the katana is defined as a mono-molecular blade, never breaking, bending, or chipping as it slices through any objects in its path.

5. Jinrai Zantetsu (Lightning Iron Cleaver)

An expanded version of Zantetsu that makes use of the Ikazuchi-Maru, a personal-armament device. By defining the katana and its wielder as one collective concept, the spell executes the entire series of actions, from enemy contact to slash, incredibly quickly and with faultless precision.

6. Mountain Tsunami

A secret sword art of the Chiba clan that makes use of the Orochi-Maru, a giant personal weapon six feet long. The user minimizes their own inertia and that of their katana while approaching an enemy at a high speed and, at the moment of impact, adds the neutralized inertia to the blade's inertia and slams the target with it. The longer the approach run, the greater the false inertial mass, reaching a maximum of ten tons.

7. *Usuba Kagerou* (Antlion)

A spell that uses hardening magic to anchor a five-nanometer-thick sheet of woven carbon nanotube to a perfect surface and make it a blade. The blade that *Usuba Kagerou* creates is sharper than any sword or razor, but the spell contains no functions to support moving the blade, demanding technical sword skill and ability from the user.

Magic Technician Development Institutes

Laboratories for the purpose of magician development that the Japanese government established one after another in response to the geopolitical climate, which had become strained prior to World War III in the 2030s. Their objectives were not to develop magic but specifically to develop magicians, researching various methods to give birth to human specimens who were most suitable for areas of magic that were considered important, including, but not limited to, genetic engineering.

Ten magic technician development institutes were established, numbered as such, and even today, five are still in operation.

The details of each institute's research are described below.

Magic Technician Development Institute One

Established in Kanazawa in 2031. Currently shut down.

Its research focus, revolving around close combat, was the development of magic that directly manipulated biological organisms. The vaporization spell Burst is derived from this facility's research. Notably, magic that could control a human body's movements was forbidden as it enabled puppet terrorism (suicide attacks using victims that had been turned into puppets).

Magic Technician Development Institute Two

Established on Awaji Island in 2031. Currently in operation.

Develops opposite magic to that of Lab One: magic that can manipulate inorganic objects, especially absorption-type spells related to oxidation-reduction reactions.

Magic Technician Development Institute Three

Established in Atsugi in 2032. Currently in operation.

With its goal of developing magicians who can react to a variety of situations when operating independently, this facility is the main driver behind the research on multicasting. In particular, it tests the limits of how many spells are possible during simultaneous casting and continual casting and develops magicians who can simultaneously cast multiple spells.

Magic Technician Development Institute Four

Details unknown. Its location is speculated to be near the old prefectural border between Tokyo and Yamanashi. Its establishment is believed to have occurred in 2033. It is assumed to be shut down, but the truth of that matter is unknown. Lab Four is rumored to be the only magic research facility that was established not only with government support but also investment from private sponsors who held strong influence over the nation; it is currently operating without government oversight and being managed directly by those sponsors. Rumors also say that those sponsors actually took over control of the facility before the 2020s.

It is said their goal is to use mental interference magic to strengthen the very wellspring of the talent called magic, which exists in a magician's unconscious—the magic calculation region itself.

Magic Technician Development Institute Five

Established in Uwajima, Shikoku, in 2035. Currently in operation.

Researches magic that can manipulate various forms of matter. Its main focus, fluid control, is not technically difficult, but it has also succeeded in manipulating various solid forms. The fruits of its research include Bahamut, a spell jointly developed with the USNA. Along with the fluid-manipulation spell Abyss, it is known internationally as a magic research facility that developed two strategic-class spells.

Magic Technician Development Institute Six

Established in Sendai in 2035. Currently in operation.

Researches magical heat control. Along with Lab Eight, it gives the impression of being a facility more for basic research than military purposes. However, it is said that they conducted the most genetic manipulation experiments out of all the magic technician development institutes, aside from Lab Four. (Though, of course, the full accounting of Lab Four's situation is not possible.)

Magic Technician Development Institute Seven

Established in Tokyo in 2036. Currently shut down.

Developed magic with an emphasis on anti-group combat. It successfully created colony control magic. Contrary to Lab Six, which was largely a nonmilitary organization, Lab Seven was established as a magician development research facility that could be relied on for assistance in defending the capital in case of an emergency.

Magic Technician Development Institute Eight

Established in Kitakyushu in 2037. Currently in operation.

Researches magical control of gravitational force, electromagnetic force, strong force, and weak force. It is a pure research institute to a greater extent than even Lab Six. However, unlike Lab Six, its relationship to the JDF is steadfast. This is because Lab Eight's research focus can be easily linked to nuclear weapons development, (though they currently avoid such connotations thanks to the JDF's seal of approval).

Magic Technician Development Institute Nine

Established in Nara in 2037. Currently shut down.

This facility tried to solve several problems modern magic struggled with, such as fuzzy spell manipulation, through a fusion of modern and ancient magic, integrating ancient know-how into modern magic.

Magic Technician Development Institute Ten

Established in Tokyo in 2039. Currently shut down.

Like Lab Seven, doubled as capital defense, researching area magic that could create virtual structures in space as a means of defending against high-firepower attacks. It resulted in a myriad of anti-physical barrier spells.

Lab Ten also aimed to raise magic abilities through different means from Lab Four. In precise terms, rather than enhancing the magic calculation region itself, they grappled with developing magicians who responded as needed by temporarily overclocking their magic calculation regions to use powerful magic. Whether their research was successful has not been made public.

Aside from these ten institutes, other laboratories with the goal of developing Elements were operational from the 2010s to the 2020s, but they are currently all shut down. In addition, the JDF possesses a secret research facility directly under the Ground Defense Force's General Headquarters' jurisdiction, established in 2002, which is still carrying on its research. Retsu Kudou underwent enhancement operations at this institution before moving to Lab Nine.

Strategic Magicians: The Thirteen Apostles

Because modern magic was born into a highly technological world, only a few nations were able to develop strong magic for military purposes. As a result, only a handful were able to develop "strategic magic," which rivaled weapons of mass destruction.

However, these nations shared the magic they developed with their allies, and certain magicians of allied nations with high aptitudes for strategic magic came to be known as strategic magicians.

As of April 2095, there are thirteen magicians publicly recognized as strategic magicians by their nations. They are called the Thirteen Apostles and are seen as important factors in the world's military balance. The Thirteen Apostles' nations, names, and strategic spell names are listed below.

USNA

Angie Sirius: Heavy Metal Burst
Elliott Miller: Leviathan
Laurent Barthes: Leviathan
* The only one belonging to the Stars is Angie Sirius. Elliott Miller is stationed at Alaska Base, and Laurent Barthes is stationed outside the country at Gibraltar Base. For the most part, their positions don't change.

New Soviet Union

Igor Andreivich Bezobrazov: Tuman Bomba
Leonid Kondratenko: Zemlja Armija
* As Kondratenko is of advanced age, he generally stays at the Black Sea Base.

Great Asian Alliance

Yunde Liu: Pilita (Thunderclap Tower)
* Yunde Liu died in the October 31, 2095, battle against Japan.

Indo-Persian Federation

Barat Chandra Khan: Agni Downburst

Japan

Mio Itsuwa: Abyss

Brazil

Miguel Diez: Synchroliner Fusion
* This magic program was named by the USNA.

England

William MacLeod: Ozone Circle

Germany

Karla Schmidt: Ozone Circle
* Ozone Circle is based on a spell codeveloped by nations in the EU before its split as a means to fix the hole in the ozone layer. The magic program was perfected by England and then publicized to the old EU through a convention.

Turkey

Ali Sahin: Bahamut
* This magic program was developed in cooperation with the USNA and Japan, then provided to Turkey by Japan.

Thailand

Somchai Bunnag: Agni Downburst
* This magic program was provided by Indo-Persia.

The International Situation
State of the World in 2096

World War III, also called the Twenty Years' Global War Outbreak, was directly triggered by global cooling, and it fundamentally redrew the world map.

The USA annexed Canada and the countries from Mexico to Panama to form the United States of North America, or the USNA.

Russia reabsorbed Ukraine and Belarus to form the New Soviet Union.

China conquered northern Burma, northern Vietnam, northern Laos, and the Korean Peninsula to form the Great Asian Alliance, or GAA.

India and Iran absorbed several central Asian countries (Turkmenistan, Uzbekistan, Tajikistan, and Afghanistan) and South Asian countries (Pakistan, Nepal, Bhutan, Bangladesh, and Sri Lanka) to form the Indo-Persian Federation.

The other Asian and Arab countries formed regional military alliances to resist the three superpowers: the New Soviet Union, GAA, and the Indo-Persian Federation.

Australia chose national isolation.

The EU failed to unify and was split into an eastern and a western section along the border between Germany and France. These east-west groupings also failed to form effective unions and now are actually weaker than they were before unification.

Africa saw half its nations destroyed altogether, with the surviving ones barely managing to retain urban control.

South America, excluding Brazil, fell into small, isolated states administered on a local government level.

The Irregular at Magic High School

[1]

The news reached Japan on April 1, 2097, at 7:00 AM. Tatsuya, Miyuki, and Minami, who had returned from Okinawa the night before, were just in time to catch it during breakfast.

"…You don't suppose this is some sort of distasteful April Fools' joke, do you?" Miyuki asked in disbelief.

"I almost hope it is," Tatsuya replied with a furrowed brow.

He grabbed the nearby remote and split the midsized dining room monitor into four screens. Each screen streamed a different news channel subtitled with the same bad news.

"…Yeah, I don't think this is a joke."

In the Santa Cruz area of what was formerly Bolivia, South America, it was currently 5:00 PM on March 31. After enduring a three-month pro-independence guerrilla campaign, the Brazilian army found itself at a disadvantage against the rebels. In its desperation, it resorted to the strategic-class spell Synchroliner Fusion.

"It looks like the explosion alone was several kilotons…but the bigger problem is where the spell was used. A grassland or mountainous region would've limited the casualties to the guerrilla fighters. On the other hand…"

"What if the spell was used near an urban area or a refugee camp?" Miyuki interjected.

"Well, given that the area has been a war zone for a while, there shouldn't have been many civilians nearby."

Just then, the news channels began broadcasting an official announcement from the Brazilian army.

"'The explosion occurred in a ghost town used by guerrilla forces as a base. Casualties were limited to armed guerrilla fighters and totaled approximately one thousand.' Right."

Tatsuya's expression darkened as he read the words moving across the screens. His complexion wasn't pale, but it was as if a cloud had cast a grim shadow over his eyes. Miyuki and Minami watched him uneasily as he continued in an uncharacteristic mutter.

"As if they would unleash a spell like Synchroliner Fusion just to take out a thousand guerrillas."

"...Do you think there were more casualties than reported?"

"I can't say how many more, but yes. And they were definitely not limited to armed combatants."

"That's awful!"

Miyuki's sudden outburst compelled Tatsuya to reach across the table and grab his sister's hand. Rather than flustering her like it usually did, her brother's touch managed to calm her down.

"Even at the best of times, it's hard to tell who's an insurgent and who isn't," Tatsuya explained. "In professional armies, even people who handle logistics are considered soldiers. But the people who provide guerrilla forces with resources and labor are usually civilians." He moved his hand to his sister's head and tousled her hair. "But there's no point worrying about it now. There's nothing we can do."

Tatsuya's grip was firm but gentle. Miyuki shot her brother an agitated look as she fixed her hair with a comb, but she seemed happy enough. Once he sensed his sister had regained some calm, Tatsuya turned back to the news.

"I'm surprised Brazil even admitted to using strategic-class magic in the first place..." he said under his breath.

He merely meant this as a simple expression of skepticism, but

Miyuki took it in a different way. To her, it sounded like a sinister premonition that soon enough everyone would be using strategic-class magic as if it were the natural response. She shivered at the thought as it sent a sudden chill down her spine.

Tatsuya, Miyuki, and Minami went to school at 9:00 AM, despite it being spring break. This didn't mean they were any less worried about the strategic-class magic incident. They just had other things to deal with first. Having been in Okinawa until just the day before, they were slightly behind schedule on preparations for the entrance ceremony.

Azusa and their other upperclassmen friends had already graduated, and in a matter of days, Tatsuya's cohort would enter their third and final year. They had already decided the changes in student council members this past October, as they had done in previous years. All that was left was to claim their school's top spot.

Tatsuya didn't feel anything special about this. Unlike Miyuki, he didn't have any additional responsibilities to get quietly enthused about. He just wanted everything to go as smoothly *as possible*.

He led Miyuki and Minami into the student council room, where he found Izumi, Kasumi, and the new freshman representative, Shiina Mitsuya, already chatting away.

As soon as Tatsuya's group came in, Izumi almost knocked over her chair in her rush to greet Miyuki.

"Long time no see, Miyuki! Wow! You're as beautiful as ever—no, even *more* beautiful than before!"

"Good morning, Izumi. Thank you for doing so much while I was away." Slightly overwhelmed by Izumi's gushing greeting, Miyuki showed as much appreciation as she could muster.

"Oh, I don't *deserve* your praise! I'm so happy I could just die..." Izumi truly looked as if she were about to faint from excitement.

"Don't be silly," Miyuki replied with a smile. She knew now not to take Izumi's theatrical declarations too seriously. She then turned to Izumi's twin.

"Good morning, Kasumi. Thank you for standing in for Yoshida."

"Good morning, President, Shiba, and Sakurai." Unlike her hyperactive sister, Kasumi bowed politely to her upperclassmen. As Tatsuya and Minami exchanged pleasantries of their own with the twins, things began to calm down, and Miyuki finally had the opportunity to greet the new freshman student.

"Good morning. You must be Mitsuya," Miyuki greeted her, smiling. "It's so nice to meet you. My name is Miyuki Shiba, and I'm First High's student council president."

"I'm Shiina Mitsuya. The pleasure is all mine." The new student bowed nervously. Her hair looked like two large tufts of cotton, except they were the color of toast, and as she bowed, they got caught on the headphones over her ears. "Oh!" she gasped, and quickly moved to take the headphones off. But Miyuki stopped her.

"Don't worry. I know all about your condition."

"I'm sorry," Shiina replied, self-consciously gazing at her feet. "I'll try not to stand out too much at the entrance ceremony."

It wasn't just Kasumi and Izumi, who had known Shiina for a while—even Shiina's older peers, who were meeting her for the first time, didn't bat an eye at her headphones. In fact, everyone in the room was well aware of her *condition*.

Shiina's headphones weren't for listening to music or podcasts. They were for noise-canceling. In fact, they worked more like acoustic earmuffs than headphones. The main difference from regular earmuffs was that Shiina's had a built-in microphone and speakers in the cups. She needed them because of her high sensitivity to loud noise.

That's not to say she had hyperacusis. She just had very acute hearing, to the point where she could hear the slightest tremors in the air that were imperceptible to regular human ears. Evidently, this was a physical manifestation of Shiina's magical powers. Much like

Mizuki's radiation sensitivity, Shiina's condition appeared to stem from magical perception.

However, unlike Mizuki's sensitivity to nonphysical particles like pushions and psions, Shiina's sensitivity was to physical sound. This made it impossible to control her sensitivity with magic.

Magic researchers who studied Shiina's condition said it was caused by her subconscious use of a type of magic that constantly heightened her hearing. But this was just a theory. Her actual magic-induced symptoms couldn't be accurately measured. What's more, any attempt to weaken Shiina's sense of hearing with magic ended up numbing her sensitivity to magic altogether. That wouldn't be a problem if she were a regular person, but she was a magician. Losing her sensitivity to magic was something she could ill afford.

Ultimately, the only thing Shiina could do was essentially block out the noise. Wearing a headset with speaker inserts that automatically adjusted sounds to a level she could handle enabled Shiina to live the normal life of a magician without making any additional sacrifices.

Whenever she went out in a public space, she typically wore headphones connected to a band that hung around her neck so they could be hidden under her hair. But the special integrated mic and speakers used to pick up and adjust the volume of ambient sounds added a considerable amount of weight. This made headphones with a band that ran over the top of the head much more comfortable to wear for long periods of time.

"You should probably wear an inconspicuous pair at the entrance ceremony," Tatsuya suggested. "But the headphones you're wearing now should usually be fine most school days. The students and teachers here won't mind them, so you have nothing to worry about."

"All right…" Shiina replied. "Thank you, Shiba."

Tatsuya only said what he did to help the meeting go smoothly. He also wanted to stress the word *usually*. While her headphones should *usually* be fine, there were no guarantees. Afraid Shiina might take this personally, he made sure to be the one to tell her this instead of Miyuki.

Shiina recognized Tatsuya's concern for what it was and bowed to him with an appreciative smile. Her poise was not quite up to par with Miyuki's, but it had its own charm. Ultimately, Tatsuya's words slightly eased Shiina's nerves, and the rest of the entrance ceremony preparations went fairly smoothly.

"This is the perfect length," Miyuki said, commenting on Shiina's speech.

"Thank you," Shiina replied with a stiff nod. She still seemed to be nervous around the student council president.

"If you don't think you can memorize the whole thing, you're welcome to glance down at it from time to time."

"Oh, I…don't think that will be a problem."

"It's true. Shiina has a great memory," Izumi chimed in, making Shiina smile.

The meeting ran so smoothly that they finished a few minutes early. This was mostly thanks to Izumi's solid planning while Miyuki was away.

It also helped that Shiina was quick on the uptake. Explain things to her once, and she was good to go. Kasumi and Izumi had clearly filled her in beforehand on the basics.

Shiina and the twins were only a year apart. Their families, both part of the Ten Master Clans, lived in the Greater Tokyo Metropolitan Area. Shiina was also the youngest of her siblings, who were all quite a bit older, meaning she got plenty of chances to see the twins at various functions. All in all, it was not surprising they were so close.

The meeting officially ended at 11:00 AM. The current student council members still had work to do at school, but Shiina was done for the day.

"Great work, Shiina. You're all good to go," Izumi chirped.

"We were hoping to have lunch together. Too bad it's still early," Kasumi added with a regretful smile. Shiina bashfully smiled back.

"Actually, I made these to celebrate our new friendship." She pulled out a wicker basket from a sports bag at her feet. It was the kind of basket often used for picnics. She opened the lid to reveal an orderly stack of pancake sandwiches, each about the size of her palm and packaged neatly in its own sheet of wax paper. The circular pancakes were folded in half to keep the cream and fruit nestled safely inside and to avoid too much of a mess.

"Wow! You always make the tastiest-looking treats!" Kasumi squealed with excitement. The pancakes' presentation and fragrance were definitely enough to whet the appetite.

"You're so good at cooking." Izumi grinned, peering into the wicker basket. "You should try one, Miyuki."

"Please do," Shiina offered shyly.

Miyuki glanced over at her brother for his approval before replying, "Thank you, Mitsuya. Don't mind if I do."

Despite the huge bite of cream-filled pancake she took, Miyuki managed to keep her lips immaculate and give Shiina an approving grin.

"I'm not sure if you're a fan of sweets, but would you like one, Shiba?" Shiina turned to Tatsuya and nervously held out the basket.

"Sure."

He picked a pancake stuffed with chocolate cream and took a couple of bites. Pixie, who came prepared with beverages, quickly handed him a paper napkin to wipe his mouth. Shiina breathed a sigh of relief. It didn't seem like he was forcing the confection down. He then turned to Minami and said, "You should try one."

As Tatsuya suggested, Minami reached into the wicker basket. Taking this as a signal, Izumi, Kasumi, and Shiina helped themselves as well.

Shiina had a hop in her step as she left the school building. The treats she worried would be a flop were a smashing success. Before meeting

Miyuki, she had been nervous and stressed. But now, she was feeling optimistic about what was in store for her this year.

Maybe she had been overthinking things, but she couldn't help it. The fact that the student council president was the Yotsuba family's heiress was nothing less than daunting.

Shiina belonged to one of the Ten Master Clans herself, but the Yotsuba were especially intimidating. While both the Yotsuba and Saegusa families were considered the cream of the crop of the magic world, the former were much more magically advanced. But since the Saegusa held several seats in the government, they theoretically stood on an equal playing field with the Yotsuba. At least, that's what Shiina heard from her elder siblings. That was why she feared deep down that Miyuki would be this terrifying witch.

Shiina knew what Miyuki looked like even before they met. She had seen the student council president at the Nine School Competition. In fact, Miyuki's beauty was so stunning, she didn't seem human in Shiina's eyes. And Shiina feared Miyuki's overpowering magic meant she was truly as inhuman as her beauty made her seem. So it didn't surprise her when Miyuki became the Yotsuba family's true heiress on New Year's. She understood completely. Who better suited to be the heiress of the infamous Demon of the East than a monstrous princess?

Shiina's impression of Miyuki did a complete one-eighty when they spoke for the first time. The student council president's beauty and striking grace, of course, more than lived up to the Miyuki in Shiina's mind. She was the epitome of a princess—or better yet, a queen.

All things considered, Miyuki wasn't as terrifying as Shiina first believed. Her stunning beauty and strength aside, Miyuki was surprisingly normal. She also wasn't as eccentric as powerful magicians tended to be. Some might even call her a bit ditzy.

This wasn't to say that Shiina could rest easy now that she no longer feared Miyuki. Tatsuya—the other member of the Yotsuba family—possessed a strangely intimidating demeanor that put her on edge.

But she didn't get the feeling he was a threat. Or at least, he wasn't as long as he wasn't her enemy. In fact, Shiina sensed having Tatsuya on her side would make her virtually unstoppable. She knew now there was nothing to fear as long as the Mitsuya and Yotsuba families didn't have a falling-out. That alone was enough to keep her anxieties at bay.

In fact, she may have let her guard down a little too much as she walked through the school gate. She almost jumped out of her shoes when someone called her name.

"S-Saburou!" Shiina managed to avoid sounding too strange, but her voice inevitably rose a few notches. Luckily, her childhood friend who had long hair didn't notice—or at least, he didn't seem to notice.

"Good work today," he said.

"Were you waiting for me all this time?" Shiina asked. "I told you to go home without me."

"You finished earlier than I thought you would," the boy replied somewhat sulkily. "Besides, as your bodyguard, there's no way I'd leave you behind."

A troubled look crossed Shiina's face. "Enough with the bodyguard thing already..."

The boy's name was Saburou Yaguruma. His and Shiina's birthdays were only two days apart, making them practically inseparable from birth. For the record, Shiina was the older of the two.

The Yaguruma family was made up of ancient magic users who had served the Mitsuya family for more than thirty years as bodyguards and housekeepers. The childhood friends' proximity in age made Saburou the perfect candidate to be Shiina's bodyguard. But plans for this relationship fell through when they both applied to magic high school. Unfortunately, Saburou's magic didn't grow as much as he had hoped. While both Shiina and Saburou would be entering First High as freshmen, Saburou had been designated a Course 2 student.

His parents had urged him to apply to a different place, since neither his older brother nor sister had attended a magic high school.

The Yaguruma family's magic just wasn't up to par with contemporary magic education. Which was why both of Saburou's siblings were taking classes with their grandparents in a rented portion of the currently operative Magician Development Institute Three.

Saburou insisted on going to First High so he could be close to Shiina and protect her. It was unfortunate he didn't have the magic ability to do so. His talent for modern and ancient magic left much to be desired.

Although he couldn't become Shiina's bodyguard, he at least wanted to be at the same high school. Luckily, her family allowed him to stay by her side.

"So how was it?" Saburou asked, ignoring Shiina's bodyguard comment. He understood it as her stating she didn't need a bodyguard, even though that wasn't what she meant. The two childhood friends started walking toward the train station.

"How was what?" Saburou's question was so ambiguous, Shiina wasn't sure what he was talking about. They were childhood friends, but they weren't always on the same wavelength.

"You know what I mean," he insisted, believing Shiina would understand without him having to spell it out. Truth be told, he was flailing for the right words. "Okay, uh… How was your meeting with the Yotsuba siblings? You were really anxious about it this morning."

"Oh, it was fine," Shiina replied. "Tatsuya Shiba will take some getting used to, but the president was very kind."

"Getting used to? Are you sure you're going to be okay?" Saburou was worried about—maybe even wary of—Tatsuya. Shiina was a pretty girl, and in Saburou's mind, no matter how beautiful their girlfriends, all guys were interested in pretty girls. So Shiina's comment about the older Shiba was an immediate red flag.

"Am I going to be okay? With the president's brother you mean?" Shiina clarified.

"Yeah. You shouldn't be seeing him alone if he seems dangerous…" Saburou said with utmost gravity.

But Shiina just giggled. "Don't worry, Saburou. I don't meet up with any boys alone. Tatsuya Shiba won't be an exception." Saburou turned red in the face and was about to snap back, but Shiina spoke first, her voice almost a whisper: "But thank you for worrying about me."

Saburou blushed and averted his gaze. "O-of course I worry about you. I'm your bodyguard."

Suppressing a smile, Shiina chose not to mention his position as her bodyguard was self-proclaimed.

The pancake snacks Shiina brought to the student council led to a lengthy early teatime and an even later lunch. When Tatsuya finally sat down to eat, he ordered Pixie to turn on the news about Synchro-liner Fusion.

Neither Kasumi nor Izumi had any complaints. It seemed everyone was interested in hearing about the aftermath. Instead of breaking up the monitor into several small screens, Pixie played the latest news on one big screen. Everyone's chopsticks paused in midair as they paid close attention.

"All news channels...are running...the same news," Pixie explained through the speakers connected to her mechanical body. The lack of improvement in her choppy speech was a result of Tatsuya's inexperience in mechanical technology. Choppiness of speech aside, Pixie was at least comprehensible. Tatsuya gave her a nod and turned back to the news.

Even without looking at the monitor, he had picked up the most important information through his ears alone. The news anchor announced new data about the victims of the incident: nine thousand dead, three thousand injured. This was significantly more than what was announced earlier that morning. It was natural for casualty numbers to increase as more information became available, but only one thousand deaths were reported on the morning news. This huge gap suggested that someone had attempted to cover things up, but it hadn't gone according to plan.

The general purpose of weapons of mass destruction was to reduce the enemy's will to resist by inflicting massive casualties. Playing down the number of fatalities was completely counterproductive. That suggested either the Brazilian government was heavily divided on the matter or the attack had killed people who would make it very inconvenient if details of the operation came to light.

Nowadays, with the exception of the Scorching Halloween, it was rare for the number of victims to reach twelve thousand people after a single day. But what most troubled Tatsuya was the unbalanced numbers between the dead and the injured. Naturally, he didn't know how exactly Synchroliner Fusion worked, but he did know what it looked like and what it was capable of.

Heavy Metal Burst, Leviathan, Tuman Bomba, Zemlja Armija, Thunderclap Tower, Abyss, Synchroliner Fusion, Agni Downburst, Ozone Circle, and Bahamut—these were the ten types of strategic-class spells the Thirteen Apostles could cast. The only one that had yet to be seen was Tuman Bomba, which belonged to the New Soviet Union strategic-class magician Igor Andreivich Bezobrazov. The appearance and/or effect of all the other spells had aleady been revealed.

Among all the strategic-class magic spells, Synchroliner Fusion was actually one of the most well-known, since it was easily recognizable. Put simply, the spell's sheer intensity made it difficult to hide. On top of that, the Brazilian military went out of their way to demonstrate the spell publicly on a regular basis.

Synchroliner Fusion was usually cast from an east and a west point several kilometers apart, and accelerated high-density hydrogen plasma clouds toward each other. These clouds would collide above the target and cause a nuclear fusion reaction, devastating the immediate area with the resulting heat and explosive force.

In order to match the strength of strategic-class nuclear weapons, it was necessary to force the millions of protons that formed in the plasma clouds to collide at essentially the same time. While there was very little information on how exactly this level of precision was achieved, the results were on par with a pure fusion warhead. Synchroliner Fusion's destructive yield was calculated by taking the cube root of the distance from the epicenter. In other words, the farther away someone was from the plasma cloud collision, the lower the chance they would immediately be killed.

And yet, during this most recent incident, the dead overwhelmingly outnumbered the injured. Despite the relatively low population density of the area, there was an immense amount of victims and casualties. This wouldn't be especially concerning if the attackers had simply been targeting a concentration of enemy forces. It would still be very problematic from a humanitarian perspective, but the magicians would at least not be faulted for their role in a military operation.

The issue in this case was that the target may have been a large refugee camp. Fighting was taking place in the Santa Cruz area of what was formerly Bolivia. Santa Cruz had formally been incorporated as a Brazilian territory during the global conflict of World War III, but it was currently occupied by independent guerrillas.

Since the area was still prone to intermittant skirmishes between the Brazilian army and the guerrillas, it was also home to a great many refugees. And those refugees had most likely become the victims of the most recent attack. In fact, there was a good chance this was actually a part of the Brazilian military's strategy. And if this wholesale slaughter of civilians was intentional, neither the one who gave the order nor the perpetrators themselves would escape blame.

It was one thing if only the Brazilian army's strategic-class magician Miguel Diez would shoulder the blame. But at this rate, it was quite possible *magicians as a whole* would be labeled as threats to humanity. This ominous thought formed a dark pit at the bottom of Tatsuya's stomach.

Once lunch was over and the news was off, a dark shadow hung over the student council room. Luckily, everyone displayed an admirable level of professionalism as the preparations for the entrance ceremony continued smoothly.

At slightly past 4:00 PM, Miyuki said, "Let's stop here for today."

"Um, Miyuki?" Izumi hesitantly walked up to the student council president as she was packing her bag to go home.

"Yes?"

"Do you know how Mitsui is doing? Maybe we could pay her a visit…"

Honoka Mitsui was currently feeling under the weather. She had immediately come down with a fever the day the group returned to Tokyo from their trip to Kumejima. Despite the warm Okinawan weather, it had probably been too early to play around outside in a swimsuit.

"I'm sure she will feel better tomorrow after some rest," Miyuki consoled. "But I received a text saying she didn't want visitors."

Miyuki would have been worried Honoka wasn't being honest about her condition if she had sent the text herself. But since it had come from Shizuku, Miyuki could rest assured Honoka's best interests were considered, and Honoka would surely feel better the next day as she said.

Besides, if Izumi were to pay Honoka a visit, that would mean Miyuki—and inevitably Tatsuya—would have to tag along. A serious illness or injury was one thing, but…

…*I would hate it if Tatsuya came to see me without warning when I was asleep with a cold*, Miyuki thought. Honoka was probably no different.

"Oh…" Izumi said, disappointed.

"But I was thinking of stopping by tomorrow if her condition doesn't improve," Miyuki added. "Would you like to come with me then?"

"Can I?!" Izumi's eyes lit up.

"Of course."

"Okay, let's do that!"

Izumi's motives seemed to have shifted from visiting a friend to visiting *with* Miyuki, but Miyuki shrugged. At least Izumi's mood seemed to have improved. In fact, thanks to her misplaced excitement, the shadow over the room seemed to have faded away.

While Miyuki and the others could temporarily distract themselves from the Synchroliner Fusion incident, those who considered magicians a threat—aka those who couldn't use magic—were a different story.

The anti-magic movements to date had often been an outlet for public grievances against the status quo. While the fear of magic was constant, part of the population also believed magicians were under government control. But when the government officially approved the use of strategic-class magic, the fears felt by nonmagic users became suddenly more real than ever.

The Japanese government never revealed the details about the devastating attack on the Great Asian Alliance naval base in late October 2095. In fact, it refused to respond to any media requests or formal inquiries from other countries through diplomatic channels, under the pretext that the situation was classified as a top secret matter of national security.

Although it was clear strategic-class magic was involved in the disaster, the Japanese government refused to admit the truth. Naturally, they intended to keep strategic-class magician and possible military trump card Special Lieutenant Ryuuya Ooguro a secret, but that wasn't all. They also weren't willing to justify the use of magic for mass carnage and destruction in battle. To disclose this information would increase the risk of strategic-class magic attacks from other countries.

Even if it was an open secret, there was logic behind not making it known. Not publicly admitting to the possession of strategic-class magic meant it was more difficult to use it openly. And even when someone *did* use it—as on October 31, 2095—there would be a strong, natural deterrent that prevented it from being used rashly.

A similar block existed for openly available weapons of mass destruction, which inhibited its users from utilizing these weapons for personal gain. In the same way, blocks like these placed restrictions on the deployment of strategic-class magic in actual warfare.

During the most recent incident, however, the Brazilian army's actions suggested their country's leaders were willing to use strategic-class magic like any other weapon. While they didn't make any specific statement, readily admitting to the use of Synchroliner Fusion made their intentions crystal clear. The lack of plausible deniability didn't fully explain why the Brazilian authorities made such a public admission. This decision implied that strategic-class magic was no longer off the table as a means of conflict resolution for Brazil.

In the military world, Scorching Halloween violently shook the psychological barriers that curbed the use of strategic-class magic. That barrier was now completely destroyed politically as well. Civilians who understood this began reacting more extremely than ever.

On the outskirts of the city of Roswell in the United States of North America's New Mexico, the local time was 3:00 PM on April 1 (April 2, 6:00 AM JST).

"There's been an insurrection in Mexico?!" Major Angelina Sirius's voice carried through the base of the USNA's special magician unit, the Stars. "That's a bad April Fools' joke, Silvie."

Ever since Japan's secret conspiracy, warrant officer Silvia Mercury First had risen through the ranks and become Angelina's aide. Lina waited impatiently for Silvia to flash a mischievous grin and throw up her hands with a *You got me!*

Instead, she said, "It's true, Major."

Lina was in shock. "...Seriously?"

"At nine fifty AM local time, a large anti-magician group instigated an insurrection in Monterrey, North Mexico. The National Guard was dispatched to suppress the riots when suddenly some of their number opened fire in the direction of their fellow soldiers. The rogue soldiers then joined the mob. Luckily, it appears there was nothing more than warning shots, and no casualties were reported." Silvia spoke in a matter-of-fact, almost robotic manner.

North Mexico was an administrative territory created when Mexico was absorbed into the USNA. What was formerly known simply as Mexico had been reorganized into three sections: North Mexico, which extended from the north of the Tropic of Cancer up into the Baja California peninsula; South Mexico, which was centered around Mexico City; and East Mexico, which stretched from the Isthmus of Tehuantepec to the Yucatán Peninsula.

"Why in the world did the National Guard just join the mob?!" Lina exclaimed.

"The problem seems to stem from the Wiz Guard being dispatched with them," Silvia explained.

"Who in the world thought it was a good idea to send those second-rate magicians in the Wiz Guard to pacify an anti-magic group?" Lina was incredulous. "You might as well dump gasline on the fire!"

The National Guard was a state-based military force made up of non-magician soldiers who were sometimes called in to maintain order. The Wiz Guard, on the other hand, was a federal military unit made up of magician soldiers who didn't make the cut to become Stars.

These two forces were widely considered to be on bad terms with each other, owing to the different types of soldiers in their ranks. Sending the Wiz Guard to suppress an anti-magic insurrection could easily be perceived as the devious work of a government official deliberately trying to make matters worse.

"Who gave the order and what the hell were they thinking?" Lina asked.

"It's not clear who dispatched the Wiz Guard or why," Silvia calmly stated. "The only thing we can say for sure is that the current situation has surpassed expectations."

Lina took a deep breath. "And what is that supposed to mean?"

Thanks to Silvia's carefully composed answers, Lina appeared to start calming down. Instead of throwing a fit, she managed to approach the situation from a rational perspective.

Silvia continued. "It seems the group of soldiers who abandoned their posts to join the mob had been holding a grudge against magicians. They most likely wanted to placate the anti-magic groups peacefully and empathetically, since both parties were more or less on the same page."

"And that's when the Wiz Guard mindlessly charged in and immediately resorted to violence?"

"Yes. Unfortunately."

"Does the Wiz Guard's commanding officer have no common sense?" Lina blurted out.

Silvia chose to remain silent, but she had been thinking the same thing.

Though their formal name, Wizard Guard, suggested they were a group of magicians who worked for the good of the people, the organization didn't live up to its name.

"The members of the Wiz Guard must have faced a good deal of resistance," Silvia reasoned aloud. "By the time they resorted to violence, anti-magic groups and locals alike began joining the riots. Now the rebels have overwhelmed the Monterrey government."

The time difference between Roswell and Monterrey was exactly one hour. It was currently 4:00 PM in Monterrey, which meant the uprising had been going on for six hours already. Neither the National Guard nor the Wiz Guard had been dispatched immediately. Since it had taken four to five hours for both forces to arrive on the scene, this meant the local government had been overwhelmed in the span of approximately one hour.

"This is insane…" Lina fell speechless for a moment. Then, with distress on her face, she looked Silvia straight in the eye. "...So does the chief of staff want *us* to suppress the riots?"

"No," Silvia replied. "Luckily, the brass know better than to give an order like that."

This news helped Lina relax a bit.

The Stars were not a law enforcement agency. While they were sometimes entrusted with the "disposal" of rebellious magicians at home, their main mission was dealing with external threats. The likelihood of the Stars being ordered to suppress a domestic rebellion was low. Still, Lina was relieved to hear she wouldn't have to possibly harm any fellow USNA citizens this day. Unfortunately, her relief came a minute too soon.

"Our orders are to extricate the currently surrounded Wiz Guard before things can get even worse," Silvia continued. "And we've been asked to avoid injuring any civilians in the process."

"Easier said than done..." Lina sighed, placing a hand to her forehead. "I'm just grateful we don't have to harm any fellow Americans."

The people involved in the riots may have originally been Mexican, but they were now bona fide American citizens. Lina was glad she wouldn't have to point a gun at her own people. At the same time, these restrictions made her job a hundred times more difficult.

"One more thing," Silvia added. "Commander Walker wants to meet with all dispatched personnel ASAP."

Colonel Paul Walker was the commanding officer of the Stars' base. Lina was the Stars' commanding officer, but Walker, a nonmagician, was the one who managed the organization.

Lina looked up in surprise. "He does? Where?"

"In his office," Silvia replied. "Major Canopus is on his way there as we speak."

Canopus was the Stars' second commanding officer and Lina's number two.

"So Ben is already in the loop. Okay. Tell them I'll be there in five."

"Yes, ma'am." Silvia saluted, then left the room.

While Lina possessed immense competence as a magician, she still lacked as a commanding officer, especially in terms of experience and skill. That's why she relied heavily on Canopus when it came to the day-to-day running of the unit. If she was being honest, Lina was powerless without Canopus's advice in situations like this. If Walker hadn't reached out to Canopus first, Lina surely would have done so instead.

She rushed to change out of her dirty training uniform and head where she was needed.

On April 3, at 5:30 PM in Japan, it was 10:30 AM on the same day in Germany's capital of Berlin.

The campus at Berlin University (short for Berlin Freedom University) was being ravaged by student protesters who were for or against coexistence with magicians.

It wasn't just the anti-magic supporters who were causing a problem. The coexistence supporters claimed that magicians should be "dutifully tolerated," and that didn't exactly sit well with magicians, either.

Professor Karla Schmidt's heart ached as, from the safety of her lab, she watched the debates turn into incoherent shouting matches. Rather than peer down from the window, she chose to observe the chaos on her computer screen. After all, who knew what might come flying through a window?

Gunfire wasn't the only thing Professor Schmidt had to worry about. Even cannonballs were a potential threat. She had learned this the hard way over the past few months.

The moment she looked away from the screen, her videophone popped up and started to ring. She manually pressed a switch on the console to answer.

"Good morning, Professor Schmidt. How are you doing?"

"Professor MacLeod..." Schmidt paused as she gazed at the man on the screen. It had been so long since she had seen his face that this call took her by surprise. But she soon relaxed enough to offer a nonchalant response. "Long time no see. I'm doing fine, thanks. Physically, at least. And yourself?"

"Well, I'm not getting any younger, but luckily there isn't anything wrong with me yet. But hold on. There's no need to call me Professor. As I've said before, I am neither a teacher nor am I affiliated with any university." MacLeod flashed a pleasant smile through the screen. He wasn't trying to pick a fight. This was simply his way of telling a joke.

But Schmidt didn't even crack a smile. "Your teaching qualifications have not yet expired in my country, Professor. We will always welcome you as a fellow academic here."

"Britain's universities would be happy to return the favor, I'm sure." Despite Schmidt's solemn demeanor, MacLeod didn't seem to take offense. But there was a tinge of mockery muddled into his light-hearted words.

He continued on a slightly different topic. *"Berlin University is experiencing a crisis, I see."*

"So you've heard." Schmidt seemed more embarrassed than surprised to hear MacLeod knew about what was happening around her.

"It's all over the news here," MacLeod said. *"In fact, the situation on the campus is being broadcast as we speak."*

"Oh?" Schmidt raised a single brow. "I was under the impression the university was declining all forms of news coverage."

Although her words were bitter, she knew MacLeod himself wasn't responsible for what showed up on the news. There was no point in getting upset with him.

"Freedom of press is one of the fundamental pillars of democracy, as they say," MacLeod stated. *"Besides, there's more than one way to capture footage on camera nowadays."*

Schmidt let out a big sigh, reminding herself once again of the futility of venting her anger at MacLeod. At the same time, she thought it unfair that this man was both taking up her precious research time and shoving a situation she was already aware of in her face.

"Professor, did you call me to argue about the rights of the mass media?"

"*My apologies. I've been prattling on for too long, it seems.*" Well aware that Schmidt's patience was nearing its limits, MacLeod sat up in his chair and got straight to the point.

"*Professor Schmidt, would you be interested in defecting to Britain?*"

She shot him an incredulous look. "Pardon?"

"*I'm serious,*" he declared. "*This is a genuine invitation.*"

"Your sincerity makes it all the more disturbing. You know very well people in our position can't just leave whenever they feel like it."

Both Karla Schmidt and William MacLeod were nationally acknowledged strategic-class magicians and members of the Thirteen Apostles, individuals who served as pillars of their respective country's defense.

The importance of their positions was made all the more clear during the Scorching Halloween incident. Schmidt could have defected at any time before October 30, 2095. But only a year and a half had passed since the incident that rattled the world. Leaving their nations was no longer an option for strategic-class magicians. Their governments would never allow it.

"*I doubt Germany is a very comfortable place for you to be right now,*" MacLeod prodded.

"...That's very brazen of you to say, Professor."

"*I beg your pardon. But I daresay you should think about yourself if you know what's good for you. Magicians are not perfect human beings. Putting up a humanitarian front, political parties claim stringent restrictions should be placed on our rights. At this rate, their support for the radical youth only gets stronger...*"

The pained look on Schmidt's face made MacLeod pause. He knew how hard it must be for her to watch her fellow Germans—especially the youth—discard all logic and give in to agitation in the most shallow and irresponsible way. But he was not about to stop.

He continued. *"Military officials claiming magic and magicians should only serve the state's interests are gaining influence by the day. Meanwhile, magic researchers such as yourself, who are earnestly trying to find peaceful ways to use magic, are gradually losing their place in the world."*

Schmidt couldn't refute MacLeod's point. He took her silence as tacit agreement.

"Fortunately, Britain was quick to shut down all radical anti-magic movements," MacLeod persisted. *"Thanks to that, there was barely any social unrest in our neck of the woods."*

"I was under the impression your country simply segregated anti-magicians from the general populace." Schmidt raised her eyebrows with as much sarcasm as she could muster, but MacLeod wasn't deterred in the slightest.

"Precisely. If you can't stand each other, living separately is the only way," he answered matter-of-factly. *"But this is merely a temporary solution. If the anti-magic activists ever decide to accept coexistence, we're happy to welcome them back to their original homes. In Britain, we believe that magicians and non-magicians alike should be given equal opportunities."*

MacLeod's words sounded syrupy sweet. But that was precisely why Schmidt could put her foot down. "...I appreciate the offer, but I'm afraid I can't leave my motherland."

She knew that when things sounded too good to be true, there was always a catch. Her current situation and the world she lived in had ingrained this lesson into her mind.

"I see," MacLeod relented. *"That's fine for now. But if you ever find it difficult to live as a researcher, please feel free to ask for help at any time. You'll receive no judgment here."*

"Again, I appreciate the sentiment. Goodbye now." Without waiting for MacLeod's answer, Schmidt quickly ended the video call. On her way back to her desk, the screen displaying the campus chaos entered her line of sight. Just outside her lab, a mob of students began throwing punches.

* * *

At 11:00 AM on April 4 (5:00 PM JST on the same day), General Leonid Kondratenko welcomed a special guest from Moscow onto the New Soviet Union's Black Sea Base.

The guest bowed. "It's been too long, Your Excellency."

"So it has, Dr. Bezobrazov." Kondratenko nodded. "Please, make yourself at home."

Kondratenko's guest had already made a name for himself as a magic researcher at the young age of forty. He was now one of the nationally recognized strategic-class magicians in the organization known as the Thirteen Apostles. His name was Igor Andreivich Bezobrazov. Though he publicly worked in the field of medicine, many said he wielded as much political influence as the secretary of defense.

At the Black Sea Base, Kondratenko was an exceptional person himself. Despite not being the base's commanding officer, he was free to use the facility's personnel and resources as he wished. The actual commanding officer was a lieutenant of equivalent rank, but Kondratenko had no obligation to follow his orders. Formally, Kondratenko was a strategic-class magician who served the armed forces, but the prime minister was the only one who could issue him an order. The New Soviet Union didn't have a presidential government; the prime minister served as the head of the state.

Kondratenko invited Bezobrazov to his personal quarters. Technically, it was the parlor of his residence built on the base. Kondratenko's residence had the stunning layout and aesthetic of a luxurious hotel suite. It was even staffed by the best manservants in the industry.

The only shortfall was the lack of women. Since Kondratenko unfortunately had no interest in men, his servants—though very handsome—gave him little pleasure.

"If my memory serves me right, you were never much of a drinker," Kondratenko said to his guest.

"Regrettably," Bezobrazov replied apologetically.

"That's quite all right. In fact, it's probably for the best. I've grown considerably weak to the stuff myself." Kondratenko smiled and snapped his fingers twice. A pair of footmen immediately brought in a small samovar used to boil tea, a pair of matching teacups, and two small bowls of *varenye*—a fruit preserve in sugar syrup.

They poured tea from the pot on top of the samovar and set a full teacup and serving of *varenye* in front of each strategic-class magician. The samovar was placed between them. After receiving a satisfied nod from their employer, the footmen left the room.

Kondratenko added more hot water to his cup before giving it a taste. He then popped a small spoonful of *varenye* into his mouth and chased it with a swig of tea.

Bezobrazov, on the other hand, tried a bit of both *varenye* and tea before supplementing the latter with more hot water. After a few minutes, the two men set down their teacups and met each other's gaze.

"Well, then. What brings you here today?" Kondratenko prompted.

"I think you already know the answer to that, Your Excellency," Bezobrazov replied.

Kondratenko frowned for the first time that day. "If this is about yesterday's riots, they have already been subdued."

"Yes, I know," Bezobrazov assured. "If I was worried about that, I would have gone straight to the commanding officer rather than yourself."

"Hmm. That's true." Kondratenko uncomfortably withdrew into his white beard. "Then what is it that bothers you?"

Bezobrazov hesitated before carefully choosing his words. "...As Your Excellency is aware, I am a magic researcher, not a member of the military police."

"Go on." Kondratenko was very articulate for his age. In fact, it was the clarity of his words that helped Bezobrazov put all qualms aside and cut to the chase.

"In short," Bezobrazov began, "I'm not in the position to question who or what started the riots. What concerns me is whether magic intervention was involved."

"Are you telling me you suspect foreign—or possibly even anarchist—elements used mental interference-type magic to incite the riots?" Kondratenko challenged.

"I don't want to jump to conclusions." The younger man shook his head. "I'm just suggesting the possibility. Out of our country's nine strategic-class magicians, the only ones who have gone public are Your Excellency and myself. It is difficult to imagine an anti-magic rebellion occurring without provoking a response from this base, where Your Excellency, a nationally recognized strategic-class magician, is present."

"I don't appreciate being equated with those degraded clones who can't even leave their sterilization rooms without protective clothes. But I understand your concern. That said, I'm afraid you're overthinking this."

"Am I?"

Kondratenko frowned at Bezobrazov's knee-jerk response. "What? You don't believe me?"

"Forgive me. I meant no such thing," Bezobrazov hastily apologized.

Quickly appeased by his guest's lack of pretense, Kondratenko responded empathetically. "Let me guess. It was Dracula's secret operations that raised your suspicions."

"Yes, Your Excellency," Bezobrazov immediately admitted. "That's exactly right."

This "Dracula" Kondratenko spoke of was the code name for a Romanian magician who specialized in assassinations and other covert missions. Since he was someone who dedicated himself to clandestine activities, no one knew his real name. Allegedly, he was secretly a strategic-class magician, but even that was unconfirmed.

The Black Sea Base, where Kondratenko and Bezobrazov were talking, was very close to Romania—the Black Sea naval base and the Black Sea Base being in different locations. That was another reason Bezobrazov immediately thought Dracula may be involved with the riots at the Black Sea Base.

"To be honest, I had my own suspicions about the matter," Kondratenko divulged.

"You did?" Bezobrazov's jaw dropped, and a chuckle escaped from Kondratenko.

"Yes, and there is no need to fear." The older man grinned. "I have already looked into a possible mastermind behind the riots and whether mental interference-type magic was involved."

"Oh, my apologies, then. It seems you were already one step ahead of me."

"Don't worry about it. I'm sure external actors simply led you and the spineless Kremlin astray... Ahem. That last part stays between the two of us."

"My lips are sealed."

Both men exchanged mischievous grins, like a pair of schoolboys, and what tension there had been seemed to fade away.

"But, Your Excellency... If the riots weren't caused by a foreign or anarchist power, doesn't it make you worry?"

"About the steadily growing tension between magician and anti-magician soldiers?"

Bezobrazov nodded.

"The anti-magic movements in places like the USNA and Japan were driven by discrimination and frustration caused by social inequality. Such inequality doesn't exist in our Soviet federation." Kondratenko shrugged.

In truth, the New Soviet Union only claimed to be an equal society; reality was a different story. But neither Kondratenko nor Bezobrazov touched on this trivial detail.

Instead, Bezobrazov ventured, "I believe something else sparked the anti-magic riots."

"Indeed," his companion agreed. "Non-magician soldiers are growing anxious, Doctor. They fear that soon enough the military will be overrun with magicians, leaving them outnumbered and alone."

Bezobrazov gave the lieutenant a knowing nod. "The truth of the matter is that armies can't be built with magicians alone. While it's possible to have purely magician units, it's impractical to build a front line with magicians alone."

Kondratenko sighed. "But our soldiers will only realize this if they have a chance to experience it in real battle."

Bezobrazov nodded again. "Then let's give them that chance."

"Interesting. Do you have something in mind, Doctor?" Kondratenko's eyes glistened with a force unbefitting of a man in his seventies.

"Unfortunately, Europe doesn't have the capacity to mobilize its current military." Bezobrazov shriveled with remorse, but Kondratenko wasn't bothered in the least.

"I'm probably more knowledgeable than you about the state of Europe's army," he boasted.

"Excuse me, you're right."

"If Europe is out of the question, the next prospective region would be…the Far East?" Kondratenko ventured.

Bezobrazov nodded wholeheartedly. "Precisely. Just the other day, there was an incident where a Hong Kong officer and his troops defected from the Great Asian Alliance."

The older man's eyes widened. "That's news to me."

"I just heard about it the other day myself. At any rate, it seems the Great Asian Alliance has joined forces with the Japanese military to catch the deserters."

"Were the soldiers trying to sabotage Japan?"

"They failed, but yes, that was their intention."

"Aha. It's all coming together now." Kondratenko nodded knowingly while stroking his long white beard. "The Great Asian Alliance and Japan were longtime rivals, but now their wars have come to an end. It seems tensions have relaxed to the point where they can be allies. It makes sense. No hostile relationship lasts forever. So you propose we interfere there, eh? All right. Let's do it."

"Then I'll return to Moscow right away and propose the idea to the Kremlin," Bezobrazov offered. "If they approve, I may need to borrow your residence once again."

"Of course. I'm sure this will serve as good motivation for the troops. Doctor, our fate is in your hands."

Unable to stand without a cane due to an injury to his left knee, Kondratenko could only lower his head from his seat. Bezobrazov was, of course, not at all offended by this. He returned the old lieutenant's gesture with a smile.

On Saturday, April 6, 2097, the entrance ceremony at the Magic University in Tokyo was off to a lively start. The Hokuriku waterfront, on the other hand, felt so tense that it was almost palpable. The culprit was a suspicious ship spotted the previous day in the coastal waters off Sado Island.

Five years prior, at the same time as the Great Asian Alliance's invasion of Okinawa, a small unit believed to be affiliated with the New Soviet Union came ashore on Sado. Although few in number, the members of this unit were powerful enough to overrun the garrison stationed there and occupy the island's major facilities. Many civilians were killed in the attack, including Kichijouji's parents, who were employed at the magician development institute located on the island.

To this day, the New Soviet Union still refused to acknowledge any involvement with the incident on Sado. But this feigned ignorance made no difference. No matter where the unit hailed from, no matter what organization it belonged to, every one of the volunteers who fought off the invaders swore they would never let anyone ravage their homeland again. And now they had gathered once again to make good on that vow.

This new volunteer unit also included some who weren't the original defenders but had lost loved ones five years prior and shared the same oath. Kichijouji, who lost his parents to the unidentified attackers, was one of them.

He was brimming with thoughts of revenge, especially when he discovered the suspicious ship almost certainly carried a New Soviet Union unit. But he was in full control of his emotions—at least on the surface.

Masaki walked up to him onshore. "Don't get too excited, George."

"Right back at you, Masaki," Kichijouji quipped back.

Masaki breathed a sigh of relief. "Looks like you'll be fine after all."

The volunteer unit's commanding officer and Ichijou family head, Gouki Ichijou, called out to the soldiers. "Is everyone ready?"

"Yes, sir!" they all yelled in unison, Masaki's and Kichijouji's voices joining the chorus.

"All right, let's go!"

"Sir, yes, sir!"

With their voices raised, 109 magicians boarded three of the Ichijou family's armored ships, which were disguised as undersea exploration vessels. The family had gathered all the male magicians they could mobilize to man them.

All three armored ships were outdated vessels with heavily reinforced hulls. Since they were civilian ships, they couldn't carry missiles or Fleming launchers. Their speed, however, didn't suffer too much, thanks to modern engineering. The only remaining disadvantage was their lack of maneuverability.

Magicians could easily defend against incoming missiles and artillery shells with magic. Dedicated firearms and melee attacks were far more troublesome for them.

Three ships set sail. Two of the three ships would land on Sado Island. The third ship was headed toward the suspicious ship at sea. Satellite cameras had captured the course of the suspicious vessel as it entered Japanese territorial waters off Sado just the day before.

The vessel's current position—in terms of territorial waters—placed it in the high seas. Since the volunteer unit didn't have a warrant, the vessel couldn't be pursued and captured unless its activities infringed on Japan's exclusive economic zone. That said, simply approaching the vessel could keep it in check. And if it opened fire, everything would change.

As soon as the ships left the harbor, Gouki spoke to the boy at his side.

"How are you feeling, Shinkurou?"

Kichijouji, Masaki, and Gouki were all on the same ship.

"S-sir! I'm well, sir!" Kichijouji replied.

"You're not afraid?" Gouki prodded.

"...I am a little, to be honest," the young man admitted.

"Good." Gouki gave him a satisfied nod. He knew that when a soldier's sense of caution was overwritten by feelings of anger and hatred, it was impossible for them to exercise sound judgments. Soldiers like that fought fearlessly, only to go to their deaths too soon. Gouki didn't want his soldiers to suffer such a fate.

He turned to his son. "Masaki."

"Yes?"

"I hope you're not letting the fear get to you."

"Don't worry. I won't let it show." Masaki was afraid, but he wasn't about to show it. His father released a valiant laugh.

"Good. It's your mission to rise above those who came before you. The Yotsuba family's Tatsuya Shiba scored a great victory in the Okinawan waters just the other day. There is no room for mistakes."

"I know," Masaki mumbled.

Tatsuya's obstruction of the potential sabotage of an artificial island off Kumejima in the Okinawan archipelago was kept a secret from the general public. The heads of the Ten Master Clans, however, had been informed of the details. Whenever any of the Ten Master Clans engaged in magic warfare, regardless of the scope, they were obliged to report it to the Master Clans Council. This policy was meant to deter the potential private abuse of magic.

While this was more of an agreement than a rule—since magic combat was covered up more often than not—the Yotsuba family immediately informed the other nine families about Tatsuya's participation in the battle, especially because it was a joint operation with the National Defense Force. Information like this was normally limited to the head of each family. In fact, Izumi, Kasumi, Takuma Shippou, and Mitsuya Shiina did not hear anything about the incident from their parents. Gouki, on the other hand, had told Masaki the night he was informed.

His goal, of course, was to put pressure on his son. Needless to say, it worked. From that day forward, Masaki became increasingly more enthusiastic about his training. In fact, he was still brimming with fighting spirit as he stood at the helm of the ship.

Theirs was one of three ships on its way to face the suspicious ship at sea. The plan was to restrict their opponent's movement and provoke an attack from the vessel. If they came under fire, Masaki's team could mount an attack under the pretense of self-defense, no matter what waters they were in.

Gouki was also aboard this ship, taking on the dangerous task of provoking a reaction. The plan was so risky, in fact, that almost all the soldiers were against it. Gouki and Masaki were probably the only ones crazy enough to want to do it. Put simply, the top two most important members of the Ichijou family were walking straight into the lion's den. Anyone who understood the importance of risk management would consider their actions reckless.

Gouki, however, refused to listen to reason. "I'm the strongest of us all and have the best chance of survival," he insisted. "What kind of leader would I be if I didn't lead from the front?" That was why he organized this volunteer unit. At the same time, it was worth noting that he had no intention of creating an army.

To Gouki, his subordinates were family. He swore to protect them with everything he had. In the military, soldiers were a resource to be exhausted for the good of the nation's citizens and interests. The Ten

Master Clans, however, was an organization that protected magicians' rights, so Gouki's subordinates were the very people he was supposed to protect. Unlike military personnel, who were considered separate from the civilians they swore to defend in times of war, the magicians who served the Ichijou family were treated as precious companions who had to be protected, even when they stood on the battlefield. At least, this was what Gouki believed. Masaki, too, inherited his father's ideals.

Gouki and Masaki's idea to lead the ship with the most dangerous mission wasn't completely unreasonable. In terms of combat power, it made sense to deploy the top two Ichijou magicians to the most critical part of the battle. On top of that, even among the members of the Ichijou family, there weren't many who had the skills to fight at sea.

Generally speaking, magic was used on a single object or zone. To lock onto and modify only a portion of a greater object or zone required a high level of technical skill. For that reason, area-of-effect spells, which modified a particular phenomenon within a larger zone, were considered more difficult than object control spells, which targeted a specific object.

The Ichijou family's forte was a spell called Burst, which vaporized liquids and made them explode. This wasn't limited to liquids inside the human body or machinery. Seawater could also easily be targeted. In this sense, the sea was like an endless storehouse of explosives for the Ichijou family.

However, no matter how skilled a magician may be, it was impossible to target the entire ocean at once. Making seawater explode required a magician to portion off a particular section of the ocean in their mind and designate that as their spell's target.

Burst wasn't the only spell that worked this way. To use seawater as a means of attack, a magician always had to designate a specific portion of it as their target. Unlike air, water was visible, making it easier to recognize its boundless expanse and more difficult to mold into a spherical projectile. So while the value of the liquid-vaporization technique was obvious, the number of magicians who could actually use it in battle was surprisingly limited.

Luckily, Gouki's ship was filled with magicians who had mastered the technique. This was one of the reasons why Masaki was on the same ship. In any case, there was no stopping the father-son plan now without causing utter chaos.

The detachment landing on Sado was divided into two ships. When they reached the island, they went around the south side and pulled in at Ryotsu Port on the eastern shore. The third ship carrying Gouki and Masaki continued northward.

They finally found the vessel of unknown origin fifty nautical miles north of the tip of Sado Island. Its considerable distance from both the territorial sea and contiguous waters made it virtually untouchable.

In any case, Gouki's vessel was officially a civilian ship and didn't have the authority to seize or conduct inspections of other ships. That's why they were prepared to use extrajudicial means—in other words, piracy. But this didn't mean they would suddenly sink the mysterious ship.

This was certainly an option, physically speaking. While Gouki's ship wasn't armed, the magicians aboard were more than powerful enough to make up for their lack of weaponry. In fact, Gouki alone could easily sink a battleship.

A strategic-class magician was defined as a magician who could use magic to destroy a city or fleet *with a single spell*. If the last part of this definition was rewritten as "in a single battle," Gouki fit the bill. The Ichijou family's Burst spell was fully capable of destroying not only human bodies but also machines. With that spell, it was more than possible to sink five or ten battleships in a row. Better yet, if the enemy didn't have any powerful magicians comparable to those of the Ten Master Clans on their side, Gouki could destroy a whole fleet on his own.

Sinking the suspicious ship from afar would have posed much less danger to his soldiers. But Gouki chose to confirm their true identity before unleashing a surprise attack.

Five years ago, the New Soviet Union feigned complete ignorance of any sort of involvement in the events at Sado Island. Since the Japanese authorities failed to capture any prisoners and no identifiable bodies were left behind, it was impossible to expose the New Soviet Union's lies. So although the invading forces were ultimately driven away, the incident ended as a diplomatic failure for Japan. This bitter memory led Gouki to select a riskier strategy this time around.

Now close enough to see the ship in question, Gouki asked for the hundredth time, "Any movement from the enemy ship?"

But the answer was the same as before: "No, sir!"

The fire control radars on the enemy ship weren't illuminated, and there was no increase in heat emission to suggest it was moving faster. There were also no signs of turrets coming online, or anything resembling a missile launch port. The suspicious ship was dead silent.

It was impossible that the enemy ship's crew didn't notice the Ichijou ship's movement—Gouki was sure of it. After all, they were already close enough to see each other without the use of telescopes.

The suspicious ship was the size of a modest charter vessel. While small, it was still larger than the average destroyer. There was no sign of onboard weapons so far, but the volunteer corps knew better than to let down their guard. Many of them had heard about the Yokohama Incident and the disguised amphibious warships that had escaped notice until it was too late. Either way, there was no point in coming all this way just to sit back and wait.

Gouki finally decided to make a move. "Dispatch the scouting party!"

Masaki, backed by four young soldiers, answered valiantly. "Sir, yes, sir!"

Gouki called this group a scouting party for the sake of convenience, but it was nothing more than a spearhead to silence enemy ships. The party's members were chosen for their proficiency in combat and defense. Put simply, they were strong enough to survive even the most extreme situations.

"Be careful out there, Masaki," Kichijouji warned.

As much as he wanted to, he wasn't about to stop his friend now that the order had already been given. He himself was entrusted with the task of feeding the reconnaissance team with relevant information from the satellite cameras and assisting in their retreat if needed.

"I'm counting on you, George," Masaki responded.

Kichijouji answered with a firm nod. Masaki flashed a little smile before pushing off the deck and jumping out to sea. But he wasn't diving into the water. In fact, his feet didn't even sink below the surface. As soon as his toes touched the waves, Masaki began sprinting toward the suspicious ship with four soldiers following behind him.

There was no sign of attack as they ran across the surface of the ocean. The five men quickly reached their destination and jumped onto the deck, Masaki in the lead. They would have been easy targets if enemies had been lurking around, but there was still no sign of attack.

Masaki was starting to feel uneasy. Standing in a position where he could retreat at any time, he spoke into his hands-free transceiver. "What's going on? Do you see anything, George?"

Kichijouji checked the information coming in from both the satellite cameras and the datalink sensors on Masaki's and his team's wrists.

"*The cameras aren't picking up a single sign of life,*" he replied. "*As far as I can tell, it looks like an abandoned ship.*"

Masaki was just about to relax, until he heard a trace of panic in Kichijouji's voice.

"*…Hold on, Masaki. Your sensors are detecting a gas leak.*"

Masaki quickly tensed at his friend's words. Before giving any orders, he checked the sensor on his wrist. Despite the sensor's small form, it was clearly detecting combustible gas in substantial concentrations.

He shouted to his team: "All hands, barriers up! Prepare to retreat!"

The gas detected was propane. It was probably chosen because of its colorless, odorless, heavier-than-air, and difficult-to-diffuse

properties. But as far as traps went, this one was subpar. Propane was only difficult to diffuse in comparison to lighter-than-air gases, such as methane. In the absence of obstacles, like here out at sea, the slightest breeze would quickly carry it away and cause it to disperse.

Even if the entire vessel were filled with the gas and it detonated, the power of the blast wouldn't be enough to break through the barrier magic cast by elite Ichijou magicians. Propane gas had a low upper explosive limit—the concentration level at which the gas would no longer explode—making it an ineffective means of attack. Its lower explosive limit was also low, meaning it ignited easily. The only way it could really be used was to intimidate foes.

All things considered, there was not much urgency in Masaki's voice. Meanwhile, Gouki and his crew were filled with anticlimactic disappointment after learning the gas was only propane. Maybe that was the real trap.

Kichijouji suddenly yelled for all to hear: *"Detecting signs of magic at sea—!"*

But there was no time for him to finish his sentence. Just moments ago, there was no sign of a magical attack. Now, suddenly, Gouki's ship was surrounded by countless magic programs projected onto the water's surface.

In a matter of seconds, the programs multiplied and detonated all at once.

"Father!" Masaki naturally noticed the presence of magic. Before he could even blink, the sea exploded.

It was as if a huge number of land mines had detonated all at the same time. Masaki and his team were thrown back by an enormous gust of wind, their bodies rolling on the waves and sinking into the sea. When Masaki finally managed to emerge from the water, his vision was clouded by the ocean spray, a hazy mist, and a deluge of briny water.

"Damn!"

He raised his entire body to the surface and created an air current to sweep away the white darkness.

"Father!"

Gouki's ship was still intact. Its outdated but heavy armor had proved its worth. The ship's stern was probably heavily damaged only because it hadn't benefited from a magical barrier. The front of the hull near the deck had suffered much less damage. The last of the many layers of magical barriers had likely held strong. Masaki had a hunch it was his father who had cast the magic.

"Masaki! Masaki! It's Gouki!"

Kichijouji's panicked voice spilled from the communication device hooked to Masaki's ear. Masaki yelled back into the microphone with a feeling of foreboding in his heart that sent chills down his spine.

"George! What happened to my father?"

"It doesn't look good. Get back here as fast as you can!"

"I'm coming!"

Forgetting to instruct his team on what to do next, Masaki ran back to the armored ship. Fortunately, there were no other signs of attack from the suspicious ship. Any remaining propane had been blown away by the impact of the explosion.

The nine magic high schools would hold their entrance ceremonies on April 7, so it was only a day away. In addition to giving a welcome speech on behalf of the current students as the student council president, Miyuki had a plethora of tasks awaiting her. She also had to manage the entire ceremony and greet guests, among other things.

Thankfully, the behind-the-scenes work could be distributed among the other student council members. Moreover, it was a given that Tatsuya would help with Miyuki's portion of the work.

Now that Miyuki was officially the next head of the Yotsuba family, she wouldn't have to entertain so many guests anymore. She had many visitors the previous year, but now that she was formally recognized as a Yotsuba magician, there would probably be fewer interlopers trying their luck.

Even so, Tatsuya intended to have her rest early, especially considering the workload she had the next day. All of this changed when a top secret e-mail arrived after dinner. After skimming through the contents in his room, Tatsuya pressed the intercom button connected to Miyuki's room.

Once everyone had gathered in the living room, he sat Miyuki down on the sofa and had Minami close the shutters. The room was already heavily soundproofed. Now it was completely blocked from both outside ears and eyes. Tatsuya's unusual caution made Miyuki sit up straighter in her seat. She knew this was serious.

"Sorry for keeping you up so late," Tatsuya began.

"Don't worry about that," Miyuki reassured him. "What news do you have from our aunt?"

A little over an hour ago, during dinner, Tatsuya had instructed Miyuki to go to sleep early. Just as she was about to take a bath, she got his call. She didn't mind, of course. Miyuki would rush over to help him anytime, anywhere, no matter what she was doing. Whether that was actually possible was a different story.

But Tatsuya never jerked his sister around on a whim. Whenever, wherever, and whatever he was doing, he always prioritized her interests first. Sure, he sometimes interrupted her plans or did things against her will. But the decisions he made were *always* based on what was best for her.

Miyuki was worried that if Tatsuya had deemed this more important than the entrance ceremony, then the current head of the Yotsuba family might be making some unreasonable demands.

"There's nothing we have to do about it," Tatsuya explained, "but I received a report from the head family."

"A report?" Miyuki asked.

What the family sent over wasn't an order, a notification, or even a message—it was a report. Ever since Miyuki was nominated as the heiress to the Yotsuba family, she had only received the most formal treatment befitting her position. Maya and the heads of the other nine clans wouldn't suddenly change the way they interacted with her overnight. A report meant the information she was about to hear was extremely important. That's how Miyuki understood it. And her interpretation wasn't wrong.

Tatsuya took a deep breath before summarizing the information. "This afternoon, the head of the Ichijou family, Gouki Ichijou, fell victim to a perilous trap. He's still conscious but completely immobile. That said, he hasn't sustained any physical injuries. Our family head thinks a magic-calculation region overload may be the cause of the paralysis."

Miyuki's hands flew to her mouth, her eyes wide and rigid. A similar feeling of shock made Minami's face go blank.

Tatsuya continued. "Ichijou's ship was on its way to interdict a vessel of unknown nationality, expected to be hostile. Upon contact with the vessel, they were hit by a powerful magical explosion. The elder Ichijou deployed a fourfold magical barrier to protect them, and the last of these barriers just barely defeated the attack. The report's conclusion is that, given the barriers were large enough to protect more than a hundred people, casting them caused serious damage to Ichijou's magic-calculation region."

"He protected more than a hundred people?" Minami asked in amazement. As a magician who excelled at barrier magic, she understood the staggering weight of this feat.

"Unlike the Juumonji family, the Ichijou family doesn't specialize in defense magic," Tatsuya reasoned. "It's impossible to expect an Ichijou magician to cast multiple barriers in such a short span of time without consequences."

"Tatsuya…"

Miyuki was suddenly worried about her brother. His tone was calm and deliberate, but she feared he might be remembering

Honami, who had similarly fallen victim to a magic overload while casting large-scale barrier magic.

Honami Sakurai was Tatsuya and Miyuki's biological mother, Miya's former Guardian, and Minami's genetic aunt. Her face was so much like Minami's, in fact, that she could easily be confused for a grown-up version of her niece. She was tragically killed while protecting Tatsuya from naval gunfire five summers ago.

Talking about a parallel situation with Honami's death in front of a girl who looked just like Honami was like prying the lid off a painful memory. Miyuki was concerned her brother must be suffering even more than she was herself.

But Tatsuya mistakenly thought *he* was the one making Miyuki suffer.

"...I'm sorry, Miyuki. I've dug up painful memories."

Was this really a misunderstanding? Or was there something else going on? Any doubts that crossed Miyuki's mind were quickly drowned out by her brother's next words.

"Unfortunately, given our position, we can't just ignore what's happening." The sudden concern in his voice made Miyuki realize he wasn't merely reminiscing about the past.

"If we're talking about magical ability, Masaki Ichijou could easily become the next head of the Ten Master Clans at any moment," Tatsuya continued. "But the head of the Ichijou family plays an important role in the defense of the Sea of Japan coast. This isn't a position that can be filled by someone who excels in magic alone."

Miyuki finally understood the weight of the situation. The key players in the fight against the unidentified invaders of Sado five years ago were now part of the volunteer corps organized by the Ichijou. That went to show how large a role their clan played in the defense of the coast from Hokuriku to Tohoku.

The Ichijou family not only excelled in magic but also in its leadership of the magicians in the regions it maintained. This leadership complemented the National Defense Force, which concentrated its strength in the northern and southern parts of Japan—namely Kyushu, Okinawa, and Hokkaido. In short, the paralysis of the top Ichijou wasn't simply the Ten Master Clans' problem; it was also potentially a major hole in Japan's national security.

Tatsuya went on. "I'm sure the Ichijou family has protocol for situations like this, where the head is temporarily absent from their duties. The Ichinokura and Isshiki clans will be there to support them, as well. In the meantime, I doubt the Yotsuba will be allowed to simply sit back and watch."

"Do we have to help, too?" Miyuki asked.

"For now, it seems sending Yuuka to help treat Ichijou is enough."

There was hesitation in Tatsuya's voice. He had a feeling this wasn't all they would be expected to do. But Miyuki didn't seem to notice. She was more interested in what he just said.

"I didn't know Yuuka could treat magicians," she wondered aloud.

"She's currently studying a phenomenon called magic-calculation region overheating in grad school," Tatsuya said. "It's what happens when overusing magic results in damage."

"Fascinating…"

Tatsuya nodded. "Our clan has actually been supporting her research for a while. This isn't purely a concern for magic performance; it's something that potentially affects the lives of brilliant magicians. It's important work."

As far as Tatsuya and Miyuki knew, Honami was the only case of a person who lost their life to magic-calculation region overheating. But there were actually several victims of this phenomenon in the Yotsuba family alone. The previous head, Genzou Yotsuba, was one of these victims. Ever since Genzou's death, the clan had been working on the development of a cure.

But the Yotsuba were not the only ones with such victims. The Juumonji family's true trump card—their magical techniques—tended to cause magic-calculation region overheating. In fact, the family's former head, Kazuki Juumonji, lost his ability to use magic because of this, providing yet another reason to research methods to prevent overheating.

What's more, the Yotsuba and Juumonji families weren't the only ones with magic researchers paying attention to this phenomenon. The magic-calculation region was a black box with many elements that were still unknown. The very existence of the region was still largely under debate. But the concept of overheating already existed as a theory. It was clear this was what had caused the severe paralysis that Gouki Ichijou was suffering.

"While many magicians in the Tsukuba family specialize in exo-typed magic," Tatsuya continued, "Yuuka excels in techniques that interfere with the mind itself. Aunt Maya must think this will help her heal Ichijou."

The magic Yuuka specialized in didn't manipulate thoughts by acting upon consciousness. Instead, it was a type of magic that interfered with the mind itself. A similar example of this was the mental configuration interference magic Miya alone once wielded. Miyuki's Cocytus and the Tsukuba family's inherited Oath were also types of magic that altered mental states.

Unlike Cocytus, which forcibly froze the mind, Oath limited the functions of the mind. If Yuuka was actually skilled in this type of magic, the Yotsuba family's faith in her made perfect sense. It was possible she might be able to facilitate the recovery of the magic-calculation region, which lay within the realm of the unconscious.

"But won't the Yotsuba clan's reputation be tarnished if Yuuka fails?" Miyuki wondered aloud.

"Well, she isn't tied to our family publicly," Tatsuya said. "As far as the Ichijou know, she's just a magic researcher and healer who has an introduction from us."

"......"

In other words, if push came to shove, the clan would throw her to the wolves. Miyuki's shock at this news proved she still retained her humanity. In fact, she was probably still too naive to be the heiress to the Yotsuba. But Tatsuya had no intention of reprimanding her for her kind heart.

He tried to diffuse the situation. "It's not like we were ordered to help the Ichijou. The treatment we're offering is completely out of goodwill. Even if it's based on a shrewd calculation of profit and loss, Ichijou has no right to blame us in the case of failure."

"...Right," Miyuki muttered.

Hearing the skepticism in her voice, Tatsuya tried to change the subject.

"Anyway, I digress. For the time being, the main family intends only to send Yuuka to deal with the situation. I don't think that'll be all, though." Nothing he had said thus far could really be considered off topic, but Miyuki didn't seem to notice. Minami, on the other hand, looked a little suspicious at this strange turn of phrase. "There's a possibility I'll be ordered to go out to intercept the intruders," he continued.

"You mean with the National Defense Force?!" Miyuki exclaimed.

But that would be a violation of the agreement between the Yotsuba family and the National Defense Force, she thought.

But Tatsuya's response was even more shocking. "I mean the order will likely come from the main family."

"But you're my Guardian!"

Tatsuya shook his head. "My role has probably changed now that we're engaged."

Miyuki whimpered. "No..."

Tatsuya's response took her by surprise. She had always felt guilty about keeping Tatsuya trapped as her Guardian. But as long as he was her Guardian, he couldn't be forced to do other work. She had used this rule as an excuse to placate her guilt for years. But it seemed things were different now. This came as a shock, to say the least. Even more so than when she heard Tatsuya might be assigned to a dangerous mission.

"Don't worry," Tatsuya reassured her. "Like I've said before, you're the only one who can really hurt me."

Tatsuya clearly misunderstood the reason why his sister had turned pale. She was more upset about no longer having an excuse for Tatsuya being her Guardian than the fact that Tatsuya would be dispatched to the battlefield. But Tatsuya's promise to stay safe did help calm her nerves.

"I still believe that," Miyuki responded. "I know you won't lose to anyone."

"I won't."

Miyuki stared fervently into Tatsuya's eyes, and Tatsuya nodded, accepting her gaze. For some reason, Minami didn't feel the usual heartburn that came on when watching the two from the sidelines. In fact, their unwavering trust dazzled her in a way it had never done before.

"But," Tatsuya continued, "I might have to leave your side more often from now on. That's why I have a favor to ask, Minami."

"Y-yes?!"

Minami's temporary distraction made her voice crack when Tatsuya called her name. He slightly raised his brow at her but otherwise ignored her overzealous response.

"I want you to look after Miyuki whenever I'm away."

"Yes, sir."

Orders or not, Minami had made it her mission to protect Miyuki. Tatsuya knew this, but the act of putting it into words touched Minami.

"Miyuki, I have no intention of taking you to war," he said.

"I know." Both her voice and face were awash in disappointment, but she was smart enough to know how her brother felt. "I respect your wishes as my brother...or should I say, as my fiancé."

In the end, she couldn't resist revealing a glimpse of her frustrations. The only reason she didn't ask Tatsuya to take her with him, she coyly implied, was because she was acting as his fiancée, not as his sister.

The Yotsuba weren't the only ones to get their hands on information about the head of the Ichijou family. If the Ichijou had wanted to keep Gouki's paralysis a secret, they weren't at all successful. By the end of the day, the news had spread among all the Twenty-Eight Families. But not every family had heard the same thing.

Mayumi had just returned to her room after learning about the incident from her father, Kouichi, when she received a video call. It was Katsuto.

"*Sorry for calling so late at night,*" he apologized.

"It's unlike you, but that's okay. I have a feeling I know what you're about to say," Mayumi replied. "It's about Ichijou, isn't it?"

"*So you already heard.*" Katsuto sighed. "*That makes things faster.*"

Since each Juumonji magician was powerful enough on their own, they had very few subordinates. The Saegusa and Mitsuya families, which were based in the same metropolitan area, had scooped up all the promising magicians. On top of that, the Juumonji family's abilities were biased toward combat, so they tended to lag behind other families when it came to information gathering. Whenever an urgent situation arose, Katsuto always used his connections with the Saegusa to learn what he needed.

"Yeah, talk about good timing." Mayumi grinned. "My dad just told me all about it. So how much do you know, Juumonji?"

"*I heard a vessel of unknown origin encroached on territorial waters,*" Katsuto replied. "*But instead of escaping, it parked itself on the open sea. When Ichijou's ship went out to intercept it, the crew was caught in an explosion, resulting in serious injuries to Ichijou.*"

The information he had was crude, but Mayumi didn't think any less of him because of it. Instead, she was reminded how unsettling it was that her father knew so much about the incident, even though it had just happened earlier that day.

She said, "Great. One correction—Ichijou wasn't physically injured. Right now, he's just severely weakened and unable to move. The Ichijou family suspects an overuse of magic may be the cause."

Katsuto stiffened. "*An overuse of magic...?*"

Mayumi's brow furrowed with wonder at the sudden fear on her friend's face. "What's wrong?"

"Ah…nothing." Katsuto shook off her question. *"Do you know anything else about the explosions?"*

Mayumi decided not to press any further, and simply answered, "Satellite sensors picked up large amounts of oxyhydrogen from the blasts. It's a mixture of hydrogen and oxygen gases. They say the gas must have been created and ignited via long-distance magic."

"Ignited?" Katsuto puzzled. *"Do you think Igor Andreivich Bezobrazov could be behind this?"*

"You mean the strategic-class spell Tuman Bomba caused the explosion? Yeah, right." Mayumi scoffed, but her expression was stiff.

"Hmm… You're probably right." Katsuto nodded. *"There's no reason to use strategic-class magic against a single ship."* But deep down, he knew there was still a possibility. Mayumi knew it, too, but shrugged it off for now.

"Yeah. You're thinking too much, Juumonji," she said.

"It looks like an unidentified magic attack, then," he corrected.

"Sure does."

"That's tough."

"You can say that again. By the way…" Mayumi hesitated before shifting to a new topic. "My older brother said he wanted to talk to you. Probably about the incident."

"Tomokazu wants to talk? …Okay. Tell him I'm available whenever."

"Are you sure? He's happy to coordinate with your schedule."

"Fine. How about tomorrow? He can choose the place."

"That should work. I'll text you where he wants to meet by lunchtime."

"Sounds good. Thanks for the info on Ichijou, by the way. I don't know what I'd do without you." Katsuto gratefully bowed his head and hung up. He seemed to be acting polite, but this was just a defense mechanism to avoid becoming the target of Mayumi's relentless teasing.

"Uptight as always, I see. And yet you still manage to be astute when it counts." Mayumi spoke wryly at the now dark screen. But a delighted smile played on her lips.

[2]

It was April 7, 2097. On this day, all nine magic high schools were holding their individual entrance ceremonies. Since they still had student council preparations to make, Tatsuya, Miyuki, and Minami arrived at school two hours early. As soon as they walked into the auditorium's break room, they were met by Mikihiko, Izumi, Kasumi, and Shiina Mitsuya.

Before Tatsuya could say a word, Miyuki greeted everyone in the room.

"Good morning."

"Good morning, Miyuki! You look as stunning as ever!" Izumi chirped in her usual fashion.

Luckily, Kasumi helped quickly diffuse her sister's excitement. "Calm yourself, Izumi. Good morning, President. Shiba. Sakurai."

Miyuki smiled, unfazed. After exchanging a few more words with the twins, she turned to Shiina. "Good morning, Mitsuya. I'm sorry to keep you waiting."

Shiina shook her head softly, like a sweet house pet. "Not at all," she said. "I got here too early."

She was on the small side but taller than the twins. She was also clearly taller than Azusa, the former student council president, but they shared a similar energy. While quiet, she didn't seem weak. At least, that was Tatsuya's impression.

Every time Shiina shook her head, her tufts of cottonball-like hair bobbed at the sides of her face, revealing the olive-brown earmuffs that covered her ears and draped around the nape of her neck. As promised, she had picked a pair that wasn't too conspicuous for the occasion. If it wasn't obvious already, this proved she was quite mature and put-together for her age.

She's clearly from a loving, well-to-do family, Tatsuya thought.

Then out loud he said, "Mitsuya, can I talk to you before the final meeting starts?"

"O-of course. What is it, Shiba?" Though unable to hide her anxiety, she looked Tatsuya straight in the eye. This made him respect her even more.

"Is that guy with the long hair tied at his neck who's standing outside the auditorium a friend of yours?" he asked.

Minami let out a surprised "Eh?" as a look of confusion crossed her face. She always paid special attention to her surroundings while working as Miyuki's escort. Moreover, it was rare to see boys with long hair nowadays. She was sure she would've have noticed someone like that right away.

Luckily, Shiina knew someone who fit Tatsuya's description.

"Long hair... Oh, do you mean Saburou?" she said carefully.

"Is that his name? He was keeping himself well hidden."

"Yes, that's definitely the Saburou Yaguruma I know. His first name is spelled with the character for 'samurai,' and his last name is a combination of the characters for 'arrow' and 'carriage.' Was he really hiding around here?" There was a mixture of embarrassment and exasperation in her voice.

"It sounds like you two are pretty close," Tatsuya noted.

Shiina blushed and looked away. "We're childhood friends."

Most people would read her actions as a sign of a crush, but Tatsuya's thoughts moved elsewhere. *Saburou Yaguruma must be the bodyguard her family assigned her*, he deduced.

Tatsuya had no intention of getting involved in another clan's business. Luckily, this helped keep his imperfect speculations to himself.

"All the nearby cafés and cafeterias are closed, and the auditorium won't open its doors for over an hour. On top of that, the main school building is only open to incoming students after the entrance ceremony. You can have him wait in here if you want," Tatsuya suggested.

He felt a strange sense of goodwill—maybe even empathy— toward the boy. In some way or other, the lack of an emblem on the boy's uniform reminded him of himself two years ago.

"That's okay." Shiina shook her head. "Saburou has always been a cunning—I mean, clever guy. He can take care of himself. I appreciate the offer, though."

"Are you sure—?"

Just then, Honoka burst into the room, apologizing profusely for running late.

"You're just on time," Miyuki reassured her.

With that, Tatsuya began the final check before the ceremony.

The entrance ceremony began solemnly and without a hitch. The school's usual buoyant atmosphere was more restrained than usual. This was no doubt because the new students, parents, and guests were anxious to see the faces of the student council members waiting below the stage. They were especially eager to see Miyuki, the student council president.

Unless the incoming students and their parents were entirely misguided, they had already done their research on First High. That meant more than half the students knew the current First High student council president was the heiress to the Yotsuba.

Miyuki's face was in all the Nine School Competition's videos. But seeing her ethereal beauty in person while knowing she was the next head of the Yotsuba family was an overwhelmingly different experience. It was impossible for the incoming students and their parents to resist the pressure brought forth by the combination of Miyuki's beauty and the Yotsuba family's image.

If that wasn't enough, Miyuki's unfathomable magic power and Tatsuya's similarly inscrutable presence at her side made it impossible for anyone to relax.

The only thing that alleviated this tension was the fact that Shiina's speech was in no way dignified or fluent. She struggled through her words, just managing to hold herself together. The moment she finished speaking, her whole body radiated a sense of accomplishment.

Unfortunately, it was a different story for the audience. It was painful to watch, even for the guests of honor, who were slightly thicker-skinned than the average person. Shiina's naïveté, though typical of an incoming student, made her seem unreliable. As a result, she was released from the stage much earlier than Miyuki had been two years ago. The situation was usually different when the student council representative was male; nothing like this happened the previous year.

As Tatsuya had predicted the night before, Miyuki didn't have to deal with too many guests. Even Councillor Ueno, who had kept Miyuki hostage for so long the year prior, was keeping his distance now. This meant she had more time to speak to Shiina.

Izumi called out to the chestnut-haired girl just as the crowd around her became sparse.

"Hey, Shiina."

"Izumi."

The guests subsequently started to disperse.

Most people involved in magic knew Izumi was the youngest Saegusa child. They also knew she was her father's favorite daughter.

The Master Clans Council imposed a strict gag order on Kouichi Saegusa's betrayal. To those outside the Twenty-Eight Families, the Saegusa magicians were only second to the Yotsuba in all of Japan. No one invited to the entrance ceremony at First High would risk angering the Saegusa.

"That was an amazing speech," Izumi gushed.

Shiina smiled shyly. "Thank you." Then she asked astutely, "Did you need something from me?"

This question didn't surprise Izumi. She knew Shiina was more clever than her gentle appearance let on.

"We wanted to talk to you for a bit. Do you have time right now?" Izumi asked.

"Sure." Shiina nodded. "Lead the way."

"Great." Izumi smiled. "Are you sure you don't want to talk to Saburou first?"

"Don't worry about him," Shiina reassured her without hesitation. "I told him I would be busy with student council duties after the entrance ceremony."

Izumi led Shiina to the student council room, where Miyuki and Minami were waiting.

Miyuki stood up from the president's chair and moved to the conference table.

"Thank you for agreeing to meet with us, Mitsuya," she said.

Izumi offered Shiina the seat directly in front of the president, who smiled and said, "Please take a seat."

The chestnut-haired girl darted a glance at Izumi before apprehensively sitting down. Minami and Izumi each took a spot at the president's side. A cup of tea was placed in front of Shiina. When she looked up to thank the person who had given it to her, she was shocked to find not a human but a 3H, or Humanoid Home Helper.

"I'm sorry. Did she surprise you? This is Pixie, my fiancé's 3H. She helps us around the office with various tasks." Miyuki grinned to ease Shiina's anxieties. Shiina was captivated by this smile for a moment or two before suddenly coming back to her senses. She then returned an awkward—but somewhat less uneasy—grin.

Miyuki quickly got down to business. "Vice President Saegusa should have informed you about how things work around here."

"Yes, she did." Shiina nodded.

In fact, Izumi and Shiina had already talked about what Miyuki had called Shiina here to discuss. Everything from this point onward was just a formality.

"Good." Miyuki smiled. "Then based on that knowledge, would you be willing to join the student council?"

"I'd be honored," Shiina agreed. "Thank you so much."

Miyuki's expression softened once again into a smile. Izumi had told her Shiina was up to the job, so she didn't have to worry about a rejection like the previous year. But it was still nerve-racking to wait for an answer. Miyuki was also keenly aware of the trouble she had caused the year she herself joined the student council. All things considered, she was relieved to hear Shiina's positive reply.

"Excellent," Miyuki continued. "From tomorrow on, you will be our student council secretary. You can speak to Sakurai if you have any questions about your duties."

Minami gave Shiina a welcoming bow. "I'm the other secretary, Minami Sakurai. I look forward to working with you."

Shiina quickly but awkwardly bowed back. "S-same here!" She then tentatively glanced up at Minami and Miyuki. "If you both don't mind, I'd like it if you called me Shiina."

Miyuki gave her a friendly smile. "Okay. Shiina it is."

"Thank you," Shiina replied with a deep sigh of relief.

Getting their ID cards put incoming students one step closer to becoming official members of the school. Even though it was Sunday, the school grounds were open to freshmen. Most of them went to find their homerooms and meet their fellow classmates. Others joined their families for a celebratory meal. While incoming students usually fell into one of these two categories, it wasn't against the rules to choose a different path. In fact, there was one incoming student who did just that.

* * *

Once the entrance ceremony wrapped up and the instructors took over, Tatsuya, Mikihiko, Honoka, and Shizuku left the auditorium. The disciplinary committee chairman, Mikihiko, had been listening to his committee members' final reports; student council member Honoka had been checking the ceremony equipment. Shizuku, meanwhile, had just tagged along because Honoka was around.

The school gate was only a short distance from the auditorium's entrance. As the group walked toward the gate, a strange look suddenly came over Mikihiko's face, and he stopped in his tracks.

Tatsuya turned to him. "Is something wrong?"

"I think someone is casting a spell."

Honoka and Shizuku exchanged quizzical looks.

"Is it old magic?" Tatsuya asked.

"Yeah, it is." Mikihiko paused. "I'm pretty sure it's Downwind Ears, a technique that allows the user to hear what's happening in a specific place from afar."

"So it's an eavesdropping technique," Shizuku suggested.

Unsure whether this was supposed to be a joke, Mikihiko replied, "Uh, yeah. I guess you can call it that." Then suddenly lifting his head, he said, "Whoever the user is, they seem well-versed in this kind of technique. Their standard is pretty high. But it's not strong at all. The user is either consciously holding back or they're not very skilled."

Tatsuya murmured to himself: "Someone who's well-versed in the technique but not very skilled, huh?"

"Do you know who it could be?" Mikihiko asked.

Tatsuya avoided the question. "Do you know where the source is?"

Mikihiko closed his eyes and slowly turned his head. After rotating his body a third from where he originally stood, he opened his eyes again and answered confidently: "The first small gym."

"But, Tatsuya." Honoka spoke up. "Aren't the small gyms closed for the day?"

He nodded. "Yeah. And all clubs are on break. We should go check it out."

Everyone agreed. As the saying went—seeing is believing.

Meanwhile, the other student council members were each enjoying a cup of coffee or tea. Shiina could have gone home by now, but she was waiting to announce her new position to Tatsuya and Honoka and ask for their blessing. She and Izumi had been reminiscing about middle school for a while when Miyuki suddenly put down her coffee cup and interrupted the lively conversation.

"By the way, Shiina..." she began.

"Yes?" She felt a lot more relaxed around the president now. In fact, maybe too relaxed.

"Is the boy trying to access this room with perception-type magic your childhood friend? Saburou Yaguruma, was it?"

"What...?" Shiina's eyes widened.

Miyuki was still smiling, but there was a sharp flicker in her eye. More than this predatorial side of her, Shiina was more shocked about what she had just said. After a few seconds of flabbergasted silence, Shiina quickly pulled off her earmuffs.

"Wh-what are you doing?!" Izumi panicked.

Before Minami had a chance to follow suit, Miyuki put a finger to her lips and stared calmly at the girl in front of her. She knew exactly what Shiina was doing.

Shiina's hearing and magic perception were not directly connected. That meant her earmuffs didn't work like Mizuki's glasses, which blocked both auras and her ability to perceive magic. But removing these noise-regulating earmuffs did sharpen Shiina's sensitivity to the magic waves around her.

Shiina couldn't function regularly without her earmuffs. Consciously adjusting her hearing with magic would only impair her perception of her own magic, and she would lose the ability to use magic properly. Wearing earmuffs didn't interfere with her use of magic, but it made her insensitive to surrounding magical interference. That's why she had been unaware of the perception magic directed at the student council room. The dilemma—or trilemma—she faced could be resolved only if the people around her were careful not to make any noise.

Shiina closed her eyes halfway and focused her full attention on listening for the faintest sound. A few moments later, her eyes popped open.

"Saburou, you jerk!" She was suddenly more angry than shocked. Angry and humiliated.

"I think you should put your earmuffs back on," Miyuki suggested. Shiina's adorable rage quickly faded and was replaced with beet-red embarrassment.

She shyly fiddled with her earmuffs to put them back on before saying in the tiniest voice, "I want to apologize for my friend's rude behavior…"

"Please don't worry," Miyuki reassured her. "Like other important rooms in this school, the student council room is protected with a rigid security system."

Shiina looked confused. "You mean like a barrier?"

"Fundamentally, yes." Miyuki nodded. "There was a bit of a scandal a couple of years ago that convinced the school to hire a special company to strengthen security across campus."

After waiting for a few seconds, Shiina responded, "Oh…"

Her older sister had told her about this scandal. If she remembered correctly, it was a big deal involving an armed terrorist group that invaded the school. Why Miyuki was downplaying it now, she couldn't say.

Before she could puzzle over this for very long, Miyuki asked, "Is Yaguruma your bodyguard?"

"Yes. I mean, no!" Shiina flustered. "Not really, anyway."

This time, it was Miyuki's turn to look confused.

Izumi sympathetically stepped in to help clear things up. "The members of the Yaguruma family work as domestic servants and bodyguards for the Mitsuya. Saburou was supposed to be Shiina's exclusive bodyguard since they were the same age, but that plan was canceled before the two entered high school. Right, Shiina?"

"Um, well..." She hesitated because she didn't want to be asked why. Even if Saburou couldn't hear her, she didn't want to admit the deal was called off because he lacked magical talent. She knew how deeply that had hurt him.

"I see... Does that mean you're not in a position to control Yaguruma's behavior?"

Miyuki's question came as a surprise, but Shiina answered, "Yes, that's right."

The president's brows furrowed. Like this was a problem. Then she said, "If that's the case, his unauthorized use of magic is at his sole discretion. We can't blame it on extenuating circumstances."

Her words were as clear as day. Shiina was speechless.

"His efforts *did* result in a failed attempt," Miyuki reasoned. "We can give him that. I'd hate to see him get suspended on the first day of school, but... What do you think, Izumi?"

Shiina continued to stare ahead in silence. She had no words.

Izumi thought for a minute. "Since I know the boy in question, my first instinct is to go easy on him. Then again, precisely because he's not a stranger, showing lenience could set a bad example. If students think anyone associated with the Ten Master Clans can get away with breaking school rules, all chaos will break loose."

"Wait! Please wait!" Shiina noisily rose from her chair. Her words were jumbled from panic, but she grabbed the student council members' attention.

"Saburou can't accept what happened!" she exclaimed. "That's why he's doing foolish things that get him in trouble!"

Miyuki responded calmly. "Do you mean he can't accept your family's decision to dismiss him as your bodyguard?"

"That's right." Shiina was suddenly overwhelmed with embarrassment.

"Let me get this straight. Yaguruma only tried to eavesdrop into this office because he's worried about your safety?" There was no hint of teasing in the president's voice.

"Yes. My family's failure to convince Saburou he wasn't fit for the job in the first place is the cause of all this. It was our duty to speak to him until he accepted reality. Then, whenever he acted on my behalf, I had a responsibility to stop him. This time, too, it's my fault for not supervising him properly. I promise to give Saburou a stern warning, so he'll never do anything like this again."

Miyuki spoke to elicit the words Shiina was too reserved to utter. "Shiina, you just admitted your responsibility for Yaguruma's supervision. You know what that means, don't you?"

Her voice, demeanor, and gaze were gentle and kind. Yet it took Shiina a lot of willpower to answer her question.

"—I do."

Miyuki turned to Izumi. "What do you think? Can we leave this up to Shiina?"

Rather than resembling the smile of her older sister, Mayumi, Izumi's smile made her look just like her father, Kouichi. "I don't mind. *This time.*"

"Thank you!" Shiina bowed deeply. The hidden meaning behind Izumi's words wasn't lost on her.

Meanwhile, Tatsuya's group stood in front of the first small gym.

"Any trace of the spell?" Tatsuya asked.

"Yeah, it's still being cast," Mikihiko responded sincerely. "The responsible party should be just beyond these walls." Then it suddenly hit him. "Wait. Shouldn't you be able to sense the spell, too?"

"I'd rather not exert any needless effort," Tatsuya said.

Mikihiko was surprisingly not upset by this. He knew Tatsuya wasn't just being lazy.

He who looks can see. These were the words of a famous philosopher; and they were true. At the very least, if one magician used perception magic on another, the former would sense the level of the latter's magical power.

If there was an overwhelming difference in the technical prowess of the two parties, it was possible for the stronger of the two to monitor the other without being noticed. That said, the risk of being discovered was never zero, no matter what kind of magic was used. Even Tatsuya's Elemental Sight could be detected if the target had the same technique. If Mikihiko could recognize the hidden student, there was no need for Tatsuya to take the risk of exposing himself, too. Honoka and Shizuku didn't understand Tatsuya's situation as well as Mikihiko did, but they trusted the disciplinary committee chairman's judgment.

"So what do we do now, Tatsuya?" Honoka asked.

"Feel like catching them?" Shizuku chimed in.

They aimed their questions at Tatsuya, but Mikihiko was the one they should really have been asking. They probably just weren't thinking.

Tatsuya glanced at the disciplinary committee president, but he didn't seem fazed. Rather than make a big deal out of nothing, Tatsuya went ahead and told the group his plan.

Someone's getting close.

Saburou Yaguruma, a new freshman student just entering First High, shifted his attention from the student council room back to his current location behind the first small gym.

There's two...no, three of them, he thought.

Perception magic didn't override eidos unless it was the type that enhanced the senses. It was also difficult to detect. But that didn't mean it left no trace at all. Saburou's family practically hammered this fact into his head.

Casting Downwind Ears at the student council room already put him in danger of punishment for the unauthorized use of magic. He didn't want to take more risks than necessary.

This meant he didn't use magic to spot the three magicians approaching him; he simply sensed their presence. Two were women—most likely students, not instructors. And they weren't hiding their presence at all. The third person, on the other hand, was skillfully controlling their presence. But it didn't seem to be a sneak attack. Saburou sensed the third person's control was happening subconsciously. The level of skill it took to do this could mean this third person was an instructor.

Saburou's magic was an old kind that wasn't easily detected by other magicians or sensors. *But First High instructors might pick up on it*, Saburou thought.

He had already ruled out the possibility that the three people approaching were simply on patrol. Unfortunately, he had failed to keep an eye—or ear—on Shiina. His Downwind Ears was unable to pierce the barriers placed around the student council room.

He begrudgingly admitted he had been wrong to think First High only used modern magic techniques. No matter how long he listened, he couldn't hear what was going on in the student council room. Thankfully, he was mature enough to know when to back off.

At least, he thought he was.

Saburou left his hiding place without a sound. Naturally, he went in the direction away from the three approaching figures. His plan was to move along the wall of the small gym and walk out onto the tree-lined path without causing a scene.

But as soon as he started moving, he screeched to a halt.

What the…?! He bit his lip to hold back a scream. But there was no point.

"Are you a new student?" a voice called out. "I detected unauthorized magic around here. Come with me. We need to talk."

Saburou recognized the face of this student who had completely concealed his presence. In fact, most new students almost certainly knew his face and name. He was a student council member, the super engineer at the Nine School Competition, and a core member of the stellar reactor experiment. Not to mention the fiancé of the Yotsuba family's heiress.

Tatsuya Shiba!

This was the last person Saburou wanted to see. He quickly untied his hair, so it cascaded down and hid his face. Then he cast the old velocity spell—Idaten—to try to escape.

"Wait." Tatsuya's voice wasn't particularly forceful, and it certainly wasn't enough to stop Saburou in his tracks.

No, what tripped Saburou was a Psionic Bullet. This bullet was infused with the counter-spell Program Demolition. The massive psionic wave that now engulfed Saburou's entire body both deactivated his magic and paralyzed him from head to toe.

He couldn't walk. He could barely even keep his balance. As he went crashing to the ground, it took all his strength to tuck in his chin and shield himself with his arms. This made his fall anything but graceful, but successfully saved him from injury.

Damn it! You need to move!

Cursing his own body, Saburou tried to regain control through sheer will. He was smart enough to understand why his limbs had gone numb. This knowledge didn't frighten him, but it did put him on edge.

Muscles contracted according to electrical signals transmitted by the nerves. This process was no different for magicians as long as they were human. But for people like Saburou, there was more to it than this.

Generally, muscles executed the commands given by the brain,

and there was a slight delay required for nerves to transmit those commands. This delay only amounted to a few tenths of a second, meaning it was usually undetectable and didn't pose any problem in daily life.

But for those who honed their mind to the point of being able to perceive that delay, the time between the command and the actual movement felt frustratingly limiting. In this span of time, lengthened by extreme mental concentration, Saburou had the vexing experience of knowing an attack was imminent but being unable to avoid or prevent it because no signal would reach his limbs in time. Maybe that feeling during this brief instant was better than the alternative—potentially, death.

People like Saburou often developed various techniques to overcome the frustrating sensation and move more freely. One such technique was to use psions to transmit intentions directly to the flesh, instead of transmitting commands to the muscles with nerve signals.

This technique functioned as a typeless magic, even though those who mastered it were not limited to magicians. All skills depended on talent; and not just anyone could master this physical manipulation technique. But those who trained correctly could learn it without any magical talent. In fact, many people used it as a martial arts technique, without realizing it was typeless magic.

Saburou wasn't blessed with magical talent, but he devoted himself to martial arts and mastered many of its highest-level techniques. With these alone, he could move as well as—or even better than—a magician using acceleration magic.

But his ability backfired this time. Since he was constantly controlling his body with psions, Tatsuya's Program Demolition canceled out Saburou's acceleration magic, and he completely lost control.

Is he going to catch me? No! I won't let him!

Saburou was on the ground, and his opponent was just a step away. He knew it was impossible to escape from a situation like this under normal circumstances. And yet he wasn't ready to give up.

Finally regaining control, he used both hands to prop his head up and look around for a rock of a suitable size. Unfortunately, there wasn't a single pebble on the permeable pavement or neatly trimmed grass. There was, however, a thick branch at the base of a nearby tree. It must have broken off somehow. The end was slightly pointed, just the way he wanted it.

Come to Papa.

Saburou focused his entire attention on the branch. He didn't want to seriously injure Tatsuya. He was just going to stab at him a bit and scare him off before making a clean getaway.

But before Saburou could act, a torrent of psions engulfed him again. A second Program Demolition. Its target wasn't the branch Saburou was aiming for but Saburou himself.

Are you kidding me?! Saburou thought. *No normal person would attack like this!*

The shock of having his body paralyzed once again caused his consciousness to fade into a haze, and he was slowly engulfed by darkness.

"...Damn. You're merciless, Tatsuya. Did you really have to subject him to Program Demolition twice?"

Mikihiko, who had rejoined the group after circling the small gym, gazed incredulously at the unconscious boy lying at Tatsuya's feet.

"I didn't have a choice," Tatsuya said. "He had a nasty skill."

"Skill?"

The word *skill* instead of *magic* confused Mikihiko, but Tatsuya didn't bother to clarify.

"I didn't expect him to lose consciousness, though. He must be highly sensitive to psions."

Honoka spoke up, concerned. "Maybe we should take him to the nurse's office."

Mikihiko agreed. "Honoka's right. Program Demolition already feels like a loud cymbal crashing right next to your ear. The effects are even worse for someone with high psion sensitivity."

"What do you take me for? I went easy on him," Tatsuya claimed. "…At least a little."

"Tatsuya!" Mikihiko couldn't believe his friend's calmness considering what he had just done.

"Fine." Tatsuya sighed. "At this point, I think he's more asleep than unconscious. But I'll take him to the nurse's office just in case."

He swung Saburou over his shoulder. Neither Mikihiko, Honoka, nor Shizuku dared to question how he could tell the difference between unconsciousness and sleep.

The first thing Saburou saw when he woke up was his childhood friend peering down at him.

"Saburou!" she exclaimed with a smile on her lips and tears in her eyes. "Thank goodness you're awake!" It was too hard for her to completely hide her concern.

"I'm fine, Shiina," he reassured her.

Truth be told, Saburou didn't know what was going on and couldn't remember how he had fallen asleep. But he stood up from the bed to show he was well. He thought it was important to ease Shiina's anxieties first.

"See? I'm not in pain, and my eyes and ears are in perfect shape."

This helped Shiina calm down. But only a little. Saburou could tell there was still some anxiety—or worry—lingering inside her that couldn't be wiped away so easily.

"Good," she said. "If that's the case…"

Maybe it was because her anxieties were making her sensitive, but Saburou felt a strange pressure coming from her. An uncomfortable sweat broke out along his back as he listened to the next words that came out of his childhood friend's mouth.

"You're not going anywhere."

For a second, Saburou thought he misheard. Not only did he not understand, her words were also wildly out of character. They didn't compute. Ignoring his confusion, Shiina swung her right hand and slapped Saburou so hard, it made his cheek burn.

Saburou had sensed her every move and could have avoided the slap. Actually, it would have been easy for him to do so. But for some reason, ducking didn't seem like an option.

"Wh-what was that for?" he asked, bewildered.

Shiina didn't answer; instead, her eyes began to water. It looked like she could burst into tears at any moment.

"I know you tried to eavesdrop on me," she said in a trembling voice. "Do you not trust me that much?"

"Shiina…"

Saburou couldn't answer yes or no. Whether he trusted her wasn't the issue. All he wanted was to protect her from danger. But if he told her this, she would take it as a lack of trust. Then again, if he said he did trust her, he would no longer have a reason to stay by her side.

After a few minutes of silence, Shiina leveled a grave stare at her childhood friend.

"Saburou…" Her voice held a note of sadness, the oblivious nature of which was enough to send pangs of guilt through a young man's heart. Saburou, of course, was no exception. And yet he said nothing. Not out of obstinance but purely because he didn't know what to say. His childhood friend glared at him, and he avoided her gaze. This continued for a few minutes. Then the first one to give up—or lose patience—was Shiina.

"I promised the student council president that I would take responsibility for your actions," she said.

That immediately struck a note.

"What?!" Saburou whipped his head up. "Why do my actions have to be your responsibility?!"

"I don't understand why you're so upset." She frowned.

Saburou fell silent again but didn't avert his gaze.

"What?" Shiina challenged. "Did you do something you don't want me taking responsibility for?"

"Well..."

"Admit it!" she yelled. "You know you were up to no good!"

There was nothing Saburou could say. Shiina had hit the nail on the head.

"Most people would get expelled if they were caught casting unauthorized magic to try to eavesdrop on the student council room. I don't want that to happen to you!"

"I know," Saburou said. "I'm sorry."

All he could do was apologetically bow his head. Deep down, he knew why he wasn't allowed to be Shiina's bodyguard. Even though he couldn't accept it on an emotional level, he did understand it rationally.

The measures Saburou took to ensure Shiina's safety were ultimately for his own satisfaction. But it didn't make sense to cause her trouble out of selfishness. Becoming a nuisance to Shiina completely defeated the point of trying to be her bodyguard.

"Should I stay away from you like your dad told me to?" he asked with a pained look.

Even though that would make everything easier, he just couldn't bring himself to do it. Then again, he decided to give up then and there if Shiina rejected him herself. But what she said next came as a surprise.

"It's too late for that," she said.

"What do you mean?" Saburou said, eyes wide.

"Like I said," Shiina replied. "I promised the student council president that I would take responsibility for your actions."

Saburou knew he was entirely to blame for what happened. He was just too stubborn to admit it.

"I never asked you to do that!" he shouted.

"I know!" Shiina shouted back with an intensity that shocked her childhood friend. "But I had no choice!" She was getting more riled up by the second. "If I hadn't said anything, you would've been expelled on the first day of school!"

Her hysteric words made Saburou fall silent.

She continued. "Like it or not, I'm responsible for you now! If you do something bad, I have to take the blame! So don't go doing reckless things like you did today! Got it?"

"Y-yes, ma'am." Saburou's voice was suddenly subservient.

"Good. Now, let's go home."

Shiina must have felt refreshed after blurting out everything she wanted to say. As if purged of an angry spirit, she now flashed Saburou her usual smile.

[3]

On April 7, 2097, the first night after the entrance ceremony, Tatsuya visited the Independent Magic Battalion's headquarters. This was the last place he wanted to be, especially because of his ridiculously busy schedule. But he had received orders the night before, and he couldn't evade the summons. Fujibayashi said there was news that was too important to convey over the phone. So Tatsuya got on his beloved electric two-wheeler right after getting home from the entrance ceremony and headed over to Kasumigaura.

The Kasumigaura headquarters had an imposing air. Despite the late hour, there were still people and cars going in and out. Even the Independent Magic Battalion's headquarters, which was usually sparsely populated, was alive with officers and soldiers alike. As he passed by the buzz of activity, Tatsuya thought, *It's as if they're preparing for war. Maybe they are.*

He knocked at the commanding officer's door.

"Please come in," Kazama said from the other side.

Am I imagining things, or does he sound almost polite? Tatsuya couldn't help but notice the slight softness in the officer's words. But he put these speculations aside as he entered the room.

"You asked to see me?" Tatsuya asked.

"Thanks for coming so late at night," Kazama said. "And on such short notice. I thought the gravity of this matter required an in-person explanation."

"By an explanation, you mean..."

"First of all, please. Have a seat."

Kazama gestured toward a convertible sofa that could accommodate three people. Tatsuya gladly took a seat on its edge and faced the commanding officer. Kazama immediately got to the point.

"Our battalion is being dispatched to Hokkaido tomorrow morning."

So I was right, Tatsuya thought. But he didn't dare say it out loud.

Kazama continued. "We'll be the first boots on the ground, and the entire brigade will follow, if need be."

Tatsuya didn't expect things to move so quickly. At this rate, he couldn't stay silent any longer. Better yet, it wasn't *right* for him to hold back.

"Are you expecting an invasion?" he pressed.

"Yes," Kazama quickly answered.

"So what happened near Sado was a diversion?"

"There's no doubt about it," Kazama asserted. "We believe the New Soviet Union's real target is Hokkaido."

"Who's we?"

"The battalion. And General Saeki."

Okay, that makes sense. Tatsuya nodded. *General Staff are probably divided on where they think the enemy will strike. Right now, it's between Hokuriku and Hokkaido, with Hokuriku in the lead. That's why instead of sending a whole division from Tohoku to Hokkaido, they're just sending the 101st Brigade, which is more of a commando unit.*

Kazama continued. "As it stands, communication between us is going to be hard for a while. Even if—heaven forbid—something like the Yokohama Incident happens again, I won't be able to help you."

"Understood."

Tatsuya agreed it would be difficult to deal with an incident of that degree without Kazama's help. On the other hand, that was simply from his own perspective. Kazama wouldn't need to call on Tatsuya for something like that.

Kazama added, "Also, depending on the development of the situation, we may need to call on you for support."

The ambiguity of this statement threw Tatsuya off guard.

"Does that mean I might need to go to Hokkaido?" Tatsuya asked.

"No, we're thinking of having you support us from here," Kazama explained.

Tatsuya suddenly understood the deliberate weight of the commanding officer's words.

"With Material Burst?"

"Not just Material Burst. General Saeki is suggesting Third Eye long-distance support magic, too."

"All right." Tatsuya simply acknowledged that he heard the commanding officer, not that he understood. He couldn't rely on the battalion, but the battalion could make good use of him. That's essentially what Kazama was saying. All militaries were probably the same. But this was a new stance that the battalion had never taken before.

Then Tatsuya added, "As a member of the Independent Magic Battalion, I'm off as soon as I get the order."

He stood up and saluted the commander. Nothing he had said was a lie. He had simply omitted the words *for now*. Kazama nodded curtly from his seat. As their eyes met, it seemed the nuances of Tatsuya's omitted phrase were not lost on the commander.

Kazama hadn't met with Tatsuya alone. His aide, Fujibayashi, had been sitting silently behind him. Once Tatsuya left the room and closed the door, so there was no danger of being overheard, Fujibayashi hesitantly asked, "Commander, why didn't you explain the situation to him in full? He might be suspicious of us now."

"Are you saying we deceived him?"

Kazama's radical choice of words made Fujibayashi flinch.

But she answered: "I doubt he feels that way, but he could suspect we're abandoning him."

"Well…" Kazama sighed. "That's not completely wrong."

"Commander…" There was a hint of reproach in Fujibayashi's tone. He was taking things too far.

"Sorry." There wasn't anyone else in the room, but even Kazama recognized what he said was inappropriate. The apology came quickly and easily.

"However," he continued, "this is how the relationship between the army and the Ten Master Clans is meant to be. Tatsuya may have returned to the fold of the Yotsuba family, but we're not about to change our policy now."

"I don't see how Tatsuya's position matters," his aide interjected. "He is a crucial pillar of our strength."

"Yes," Kazama said agreeably but firmly. "There are only two strategic-class magicians in Japan, and no more than fifty in the entire world. As one of those few, Tatsuya plays an essential role in Japan's defenses. That's all the more reason to keep an appropriate distance from him."

Fujibayashi's body language betrayed her disapproval. This wasn't the first time they'd had this conversation. In fact, they'd had it many times before with Sanada, Yanagi, and Yamanaka in the same room.

Kazama spoke up again. "We're already too friendly with him. I realized the repercussions of this during the Okinawa operation a few days ago. He is supposed to be our wild card, a resource we use only in the most dire situations. And yet our close relationship with him has made us rely on him too much. Without Tatsuya, we wouldn't have been able to locate and neutralize the enemy's main forces as easily as we did in Okinawa."

"Isn't that all the more reason to remain on friendly terms?"

"That was all fine and dandy when the Yotsuba family was indifferent to his existence. But now they have accepted him and treat him as a prime military asset. That means he could abandon us at any moment. If the interests of the Yotsuba and the National Defense Force ever conflict, how can you be sure he will side with us?"

Despite the potential holes in her argument, Fujibayashi held her ground. "Tatsuya knows the Yotsuba cannot exist without the protection of the state. I don't believe he will choose a path that leads to open confrontation."

"That only stands if the interests of the state and the military remain on the same page," Kazama retorted. His subordinate fell silent, so he continued. "A preemptive strike via strategic-class magic, for example, would undoubtedly be in the military's interests. But it wouldn't necessarily be in the interests of the state. Material Burst is certainly a weapon with superior power, speed, and range, but destroying enemy forces could make a diplomatic situation worse rather than better."

This wasn't just a theoretical possibility. In South America, for example, the Brazilian military had won so many battles against surrounding countries that virtually all other South American countries had collapsed. To date, the continent was still embroiled in endless regional warfare. This was why people said the Twenty Years' Global War Outbreak still raged in South America.

Kazama sighed. "My biggest fear is that a friendship with Tatsuya will lead to the National Defense Force leadership thinking they can use Material Burst whenever they want. If we don't distance ourselves from him, there will always be those who want to use his power."

The way he spoke was like a teacher to his student.

"Isn't that all the more reason to tell Tatsuya our true intent?" This was Fujibayashi's only possible counterargument, as her concerns echoed Kazama's.

"And make him lose his trust in us? I don't think so," Kazama said firmly. "It's in our best interest to accept the way things are, rather than to risk instilling a bad impression of the National Defense Force as a whole."

Like all their discussions over the past few days, this one ended here.

While Tatsuya visited the Independent Magic Battalion's headquarters, Katsuto was secretly meeting with Tomokazu Saegusa in a high-end downtown restaurant. It was the kind of place frequented by big-name politicians and prominent businessmen, but Katsuto seemed completely at home, seated elegantly on the tatami-mat floor. He was there for only about a minute when Tomokazu showed up.

"I'm sorry to keep you waiting." Tomokazu bowed apologetically before clumsily taking a seat across from Katsuto. He was clearly not as accustomed to kneeling on the floor as his companion.

Katsuto quickly offered, "Please. Feel free to sit comfortably."

"If you really don't mind. Thank you."

Tomokazu unfolded his legs from beneath himself and sat cross-legged on his cushion. Since Katsuto remained seated on the soles of his feet, he ended up slightly looking down at his companion. Neither party seemed to mind this, however. At least at surface-level. They exchanged pleasantries, each ordered a nonalcoholic drink, and then naturally dove into the topic at hand.

"Your sister told me you had something you wanted to talk about," Katsuto began.

"Right. Let me get straight to the point," Tomokazu said. "I'd like to ask what you think should be done about the current climate of hostility toward magicians."

Katsuto raised his brow. He wasn't expecting a question like this.

"You don't want my opinion but an actual solution? I assume you think we need to take effective action against the anti-magician movements, then."

"That's right."

Tomokazu neither hid his intentions nor minced words. This side of him was the polar opposite of his father, Kouichi.

He continued. "At this rate, it's not enough to take action after the damage is done."

"Are you saying unchecked smear campaigns against magicians could lead to irreversible consequences? What kinds of consequences are we talking about exactly?" Katsuto prompted.

"I fear terrorist acts worse than the Hakone incident. Even kidnappings of young children and babies who still can't use magic," Tomokazu claimed.

"So serial crimes perpetrated by non-magicians."

"Right." Tomokazu nodded and repeated his initial question. "What do you think we should do to stop this from happening?"

"I can't think of a solution off the top of my head. Actually, I doubt I could ever come up with a solution on my own," Katsuto replied honestly. Those who knew him wouldn't have expected any other answer.

Tomokazu's own flat resignation, however, came as a surprise. "I'm at a loss myself."

"It's too big of an issue," Katsuto consoled. "Even if you did come up with the perfect solution, it's definitely not something a single family could carry out."

"You're right. The current state of anti-magic activities isn't something one person can tackle on their own." Tomokazu let out a small sigh of relief, and it didn't seem to be an act.

When it came down to it, Tomokazu wasn't as tough as his father. In that respect, Katsuto felt he could be trusted.

Tomokazu continued. "I don't think this issue should be tackled by the Juumonji alone. We should gather knowledge from a much larger group of magicians and try to reach an agreement about what to do."

"Do you think we should bring it up with the Magic Association of Japan?" Katsuto asked.

"No." Tomokazu shook his head. "Discussing this kind of issue with such a big group would just lead to a generic answer. Besides, putting the clan heads together would spark a war of words where nothing would ever get solved."

"But if the representatives of each clan don't participate, any decisions are more likely to end up mere speculative ideas without any decisive action to back them up."

Tomokazu nodded in contented agreement. "That's exactly what I was thinking. Why don't we call on the younger generations? Not the current heads but the *heirs* to the clans. We'll start with the Twenty-Eight Families, then invite the Numbers, and finally the Hundred Families. What do you think?"

That's not a bad idea, Katsuto reflected.

He realized that after assuming the position of clan leader, his approach to matters had noticeably changed. He now prioritized what was feasible rather than what was optimal or best. In that sense, clan leaders were less flexible.

That said, idealistic thinking that completely ignored practicality ran a high risk of complicating the situation.

Heirs, he considered, *must be conscious of reality but aren't bound by it as much as the head of the clan. If we gather them together to share their wisdom, we may be able to generate constructive proposals for the Master Clans Council.*

It wasn't a bad idea. But it was also too abstract.

"You know," Katsuto started, "I wouldn't be involved if you just gather the immediate family heirs."

Tomokazu faltered. "Y-you're still young! If we stick with the idea of gathering young clan members—"

"So you want to divide people up by age?" Katsuto prompted. "What's the range we're talking about accepting here? You'll want to include yourself, of course."

A sweat broke out on Tomokazu's forehead. "O-of course. I was thinking…everyone thirty and below?"

"Thirty? I hope you know that will mean that the head of the Mutsuzuka will be able to participate while the head of the Yatsushiro will not."

"You have to draw the line somewhere. Yatsushiro has a younger brother he works with closely, so that should be fine."

"Very well. I do agree that having some sort of limit is important." Katsuto nodded solemnly—if not ambiguously. And then he said, "I'm not sure what good it'll do, but I'm happy to help."

All at once, Tomokazu breathed a sigh of relief.

On the day after the entrance ceremony, First High was generally calm, except for some nervous new students losing their footing. It would be a lie to say Tatsuya wasn't bothered by the stares of the new students who came to observe classes. Then again, two years ago, he was in these students' shoes. With this in mind, Tatsuya decided to be patient. The students bothered him only while he waited to perform his experiment. Once it was his turn, they would naturally disappear from his mind.

The Department of Magic Engineering, which Tatsuya was a part of, had been around for only two years. The curriculum hadn't been completely finalized the previous year, so instructors weren't assigned to students until just before the start of the school year. Because of this, there were practically no classes for the previous year's freshmen to observe. This year was the first time they could welcome curious students, but Tatsuya didn't expect so many to show up.

First High had always maintained a good balance of aspiring magicians and aspiring magic engineers. It was merely a coincidence that the latter group was so small during Mayumi and her cohorts' generation. A "good balance" meant neither group significantly outweighed the other. But the number of aspiring magic engineers with magical abilities was still less than the total number of students who didn't specialize in magic engineering.

Not all the freshman observers on this day were aspiring magic engineers. But it was incredible to see how much interest the Department of Magic Engineering was attracting. This was clearly a result of the previous year's stellar reactor experiment.

While these thoughts spun through his head, Tatsuya's turn finally came around. His task was to build a tin sphere using a magic program students had constructed in advance without modifications. This assignment worked as a practical exercise to teach students how to construct a magic program that showed all their work.

The procedure for making the true sphere was also fixed. Students melted tin, neutralized by gravity, which then formed a sphere via surface tension. The spherical liquid tin was then cooled and solidified so it wouldn't distort. That was all there was to it.

The tricky part was that the gravity students neutralized didn't only come from Earth. While it was possible to ignore the gravitational pull of the mass of the students experimenting or observing the experiment, the gravitational pull of the moon and sun was a different story. These forces were counteracted with a rotational movement that completely blocked Earth's gravity. So students had to follow this movement while adjusting their sphere according to by-product distortions. To prevent the spheres from warping due to air currents, students had to create a vacuum around the liquefied tin. If the cooling process wasn't even, the sphere could shrink at different rates, which could also potentially cause deviations. In other words, this exercise was an advanced one that provided students an opportunity to acquire precise control over their magic. Creating a true sphere involved mastering a step-by-step procedure rather than simply having a magic program create the sphere for them.

There were five experimental devices in total, and each student was given ten minutes. Within that time, students had to assemble the magic program in the editor, program it into the CAD, perform the spell, and complete the sphere. A module was provided to create the initial magic program, but whether students used it was up to their own discretion.

Since the students were told about the task in advance, they had time to prepare the magic program before class started. However, they were not allowed to bring their prework into the lab; they had to re-create the program based on their memory and extemporaneous inspiration.

The screen of the editor where students created their magic programs was projected onto a large screen suspended from the ceiling. This might make it seem easy to cheat. But the instructors had thought this through. The order of the experiments was set so students with the highest grades came last. Even if a student tried to imitate someone else's magic program superficially, a logic failure would occur and the magic wouldn't work. That said, instructors believed a student with the ability to imitate at an advanced level should be evaluated just as highly as someone who worked from scratch.

Tatsuya was part of the last group. For forty minutes straight, he just watched his classmates run their experiments. It wasn't as if there were no students who could be helpful references, but he had already finished his own magic program the day before. Any thoughtless tweaking now would only make things worse.

After the previous group finished submitting their tin spheres— the finished product was the most important factor in scoring—Tatsuya headed for an experimental device. He cast a perfunctory glance at the observation deck. Maybe it was his imagination, but there seemed to be a noticeable increase in the number of new students.

An electronic chime signaled the students to begin the assignment. Speed wasn't a factor in the evaluation as long as the sphere was finished in time. But to ensure fairness, the editor was locked until the chime rang.

Tatsuya started typing his magic program on the stand-alone keyboard, as usual. He wasn't in any particular hurry. He knew he could complete the task with plenty of time to spare. The long string of magic program code streamed onto the monitor in front of him. Meanwhile, the same data appeared on the large public display in real time.

A quiet murmur spread through the crowd. No one was foolish enough to shout, but talking in general wasn't very good manners.

Tatsuya heard the instructors whispering a few words of warning. It wasn't only the freshmen observers who were talking. The voices of some of Tatsuya's classmates also mingled in the crowd. But this was strange. They had seen Tatsuya write magic programs countless times.

Maybe they're being influenced by the freshmen, Tatsuya thought briefly before shutting out all unnecessary stimuli and focusing completely on his magic.

Tatsuya's fingers came to a halt on his keyboard. The large screen monitoring the activity on his experimental device displayed a 3D bar with the magic program data being copied from the editor to the CAD.

He was the first of the final group of five to have his magic program ready to activate. From two devices over, Chiaki Hirakawa's aggravated gaze bored into him. But Tatsuya completely ignored this and activated his CAD.

Again, the skill required for this assignment—as was common with all magic engineering assignments—wasn't speed, magic capacity, or even event interference. It was the ability to construct complex magic programs with precision.

This, of course, didn't mean capacity or interference played no role at all; they could definitely provide an extra boost. This would make the magic program longer (not bigger), but since students weren't really competing against time, the extra time it took to write out the program wasn't a problem.

Two meters away from Tatsuya, a tin trial piece emerged, melting and losing its contour. The liquefied metal soon amassed into a spherical shape. The freshmen watched the process intently from the observation deck. Though the other four students in the final group had also activated their magic, everyone's eyes were focused on Tatsuya's work.

A soft clink signaled that someone nearby had finished molding their tin into a sphere and dropped it gently onto the presentation platform. Tomitsuka was the first to complete the assignment. Tatsuya's experiment, meanwhile, was still cooling.

Chiaki finished second. But Tatsuya was still in no hurry. The assignment couldn't be modified halfway. So once the magic was activated, the student could only watch and wait. Tatsuya stared at the ball of tin solidifying in the weightless vacuum.

Once the process was complete, Tatsuya's tin sphere dropped silently to the presentation platform. The lack of even the slightest clink was proof that Tatsuya had completely controlled his sphere's descent with magic. Tatsuya was the third of his group to finish, with one minute and thirty seconds remaining.

Jennifer Smith was once again the practical instructor for the Class E seniors. The experiment was completed before the end of class time, and Jennifer immediately called Tatsuya to the staff room.

"I know you're busy with student council duties, so this will only take a minute," Jennifer reassured him.

Fifth period was about to end, followed by after-school activities. Like Jennifer said, the student council would be waiting for him soon.

"It's a bit early, but I wanted to ask about the theme you were considering for the Thesis Competition," she prompted.

The Thesis Competition—short for Japan's All-High Magic Thesis Competition—was held every year on the last Sunday of October. This year, it would be on October 27. While that felt like ages away, each school elected its representatives for the competition in June. All things considered, Jennifer's question wasn't that unexpected or early.

"I haven't decided yet," Tatsuya replied curtly. He opted not to tell her he hadn't made up his mind whether to participate in the competition in the first place. Magic engineering students were required to apply, but they could always decline if chosen.

"That's great to hear," Jennifer said.

"It is?" Tatsuya was puzzled. This wasn't the reaction he was expecting.

Meanwhile, Jennifer seemed to expect Tatsuya's confusion. This seemed to be an unnecessary way to go about this conversation, but she probably had her reasons.

"Absolutely." She nodded. "I have something to tell you, you see."

"Does it have something to do with the Thesis Competition?" Tatsuya asked.

"It sure does."

Two possibilities immediately came to Tatsuya's mind. Jennifer would either tell him to write about the stellar reactor—aka the gravity-controlled thermonuclear fusion reactor—or declare the same theme off-limits.

She said, "I'd like you to write about anything other than the stellar reactor."

Tatsuya was right.

"All right," he agreed.

Jennifer seemed surprised by his quick answer. "Aren't you going to ask why?"

"No. I already know something as dangerous as the stellar reactor isn't the best topic for the Thesis Competition."

"Oh, well…" She looked relieved. "It looks like I was worried for nothing."

Truth be told, Tatsuya had an entirely other reason for agreeing to Jennifer's request. He did believe the stellar reactor wasn't an appropriate topic for the competition, but not because it was dangerous. The reactor was the key technology for his magician liberation plan. He didn't want others potentially imitating it and claiming a patent on it first.

He tried to change the subject. "By the way, it looks like Kento got accepted into the magic engineering department. Congratulations."

This made it seem as if he had just heard the news. In reality, his position on the student council gave him access to Jennifer's son's exam results in early March.

"Thank you." Jennifer's usually nonchalant face melted into the smile of a proud parent.

She continued. "The competition this year was nothing to be scoffed at, but it looks like things are going to get even more heated in the year to come. We might need to increase the number of magic engineering classes we offer."

This was news to Tatsuya. His curiosity was piqued.

"The entrance ceremony just ended, and you're already making predictions about next year?"

Jennifer displayed the slightest hesitation, a nervous gesture that betrayed this was information she wasn't supposed to tell students. But Tatsuya quickly felt her calmness return. Maybe she realized it wasn't necessarily a secret.

"This year's entrance ceremony saw more high scores in magic engineering than ever before," she explained. "A higher percentage of incoming students also excelled in magic engineering technology than in previous years."

Tatsuya immediately realized the large numbers of onlookers he sensed during the experiments hadn't been his imagination. Before he could come up with a possible explanation, Jennifer offered: "I'm sure it's in no small part thanks to the stellar reactor experiments from last year. Even the kinds of kids who usually apply to Fourth High decided to come here instead. Thanks to that, our admissions are off the charts."

"I feel like this is my fault." Tatsuya hesitated. "But I guess it's a good thing."

"It definitely helped the quality of admitted students skyrocket."

Tatsuya wasn't sure if this was a joke. Before he had time to think about it, Jennifer said he was free to go.

The time Tatsuya spent speaking to Jennifer wasn't that long. When he walked into the student council room, only Pixie was there.

Since Pixie was connected to the security system of the office—and other rooms—she should have sensed Tatsuya enter. But she didn't acknowledge his presence. Not even a *Welcome home, Master.*

Tatsuya walked over to his chair and activated the terminal on his desk. As soon as it turned on, he immediately got to work.

Pixie made sure he didn't have any commands for her before gliding over to the dining cart. A 3H's original job was to function as a human-shaped home automation interface, helping with cleaning, cooking, and managing the house. It could also be updated with management software to expand the scope of its duties to work in spaces like restaurants. The dining cart in the student council room was commercial size, but Pixie could easily control it remotely. In fact, she activated the cart as soon as she got to her feet.

The cart produced a cup of coffee, which Pixie placed at Tatsuya's side. Although the cart worked automatically, it functioned like an extra set of Pixie's hands. As a result, Tatsuya received a cup of coffee that was carefully tailored to his taste. He took a sip. Since he didn't ask for anything else, Pixie returned to her seat.

A few minutes later, Izumi and Minami walked into the room. Izumi saw Tatsuya at his desk and presumed Miyuki was with him, only to be visibly disappointed when she found the president's seat empty. Minami was similarly upset to see a coffee cup on Tatsuya's desk. Luckily, these negative feelings faded quickly as Miyuki and Honoka appeared before the juniors had a chance to sit down.

"You're early, Tatsuya," Miyuki said.

"Izumi and Minami, too," Honoka added.

Before turning on her terminal, Minami moved to make tea. Pixie controlled all the apparatuses in the student council room, except for the information equipment. But she could operate them if she wanted to; they weren't locked. Minami made tea for four people, including herself. This wasn't an intentional jab at Tatsuya's coffee—or maybe it was. Meanwhile, the student council's—and school's—new member seemed to be running late.

◇ ◇ ◇

Shiina's tardiness wasn't because of a class running overtime. This day and the next were dedicated to observing specialized courses featuring magic experiments and practical skills. Since Course 2 students didn't have instructors, they were usually free to observe classes as they pleased. Course 1 students, on the other hand, were typically instructed by their teachers to observe particular classes. Although this wasn't a fixed rule, no one—at least in Course 1—wanted to go off the rails at the beginning of the school year.

Classes A through D had their observations controlled by their supervising teacher, so they didn't go on for too long or eat into the next item on the schedule. In fact, rotations were often cut short so students could return to their classrooms and have free time to reflect on what they experienced.

The last class period of the first day of school followed this pattern. Class A was even granted an extra ten minutes of free time. Normally, an early dismissal meant Shiina could head to the student council room earlier, but as it turned out, the extra time was a detriment.

The day before, Shiina was invited to the student council room immediately following the entrance ceremony. After agreeing to join the student council, she and Saburou went home together. This meant her classmates didn't have a chance to talk with her. Shiina had lunch with her classmates this day, but it was just a normal meal in the cafeteria—not a formal gathering. So once again, she didn't have the opportunity to talk to many people. It also didn't help that she was worried about drawing attention to herself if she made too much noise.

At the same time, Shiina's Class A classmates were itching to get to know her. She was this year's general student council representative, and the only new student this year who was a direct heiress of one of the Ten Master Clans. But the biggest reason why all of

Shiina's classmates flocked to her was because she was the type of beautiful, friendly person who even other girls found endearing.

For freshman students, Miyuki wasn't just the Yotsuba family's heiress—she was also too beautiful and awe-inspiring for them to approach. Just making eye contact paralyzed them with reverence and fear. Even Kasumi and Izumi weren't very approachable. Izumi, in particular—despite her friendly appearance—was on the intimidating side. Shiina, on the other hand, gave off a much more amicable air.

As soon as the instructor left the classroom, Shiina was surrounded by her classmates, unable to move until the end of the school day.

Shiina was, of course, concerned about the time. She had in no way forgotten about her student council duties. For better or for worse, she was a people pleaser by nature—an unusual trait for a member of one of the Ten Master Clans. Maybe it was because she was the youngest of seven siblings.

Shiina was initially worried about being shunned at school because of her position. So being surrounded by her classmates like this made her happy. In all honesty, she'd rather not be the center of attention. But apart from that, her current situation was close to the ideal high school life she had envisioned.

I don't want to be canceled for being insensitive, Shiina thought and couldn't find a natural way to bring up the student council. It was her loyal childhood friend who rescued her from her prison of good intentions.

His loud voice resounded from the classroom entrance: "Lady Shiina!"

Both Shiina and the other Class A students around her whipped their heads toward the sudden noise. They all looked startled. But Shiina was the most surprised of them all.

Saburou raised his voice again. "You need to go to the student council *now*!"

Shiina was still shaken by his sudden eccentricity, but these words struck a chord. She panicked. "The student council? …Oh, I'm late!"

Her classmates finally realized they were holding her back.

"We're so sorry for keeping you so long, Mitsuya," one apologized. "Come on, guys! Out of the way!"

"Sorry, Shiina," another said.

They weren't holding her there out of malice. They were just absorbed in conversation. New freshmen didn't have the guts to interfere with student council activities.

"That's okay. It's my fault, too," Shiina said. "I'll see you tomorrow."

She waved affectionately, slipping out of her classmates' circle and hurrying to join Saburou at the classroom door.

Shiina ran up the stairs at a short trot, Saburou skipping steps at her heels. Only when they arrived at the landing between the third and fourth floors did Shiina turn back to speak.

"Hey, um…thanks for helping me back there."

"Don't worry about it," he replied. "I know it's hard for you to deal with strangers."

"Well, you're not wrong…"

But Shiina wasn't happy with Saburou's answer. Her cheeks looked as if they were about to puff with anger at any minute.

"By the way, why did you call me that?" she asked. She was blatantly changing the subject, but the name Saburou had shouted out did bother her.

"Call you what?" he asked.

"Lady Shiina."

"What's the big deal?" Saburou replied, and he wasn't playing dumb. "You're a lady, aren't you?"

To him, calling his childhood friend "Lady Shiina" came as naturally as calling her "Shiina." His parents didn't forbid him from becoming friends with Shiina just because she was the daughter of their employer. But they were also careful to teach him the importance of knowing his place.

Shiina wasn't satisfied with Saburou's answer, but she couldn't come up with the words to challenge it. Deep down, she knew she was nothing more than the daughter of a well-to-do family in magician society. The powerlessness of it all added another layer to her anger. But, realizing it was childish, she refrained from actually letting it bubble to the surface. Instead of expressing her frustrations on her face, Shiina decided to use tone and actions.

Right before reaching the fourth floor, she said, "Anyway, thanks for your help. I can go the rest of the way on my own."

She then spun away from Saburou in a huff and headed toward the student council room, deliberately refusing to turn back around.

Left behind in Shiina's dust, Saburou paused in the middle of the stairwell and sighed. He usually loved Shiina's childishness. It made him happy that—apart from her family—she showed this side of herself only to him. It was a sign that she trusted him. But now, it only puzzled him.

Shiina had left without any instructions. That meant he was free to do as he pleased. But for Saburou, this so-called "freedom" was generally a hassle he didn't know what to do with.

Someone who couldn't act without orders was no better than a slave or a robot. Saburou knew this wasn't good. It wasn't that he followed orders twenty-four hours a day, seven days a week. In fact, it was the opposite. When he was still in middle school—basically just the other day—the only obligation he had been given, other than a few rare jobs, was training.

Still, as long as Shiina was within sight, he never had trouble finding a way to use his spare time. Saburou was always thinking about how he should act as Shiina's bodyguard. Some might even say being Shiina's bodyguard was a core part of his identity. Until six months ago, that is.

Saburou was disqualified as a bodyguard because of his lack of magical talent. There was no one to blame. Resenting his parents was meaningless. In fact, it was completely out of line. If he had been born to a different family, he would never have met Shiina in the first place.

Despite the circumstances, Saburou wasn't ready to give up. He knew he still wasn't strong enough to be by Shiina's side, but he also believed talent didn't equal ability. If he lacked strength, he would just have to hone his skills to compensate. And he made up his mind to do just that.

That said, he didn't exactly know *what* he should do. It could all just be a juvenile ambition. But his parents believed he was admirable enough for not losing heart after his very identity was disavowed. This was the reason why they allowed him to attend First High.

For now, Saburou's goals still existed only in the realm of possibility. In the real world, Saburou wasn't allowed to stand by Shiina's side, so he decided to watch her from afar. That's when he made a huge mistake.

Unsure what to do next, Saburou plodded up the steps. The option of going home without Shiina never crossed his mind. Accompanying his childhood friend to and from school was one of the few privileges he had left. Until then, he needed a place to kill time. Saburou headed to the rooftop.

There was a garden on the rooftop of First High. In the winter, various flowers and herbs that repelled bugs were planted in tiered flower beds inside a greenhouse.

It was sunny and still on this day, and despite it being an early April evening, the rooftop was neither hot nor cold, but comfortably warm. Like being immersed in a pool of lukewarm water.

It was precisely this sunny weather that must have lulled her to sleep—a pedigreed cat was napping on a rooftop bench. Saburou couldn't help but stop and stare at the cat's unusually striking appearance. She had a long, slender body and light semi-long hair that curled at the ends. Even with her eyes closed and her arms half-buried under a pillow, she clearly had a well-defined face. In every respect, she was truly a thoroughbred. Of course, this cat was actually a First High student.

The girl's face was more mature than Shiina's. Saburou assumed she was a couple of years older. She was lying on her right side, meaning the left shoulder of her uniform was visible. Just like Saburou's uniform, it didn't sport an eight-petaled emblem. In other words, this girl was an older Course 2 student.

After admiring the girl in her sleep for about ten seconds, Saburou suddenly came to his senses. His first thought was, *Maybe I should wake her up.*

Spring had just begun. It may be warm now, but the temperatures would almost certainly drop as the sun went down. The wind could even pick up. Lying on the rooftop at this time of year was a surefire way to catch a cold.

But just as he was about to shake the girl's shoulder, he began to worry his intentions might be misunderstood. Right now, the two of them were the only ones on the rooftop. When she woke up, she might mistake him for a pervert. Or a Peeping Tom who enjoyed watching girls sleep.

Saburou stopped in his tracks, then slowly backed away. Once he decided he was far enough away to avoid being mistaken for a pervert, he ripped his eyes away from the older girl and turned toward the rooftop door.

"You don't have to run away."

A voice called out from the bench he had just been watching. Saburou stiffened, as if he had just been caught in a mischievous act. Barely turning his head back around, he saw the girl pushing herself up.

Ignoring Saburou's suspicious behavior, she stretched her arms into the air. Again, just like a house cat. But when she lowered her arms and gazed at Saburou, her eyes had an intensity more akin to a tiger or panther.

"Relax. I don't think you're a pervert. You tried to wake me up so I wouldn't catch a cold, didn't you?"

"U-um, maybe…" Saburou replied sheepishly.

The girl had both taken him off guard and known exactly what he was up to. The shock of it all made his tongue and entire body feel rusty.

"Hmm…" The girl studied him, nodding perceptively.

Saburou, meanwhile, felt extremely uncomfortable. Now that the girl was awake, she was ten times more beautiful than he imagined, emanating vitality and youthful charm. Just having her eyes fixed on him made him squirm in place. She wasn't only beautiful; she also had the kind of gaze that seemed to pierce bone.

She wasn't exactly a mind reader who could see into the depths of his heart. She just had eyes that seemed to be analyzing Saburou's mannerisms, strengths and techniques, all in one glance. Saburou suddenly had a light bulb moment.

Is this girl who I think she is? he wondered.

"Excuse me." He spoke up.

"What is it?"

"Are you Erika Chiba?"

The girl's eyes went wide for a moment before an amused smile twisted her mouth.

"So you've heard of me. And you are?"

"Oh, sorry!" Saburou reflexively straightened, not because Erika was older than him, but because his body told him to.

"My name is Saburou Yaguruma. I'm a freshman in Class G."

"A freshman, huh?" she replied. "You guessed it—I'm Erika Chiba. If you know me, that means you must do *kenjutsu*. Let me guess. Your forte is short weapons, like knives."

Saburou was more impressed than alarmed by Erika's accuracy. Her ability to recognize his techniques with a single glance definitely made her better than his fighting instructor. But given his familiarity with Erika's reputation, this was nothing surprising.

"You've seen right through me," he said stiffly. "That's correct. I practice the art of self-defense and specialize in short weapons, such as collapsible knives and traditional *jitte* blades."

Erika grimaced uncomfortably. "You're a pretty stiff guy. The way you speak is enough to make my neck ache."

"I'm…sorry."

"You don't have to be so polite around me," Erika said. "Where's that rough speech you always use? Just be yourself."

"How did you know about that?" Saburou wondered aloud.

This was actually just one of Erika's wild guesses, but she didn't say so, mostly because she was focused on asking the next question: "And another thing. You don't look like you specialize in self-defense. It might be called 'self-defense,' but you only defend people other than yourself. What you practice is a concealment technique, becoming a shield for your master. Am I wrong?"

"How did you know about that?" Saburou repeated. The first time, he was just surprised. Now he was filled with perplexed disbelief.

Erika, on the other hand, frowned for a moment at Saburou's answer but quickly shrugged it off. She explained, "I teach the same technique to students."

Saburou's eyes suddenly lit up—flared, even—with excitement. "If it's not too much to ask, could you be my instructor?"

The insatiable hunger in his eyes made Erika sit up. This suddenly straighter posture instilled a renewed sense of elegance that put Saburou on guard.

"What do you want me to teach you?" Erika asked.

Saburou finally managed to untangle his tongue. Now the only thing preventing him from speaking was a stress-induced thirst. He swallowed a mouthful of saliva to quench his parched throat and mustered up an answer: "How to be strong."

"Why do you want to be strong?" Erika pressed.

Saburou tried to swallow again, with a throat that was getting drier by the second. When he opened his mouth to speak, his voice was painfully raspy. "I want to protect someone with my own two hands."

"With your own two hands, huh?" Erika closed her eyes, her mouth twisting wryly. "I like your spunk."

Her eyes popped open, and she flashed an amused grin. "All right. I'll teach you."

She hopped off the bench, headed for the rooftop entrance, then swiftly turned her head back at a flustered Saburou. "Come on."

Erika led the way to the second small gym—aka the arena—which featured a raised wooden platform at its center. The *kenjutsu* and kendo teams were practicing there together.

"Let's see…" Erika glanced around. "Aha, there he is! Aizu!"

Her expression brightened when she found the person she was looking for in a corner of the room. She bowed to him, stepped onto the wooden platform, and strode toward him along the outer rim to avoid interrupting the team practice. Following her lead, Saburou bowed and trailed behind Erika in the same polite way.

"Hey, Chiba," Aizu greeted. This was the *kenjutsu* team's captain, Ikuo Aizu. He turned only his head toward Erika—acknowledging her with his eyes—before turning back to the *kenjutsu* practice.

"Mind if we take up a smidge of your space?" Erika petitioned. "A corner would be enough."

"That's fine," Aizu answered. "But could you join our team first? The disciplinary committee and school admins get on our case whenever an outsider comes around and someone gets hurt, and I'm getting sick of covering it up."

"You don't have to cover it up," Erika teased.

"That's what you think." Aizu sighed. "We, on the other hand, have a reputation to keep."

"Yeah, yeah. Save your sob stories for later." Erika waved at the air before revealing the boy behind her. "I brought someone to join your team."

"What?" Saburou's eyes widened with surprise.

Aizu looked at him incredulously. "He doesn't seem very excited about it."

"That's not—" Saburou panicked.

"Is there any other club you want to join, Yaguruma?" Erika pushed.

"No." Saburou fumbled to find words. "But I have work at home, so—"

This wasn't an excuse. He may have been rejected as Shiina's bodyguard, but he was still a Mitsuya servant. It was more than possible to get assignments he couldn't mention in public.

"That's not a problem," Aizu said. "Yaguruma, was it? Are you a new student?"

"Y-yes."

"A lot of our *kenjutsu* members juggle team practice with housework. We don't mind if you miss a few days of practice as long as you let us know in advance."

Saburou squirmed in place. Now it felt like he *had* to join the team.

As if sensing his discomfort, Aizu assured him, "Don't worry. I won't force you to make any immediate decisions or join the team at all. I'm sure Chiba brought you here without any explanations. Take all the time you need."

"Thank you..." Saburou was relieved the team captain was a rational guy.

But this relief was short-lived. A voice suddenly interjected from behind: "Aizu! You're way too nice!"

This voice didn't belong to Erika, but it was very nearby. Saburou whipped around to find a petite girl in a kendo uniform had sneaked up on him unawares. The girl tilted her head in confusion at his surprise. She didn't seem to have any malice or hostility toward him. Maybe that's why he didn't notice her approach. Chalking it up to his own carelessness, he ground his teeth in frustration. The girl briefly scrutinized him before turning to Aizu.

"How can you call yourself our captain when you let potential members slip through your fingers?" she accused in a tone of voice a little too young for a high school student.

"But, Saitou…" Aizu retorted. "It's not like I can force the kid to stay."

The girl was Yayoi Saitou—the *kenjutsu* team's second-in-command and captain of the female team. She shook her finger at Aizu in an accusatory way.

"You silly boy!" Yayoi chided. "You really don't get it."

Erika rolled her eyes. "What a pain in the—"

"I can hear you, Erika!" Yayoi interrupted Erika's reproach before whirling back to the *kenjutsu* team's captain. "Anyway, Aizu. You don't have to force him to do anything. Just ask him to join! Give 'em the captain's passionate invitation, and it's hook, line, and sinker!"

"Are you sure that actually works?" Aizu asked skeptically.

"Absolutely!" Yayoi asserted before whipping back to Saburou. He tried to retreat a step, but a wall was in his way. Yayoi pressed forward. "All right, rookie! Uh, what's your name?"

"Yaguruma."

"Okay. Yaguruma." She grabbed his hand, and he didn't stop her. Saburou was more than overwhelmed by now.

Yayoi's eyes widened with joy. "Ooh, you seem promising! We'd love to have you join us."

This girl was honestly more than Saburou could handle. He would have easily pulled away from her grip and run away if she were an enemy. But not only was she his senior—she also didn't mean any harm. He wasn't about to do something that could hurt her.

Erika stepped between the two, easily swatting Yayoi's hands away with a single sweep. "You know the rules. No soliciting new club members until the day after tomorrow."

For a second, Saburou didn't know what had happened. But Yayoi paid no mind to Erika's high-level move. She narrowed her eyes. "Like you can talk. When's the last time you cared about rules?"

"Say whatever you want," Erika replied. "I've come here to practice *kenjutsu* with Yaguruma. You can save your complaints and invitations for another day."

Yayoi scowled like a small child. "Practice *kenjutsu*? Aren't you on the tennis team? If you have time to hang out with freshmen, why don't you fight me instead?"

"Aizu already gave me permission," Erika retorted.

Yayoi whirled on Aizu, who just shrugged. It was much too late to question Erika's presence around the *kenjutsu* team at this point.

"Besides," Erika added calmly, "Yaguruma and I aren't just hanging out."

The sound of her voice sent a chill down Saburou's spine. A grim look passed over Yayoi's face.

Aizu sighed, a wrinkle in his brow. "Just avoid sending him to the hospital."

"You never know," Erika said. "I might be the one who needs an ambulance."

Saburou suddenly felt all eyes on him. He didn't know why they were staring, but he felt like he needed to deny whatever it was. He violently shook his head.

"Come on, Yaguruma. It's time to get ready." Erika pulled off her socks and walked barefoot to an open corner of the gym. Then she lifted a bamboo sword off the wall and gripped it in both hands. Saburou quickly followed suit, choosing a bamboo sword about half the usual length. This was still too long for him, but he figured he shouldn't go all out anyway. Even with someone as strong as Erika.

"Aren't you going to take off your blazer?" she asked, facing Saburou with her sword.

"Things might get a little crazy if I do that," he replied. "But what about you? Are you okay fighting in that skirt?" He didn't mean this in a demeaning way; he was completely serious. The girls' uniforms for First High—in fact, all the magic high schools—consisted of dresses that clung to the knees, and they weren't easy to move around in. But Saburou's concern fell on deaf ears.

"Aw, you must be pretty confident if you have time to worry about me," Erika said quietly, as if speaking to herself. An instant later, she disappeared. At least, that's what it looked like to Saburou. He couldn't read her preliminary movements, so his mind couldn't keep up.

Suddenly, he heard her voice on the left: "Over here."

He hastily raised his sword into the air, and it received a powerful jolt. In a matter of seconds, he locked his joints, hoping to push back.

He heard Erika's voice again: "That's not very nice." Before he could react, a sudden burning sensation ran across Saburou's back, and he fell to his knees.

"That's a high-level skill," Erika commented, "but are you sure it's your style?"

Enduring the pain, Saburou whipped around and found Erika looking down on him with her bamboo sword over one shoulder.

"Game over?" she asked.

"Not yet!" he yelled.

The pain in his back was quickly beginning to fade. Saburou realized Erika must have hit him in a way that caused only pain, not injury. He had experienced something similar during the Mitsuya clan's training camp. If this were a serious fight, he would have been knocked out cold with that single blow. In fact, there was a good chance he would have died.

Then again… Saburou thought. *In this battle, we're only using bamboo swords. It's pointless to think about what would have happened in a real fight. What's important is I can still fight!*

Rather than standing straight up, Saburou jumped directly at Erika from a crouched stance.

"Did he just leap?!" someone exclaimed.

Then someone else: "No, that's—!"

The circle of *kenjutsu* team spectators that had formed around them at some point started to buzz. Then almost simultaneously:

"A leap spell?"

"But there was no sign of magic being activated!"

Their eyes were sharp enough to analyze that magic had not been used.

Sure enough, Saburou leaped toward Erika using a physical-enhancement technique that didn't involve magic. Instead of attacking from above, he flew almost parallel with the floor, aiming for Erika's legs from below. It was a surprise attack on a part of the body rarely targeted in kendo or *kenjutsu*.

But Erika easily smacked him away. Literally. She used the entirety of her short bamboo sword to knock Saburou to the floor. The strike had so much force, it was a mystery how her slender arms could pack such a punch. To clarify, her bamboo sword didn't hit Saburou's body. She just took a big step to avoid his lunge and swatted the top of Saburou's bamboo sword, which had been aimed at her torso.

The impact spread down his arms and through his chest. It was thanks to pure willpower that he didn't drop his sword as he dove to the floor. While there was pain, he received no direct damage from the strike. He tried to quickly get his feet under him and prepare to continue the fight. But just as he looked up, he heard a bamboo sword thrust toward the floor at his side. It was a quiet sound, but its meaning was clear.

"...I give up."

Saburou stopped trying to rise, announcing his own defeat with his eyes to the ground. Erika pulled back her sword, and Saburou stood up with a single bow.

"That movement skill was pretty good," Erika said from above him.

Saburou looked up and met her gaze. She continued: "But it doesn't work in a fight."

These were harsh words. But Saburou neither dismissed nor challenged them. He had asked Erika for instruction because he knew the opportunity to receive advice from someone stronger than himself was valuable. In an actual battle, there was no guarantee he would live to face a stronger opponent again.

"Geez." Erika sighed. "You really don't get it, do you? That was just a practice match."

Her tone was noticeably more relaxed. Saburou felt it was a lot more comfortable when she talked this way.

"Sure, it's important to take each battle seriously," Erika explained. "But it's also important to recognize when it's okay to lose."

"Are you saying I was trying too hard to win?" Saburou asked.

"You were trying too hard to fight."

Saburou was smart enough to know what Erika meant. His leap skill was an all-in kind of attack—the type that staked the attacker's own life against an enemy with the upper hand. Now that he thought about it, it wasn't the kind of technique used in a training match, where the point was to learn from losses and mistakes.

Erika went on. "Even if this had been a real battle, that last attack cost you points. You didn't make the most of your physical abilities at all."

"I'm sorry." Saburou hung his head.

"You don't need to apologize to me."

Saburou knew this was true, but he still felt the need to ask for forgiveness.

I should leave, Saburou thought. At this point, there was little to be gained from sticking around. He had only been made aware of his own weakness. He wasn't bold enough to ask for another lesson after such a pathetic display.

But just as he was about to apologize again, Erika spoke. "But I have to say. You show promise."

"What?" He didn't understand.

"If you ask me," Erika said, "I'd say you have some serious hidden potential. Depending on how it pans out, I know you could become stronger."

The words *you're wrong* balanced dangerously on the tip of Saburou's tongue. But he stopped himself from saying them. He knew he had abilities that no normal magician could use. Then again, they were low in power and only practical for surprise attacks or assassinations. They couldn't be used to protect. That's why he washed his hands of those abilities and focused on polishing his martial arts.

Erika looked straight at him. "Don't you want to become stronger?"

Saburou couldn't resist the words that cut so deep. Their sweet temptation melted away his stubborn self-doubt.

"Hey, Aizu." Erika called out to the *kenjutsu* team's captain. "Could you help Yaguruma practice? I'll swing by to check up on him now and then."

"If he joins the *kenjutsu* team, I'd be happy to help," Aizu replied. "But this is rare, Chiba. It's not every day you show interest in taking someone under your wing."

"I would say I'm only doing this on a whim, but it's more like a change of heart. Let's just say there's someone I want to get back at."

"I feel bad for whoever that is." Aizu didn't understand how training a new student would help Erika get back at this mystery opponent, but he convinced himself that Erika was Erika. He then turned to Saburou with an empathetic look.

"Yaguruma, team recruits don't begin until a week from the day after next. But that rule doesn't apply to students who want to directly join a team of their own volition. If you say you want to join the *kenjutsu* club, we'd be happy to have you."

"Can I talk to my household about it first?" Saburou used this excuse to avoid giving an immediate answer. He hadn't been expecting all this to happen when he met Erika on the rooftop a few hours ago. It wasn't that he really intended to talk to anyone in particular; he just wanted some time to think on it.

"Sure. We'll just say you're a potential member for now," Aizu replied good-naturedly.

Erika, on the other hand, had no patience for Saburou's hesitation. "Have Aizu teach you what he knows. At this point, I'm willing to bet you'll learn a lot more from him than from me."

Saburou couldn't deny the truth in her words.

"Anyway," Erika continued, "I'm done for today."

"Hold on, Erika!" Yayoi spoke up. "What about our battle?"

But Erika had already spun around, headed toward the door. "Next time."

"Really? You mean it?" Yayoi squealed excitedly. "You better keep your word!"

Without turning back, Erika lazily waved her hand and left the small gym.

Unbeknownst to Erika, she was considered the second or third most beautiful girl at First High. She didn't make first place because there was another girl in a class of her own.

Naturally, Erika's movements were monitored, mostly by the male student body. Rumors of Erika calling dibs on a freshman boy quickly circulated First High before the day was over. It even came up over the dinner table at the Shiba household that night.

"Tatsuya, did you hear what Erika did?" Miyuki asked.

"You mean the rumor about her training Yaguruma in the second small gym? The *kenjutsu* team's captain, Aizu, claimed it wasn't head-hunting."

"Already? He's so cautious."

Aizu had never been selected as a player for the Nine School Competition because of the quirks in his specialty magic. But his skill with the bamboo sword was well-known—he was always one of the top performers in *kenjutsu* tournaments. Naturally, he and Tatsuya knew each other. Tatsuya even talked with him fairly regularly because of their mutual connections with Erika.

Tatsuya sighed empathetically. "Yeah. He would be able to relax if the vice captain helped out more."

Miyuki giggled. As student council members, both Tatsuya and Miyuki were familiar with Yayoi Saitou. They didn't interact with her much, but they knew she regularly made trouble for the disciplinary committee. At least she didn't break any serious school rules.

"It's rare for Erika to find someone she likes," Miyuki commented.

Tatsuya agreed. He also doubted her interest was just surface-level. "She must have sensed something special about Yaguruma."

"Something special?" Miyuki asked. "What do you think?"

She knew her brother had been the one to catch Yaguruma casting unauthorized magic. If Yaguruma had some outstanding potential, Tatsuya would have been able to sense it then with his ability.

"He was well trained," he replied. "But aside from his telekinesis, his abilities weren't anything to write home about."

"Yaguruma has telekinesis?" Miyuki probed.

"Mm-hmm," Tatsuya affirmed. "One part of his magic-calculation region is occupied by movement-type magic that he controls himself. It's no wonder he finds it difficult to use other magic. As someone with the same handicap, I can't help but empathize."

"But it's just one part, right?" Miyuki asked.

"As far as I could tell."

"That doesn't sound nearly as difficult as having it fully occupied like you." Miyuki said this, but the amount of space occupied didn't change how much it painfully limited the user's powers. Then again, Tatsuya didn't want to say anything when his sister was looking at him with such compassion.

"I guess," he conceded.

"Now I'm really curious why Chiba showed interest in Yaguruma," Minami interjected. She didn't usually interrupt the siblings' conversations. This time, it was definitely to distract Miyuki from Tatsuya's deflection.

"Telekinesis can be a powerful weapon when combined with traditional martial arts," Tatsuya offered. "It's like having one more invisible hand in close combat."

Miyuki didn't seem to understand right away, but Minami had gone through harrowing Yotsuba clan training and knew how useful an extra hand could be.

Tatsuya continued. "I don't know how aware Erika is of Yaguruma's telekinesis. But I'm sure she can instinctively sense it in her own way. That's why she wants to train him."

Understanding this much, Miyuki nodded. She knew how often Erika based her judgments on instinct.

A bell rang just as the conversation reached a stopping point. But it wasn't the doorbell or a phone. It was the bell to notify the arrival of a package or letter.

"I'll go see what it is." Minami stood up from her chair before Miyuki could stop her. Miyuki and Tatsuya put down their eating utensils until Minami returned.

"You got a letter," Minami announced. "Addressed to both of you."

Many experts had predicted letters would disappear with the advancement of electronic networks. But this ended up not being the case. What they didn't expect was logistics networks advancing at the same—or even higher—rate as the electronic networks. Now domestic mail could be delivered within twenty-four hours in Japan. And now that it was all automated, labor costs were not as high as in the past. Both in terms of speed and cost, the postal system remained at a high enough level to be of practical use. That helped it survive as an active service, if only as a formality.

"Who is it from?" Tatsuya asked.

Minami flipped over the letter. For the sake of Tatsuya and Miyuki's privacy, she hadn't initially looked at the sender.

"A Mr. Juumonji."

"As in Katsuto Juumonji?" Miyuki asked in surprise. Minami held out the letter to make it easier to see, but Miyuki motioned with her eyes to Tatsuya. Without the slightest hint of disappointment, Minami handed over the envelope and a letter opener.

It was still dinnertime, so Tatsuya wasn't sure if he should open the letter right away. But the looks of anticipation on Minami's and Miyuki's faces forced his hand. He slid the letter opener under the envelope flap and sliced it open.

The letter wasn't that long. Tatsuya skimmed it quickly, then announced, "It's an invitation to a meeting discussing countermeasures against anti-magician movements."

"Why is he sending this to us and not Aunt Maya?" Miyuki posed a fair question.

"It looks like a meeting for just the young members of the Twenty-Eight Families. Juumonji says he eventually wants to include youth from the Numbers and the Hundred Families, too."

"I hate to sound rude," Miyuki commented, "but this scheme doesn't sound like Juumonji at all."

Her use of the word *scheme* brought a grim smile to Tatsuya's lips. She had clearly been poisoned by one too many conspiracies.

"I don't think he's necessarily planning anything bad," Tatsuya ventured. "Maybe he genuinely wants to create a space for sharing opinions."

Miyuki blushed at her brother calling her out on her negative judgments.

"Y-you're right," she conceded. "Juumonji must be trying to create a community for the next generation of magicians."

"Then again, I doubt this 'scheme' was entirely his idea."

"Tatsuya..." For a second, Miyuki thought her brother was teasing her. But then she realized what he meant. "Wait... You think Juumonji might not be working alone?"

"Right. In fact, I agree—this invitation doesn't sound like Juumonji at all." Tatsuya sounded confident, despite his soft tone.

"Then who else could be behind this?"

"It sounds like something the Saegusa would cook up. But it's not sophisticated enough to have come from Kouichi himself." Tatsuya showed a surprising lack of qualms in speaking frankly about a man his own father's age. It was probably because Kouichi wasn't in the room. "Well, this is all just a theory. There's no point in speculating about something without any concrete answers."

He handed the invitation to Miyuki to see if she wanted to read it. But she shook her head. Instead, she said, "So? What will you do?"

She was clearly more interested in Tatsuya's response than the contents of the letter.

"I'll go to the meeting." His response was immediate.

"By yourself?" Miyuki asked.

"It's better if you don't come with me." Tatsuya didn't say why, and Miyuki didn't pry.

"All right."

Minami seemed to expect an explanation, but Tatsuya only said, "The meeting is next Sunday at the International Magic Association's east branch building in Yokohama at nine AM. I want you to stay at home that day, Miyuki; Minami, I'm counting on you to protect her."

The two girls didn't put up a fight.

"All right." They nodded in complete unison.

The Shiba family weren't the only ones Katsuto had sent an invitation. Since ground mail physically had to travel from place to place, the invitation was delivered at different rates. But the Mitsuya family in Tokyo received it at about the same time as Tatsuya did.

Shiina Mitsuya had little to do with this invitation. She had six older sisters and brothers, so she was rarely involved in public interactions among the Twenty-Eight Families. Her oldest sister and three older brothers were the ones who took it upon themselves to quickly discuss how to respond to the situation. Shiina wasn't even included in this discussion.

She was the youngest of all her siblings—by a lot. Even her triplet siblings, the closest to her in age, were an entire eight years older. Shiina was used to being treated like the baby at times like this. But this time, she felt less alienated since she wasn't the only one left out.

After dinner, Shiina was enjoying some free time in her room—more specifically, enjoying the chance to just lay around—when she decided to practice magic.

The Mitsuya family's mansion was a fair distance from the still-active Magician Development Institute Three—a place equipped with magic training facilities. It didn't include any experimental facilities, but the range of training equipment was as good as any magic high school. By car, it was a quick drive to the institute, but since it was already late, Shiina decided to head for her family's training grounds instead.

Needless to say, these training grounds were used only by those who lived in the Mitsuya mansion, and family members had priority. Not wanting to get in their employers' way, most servants went all the way to Institute Three whenever they trained. As a result, there were quite a few hours when no one was using the mansion's training grounds. Shiina often thought it a waste to leave such a splendid facility unused. This night, though, there was a visitor.

"Saburou? What are you doing here?"

Saburou froze, standing on the mats. He barely glanced at Shiina before saying, "What does it look like I'm doing?" And he immediately continued what seemed to be an enigmatic exercise to Shiina's eyes.

Saburou kicked his leg into the air, immediately falling back-first onto the mats. Then he quickly got to his feet, did a flip in the air, and fell flat on his stomach. He groaned with each fall, so there was no doubt it hurt.

Shiina immediately conceded. "I have no idea." She didn't even want to guess what her childhood friend was trying to do.

Saburou lifted himself up. Sitting with his legs outstretched on the mats, he looked up at Shiina. "I'm practicing being thrown. I thought you would know that, since you did aikido."

"That was back in elementary school," Shiina said in her own defense.

It was true she had practiced aikido, but only until the age of ten. Back then, she was able to endure the pain without having to cover her ears. It was impossible to do martial arts now that she wore earmuffs.

"But, Saburou," she continued, "you weren't falling very safely." Even if she had nearly no experience in martial arts, she learned enough from watching her older brother and Saburou practice.

Saburou didn't deny it, but he did say, "There's no guarantee your opponent will let you fall safely. I'm studying how to fall with the least damage possible, using these soft mats to practice."

"What brought this on?" Shiina asked, sighing.

Annoyance suddenly crossed Saburou's face. "Aizu, the *kenjutsu* team's captain, let me train with his team," he explained. "But he threw me to the ground so many times, I didn't even have time to counter."

Despite the irritation on his face, Shiina thought he sounded almost happy.

"My martial arts teacher always told us being thrown is much more painful than being punched or kicked outdoors," he continued. "I really understood that today."

"This is *kenjutsu*, right?" Shiina murmured, perplexed.

Saburou understood her confusion. Team members usually didn't throw each other in *kenjutsu*, a typically sword-centered martial art.

He quickly elaborated: "Among all the sword-fighting techniques, *iaijutsu*—the art of drawing the sword—derives the largest number of techniques from advanced jujutsu. Plus, Sekiguchi-ryu—one of the Kishu Tokugawa family's five schools—is a combination of jujutsu, *kenjutsu*, and *iaijutsu*, so it's not surprising that the *kenjutsu* team is well-versed in throwing techniques. Especially since Aizu seems to be skilled in *iaijutsu*."

This enthusiastic description was meant for Shiina's benefit, but she unfortunately didn't seem very interested. She would have been satisfied with the simple answer that throwing techniques weren't a rare skill for *kenjutsu* teams. So while her childhood friend was talking, Shiina's mind was somewhere else.

Once he finished, she called his name: "Saburou?"

"Huh? What's up?" Shiina struggled to put her question into words. She started to fidget, and Saburou gave her a puzzled look.

"Is it something hard to say? You know you can talk to me about anything, Shiina."

Encouraged by Saburou's words, Shiina took a deep breath and spoke. "Is it true you hit on Chiba and had a training date in the small gym?"

"What?" Saburou probably would have slid out of his chair if he hadn't already been sitting on the ground. "H-hold on! Where the heck did you hear that? Weren't you in the student council room for the rest of the day after classes ended?"

"I was." Shiina nodded and easily revealed the responsible party's names. "Kasumi and Izumi were talking about it."

"Those crafty devils…" Saburou muttered. He knew the Saegusa twins through Shiina. The thought of their identical smiles on their melon-like faces gave him a headache.

"Don't call them that," Shiina chastised. "Like it or not, they're older than you."

Saburou wanted to yell about how the twins had fooled her. But he couldn't bring himself to say it. He knew how Shiina thought of Izumi and Kasumi as sisters, especially because they were much closer in age than her real older siblings.

Instead, he calmed himself and mounted a defense. "…Anyway, whatever they told you isn't true."

Unfortunately, this wasn't enough to convince Shiina.

"But you *did* train in the second small gym, right?" she asked.

"…I wouldn't call it training." Saburou defended himself. "It was more of a spar. As I said before, I only started training with Aizu." With his eyes to the floor, he reeked of guilt. No one would have believed him with the way he spoke.

"Is it true you were with Chiba, then?" Shiina pressed.

"…Yes," Saburou admitted.

"I heard you walked into the second small gym together."

"That's true, too, but—" Realizing it was ridiculous to look away, Saburou suddenly made direct eye contact with Shiina, ardently denying the unscrupulous rumors. "But it definitely wasn't a date!"

Shiina forlornly forced a smile and said, "Don't get me wrong. I'm not against the two of you going out at all. It may be a bit fast, but if you take all the right steps, a two-year age gap isn't an issue."

"I'm telling you—*you're* the one who's got it all wrong," Saburou insisted. He was overwhelmed with an exasperating desire to stomp off in a huff. But he was afraid he would regret it if he gave up now. Though he wasn't exactly sure what he would regret, the feeling was enough to make him stay.

Shiina's eyes began to wander nervously. "Then explain to me why you ended up going to the small gym with Chiba. When did you even meet each other?"

Saburou suddenly tensed, despite himself. "...On the rooftop. Completely by chance."

"So you met by chance, and she immediately invited you to train?" Shiina asked.

"That's not..." Saburou sounded like an unfaithful boy making up excuses to his girlfriend. But neither he nor Shiina realized this.

"That sounds completely unlike the Chiba I've heard about." Shiina didn't know Erika personally—or rather, she didn't pay her much mind. But after the Yokohama Incident, Erika Chiba made a name for herself apart from the Chiba family, and that reputation had spread far and wide.

The National Defense Force and security forces with access to the details of the incident spoke highly of Erika literally crushing a unit of mechanized infantry with a giant sword. Her bravery, coupled with the fact that she was a daughter of the Chiba family, earned her high prestige.

On the other hand, the Chiba family—including Jouichirou, the family head—were reluctant to promote Erika's name. In fact, they even seemed to be trying to hide her. This gave rise to her moniker as the Chiba's "secret weapon" and "mythical sword princess," which were only half jokes.

The Ten Master Clans also knew more about the Yokohama Incident than the general public. Gen Mitsuya, who doted on his youngest daughter, as most fathers do, told Shiina all about Erika as part of the background knowledge he deemed necessary for her to know before entering First High. Saburou had listened to this story with her, no doubt hoping to aid the seemingly unreliable Shiina. In fact, Shiina helped Saburou more often than the other way around.

Shiina's source of information wasn't always her father or the Saegusa twins. Mayumi would sometimes fill her in on things, too. Since Mayumi was best friends with Shiina's big sister, she made a point to spoil Shiina.

Shiina's acquaintances were also not limited to the Ten Master Clans; they extended into the Hundred Families. On top of that, Shiina had groups of Numbers girls who—although too informal to call her a part of their social circles—provided even more information than her father through chat groups.

From what she had heard about Erika's personality, the older girl didn't seem the type who went out of her way to reach out to a lowerclassman. In general, Erika was someone who pretended to casually mind her own business, but when asked to do something, couldn't say no.

"I asked her to train me," Saburou admitted.

Shiina threw him a cold look, as if she knew it all along.

"But I wasn't hitting on her, I swear!" Saburou insisted. "I honestly just wanted her guidance, knowing how strong she is."

"Chiba is a pretty girl. Wouldn't you agree?" Shiina tested him.

"Well, yeah… But that's a completely different story!" No matter how much Saburou made excuses, his childhood friend continued to give him a cold stare.

Even after advancing to his third year of magic high school, Tatsuya continued to visit Yakumo's temple every morning whenever possible. When he first entered high school, he would lose every battle Yakumo challenged him to. But now his success rate was 50 percent.

That wasn't to say that Tatsuya believed his abilities were on par with Yakumo's. They each had their different strengths. Tatsuya did feel his abilities weren't too far behind Yakumo's in terms of routine skills like intelligence gathering, infiltration, and single combat. But this was only the case in a structured type of battle. In a fight to the death, Tatsuya may come out on top, but he would lose a lot in the process. There was no point to winning by simply killing his opponent.

That said, Tatsuya didn't visit Yakumo with the expectation of learning techniques that taught him the meaning of fighting. He was less Yakumo's disciple and more a training partner. Yakumo had been training him thus far only because Tatsuya was the weaker fighter. Once their fighting skills were on par, they finally became training partners who could benefit from each other.

After losing the last match of the morning, Tatsuya said goodbye and was about to head home. But before he could leave, Yakumo called out to him: "Wait a minute, Tatsuya."

"What is it?" Just as Tatsuya spoke, the air around him seemed to change. And the change wasn't metaphorical. A wall of air had formed around Tatsuya and Yakumo, impenetrable by sound.

A soundproof boundary… This is different than the activation sequence I'm familiar with, Tatsuya thought. He was filled with a sudden urge to analyze the program when Yakumo interrupted his thoughts.

"You got the invitation from Juumonji, right?" he said. "Which of you is going to attend?"

"So you already know," Tatsuya muttered. He had only received the invitation the night before. Barely half a day had passed. At the same time, he knew how good Yakumo's information networks were, so he wasn't surprised. He just shook his head in amazement.

"Of course I know," Yakumo replied with a delighted grin. "I'm a ninja."

This explained nothing, but Tatsuya didn't bother putting effort into asking questions he knew would be a waste of time.

Instead, he answered Yakumo's original question. "I haven't confirmed with the main family yet, but I'm planning on going alone."

"I see. That's probably for the best." Yakumo seemed strangely satisfied.

"Do you sense trouble brewing?" Tatsuya asked.

"As of this moment, nothing that would cause any direct harm." Clearly, there was something on his radar.

"Are you saying there's someone planning an indirect attack?" Tatsuya knew Yakumo wouldn't give him any answers, but he at least decided to try.

"I don't think there will be any attack," Yakumo replied.

"I see." Tatsuya felt as if he somehow understood what Yakumo was trying to say. But wary of the risk of being wrong, he decided not to voice his baseless speculations.

Then Yakumo added, "If anything dangerous were to happen, it would be after the meeting."

"Thank you for letting me know. I'll be careful."

Tatsuya was indifferent about anything that might attack him personally. What worried him was the possible need to call for the Yotsuba family's support to strengthen the security around Miyuki.

"Tatsuya, I suggest you don't take the situation lightly," Yakumo added abruptly, caution in his voice. "The monster we call society may not have fangs and claws, but it can easily devour a person or two."

Tatsuya felt like a bucket of ice water had just been poured over his head. Unsure what Yakumo really meant, he answered almost mechanically.

"I'll keep that in mind."

Maya Yotsuba's mornings didn't start particularly early. Thanks to the modern popularity of flexible hours and work-from-home policies, even office workers no longer had to get up at ridiculous hours.

Still, compared with the average office worker, Maya had fairly easy mornings.

This particular morning, she woke up at a leisurely 8:30 AM and was finished with breakfast about an hour later. Right when she was done, Hayama spoke behind her in a reverent tone.

"Ma'am. You have a video message from Tatsuya."

"Really? At this hour?" Maya inquired, eyes wide.

Needless to say, Hayama respectfully refrained from telling her it wasn't early at all.

"It arrived last night after you went to sleep, ma'am."

"I take it that means it's not that urgent, then."

"That's correct. Master Tatsuya said it could wait until this morning." Hayama's answer piqued Maya's interest.

"All right. I'll watch it here."

Hayama retreated into a corner of the room and signaled to the maids. A veteran waiter cleared the breakfast dishes while a younger maid set up a screen in front of Maya. Once everything was ready, the maids lined up and bowed. Maya nodded, a signal for Hayama to order the maids to leave. He then went around the room, locking all the doors and flipping a switch to lower a set of soundproof walls. Finally, he inserted the memory card with Tatsuya's decoded message into a wireless playback machine.

The video was a brief three minutes. Once it was over, a giggle escaped Maya's lips.

"So Tatsuya feels he has to ask my permission for the most trivial thing. How surprisingly adorable." She glanced at Hayama for affirmation.

But instead he said, "You seem pleased, ma'am."

"I guess I am," she conceded. "At the same time, I meant to give him more freedom when I accepted him as my son. Maybe he didn't understand that."

Anyone could tell she wasn't being sincere from the way she slightly tilted her head.

"I'm sure Master Tatsuya is simply adhering to the mindset expected of a member of the Yotsuba clan," Hayama offered.

"I guess you could say that," Maya responded coldly. She seemed to be annoyed about Hayama not agreeing with her joke this morning.

"By the way, ma'am," Hayama continued. "How would you like to respond to Tatsuya's request?"

"I'll accept it, of course," Maya replied, referring to allowing Tatsuya to attend Katsuto's meeting. "He has that discretion as my son."

"Then I will tell him."

"Oh, and let him know he doesn't need to ask my permission for matters of this caliber in the future," Maya added dismissively.

"Yes, ma'am." Hayama bowed compliantly.

The letter from the head of the Juumonji family arrived at the Kudou house just before noon the day after Tatsuya received his. Minoru Kudou stared blankly at his brothers fussing over the unexpected invitation, as if he were mindlessly watching TV.

Today was a weekday, and school had already begun. But Minoru had been running a fever since last night and decided to take the day off. He was the vice president of Second High's student council. His sudden illness was clearly from the exhaustion of organizing the entrance ceremony.

Minoru felt ashamed about being absent at the beginning of the new term, especially given his position on the student council. He was never told why his body was so weak and knew it was no one's fault, not even his own. Since he didn't know why he was born so frail, he didn't resent anyone for it. He couldn't even hold a grudge.

But precisely because he couldn't shift the blame on others, Minoru couldn't help blaming himself, deep down. His magic abilities were at a level worthy of the Ten Master Clans, but he couldn't cast magic often because his weak constitution caused him to fall asleep at the slightest effort. To Minoru, this was worse than not having high-level magic at all.

The Kudou family's falling from the Ten Master Clans' ranks also added to his low self-esteem. Of course, Minoru had nothing to do with his family's loss of status. He wasn't responsible in any way. But he sometimes wondered if he could have saved his family's status if he had been named heir and played an active role in major events, like the Nine School Competition. So he simultaneously hated himself and unintentionally looked down on his older siblings. He saw his grandfather Retsu Kudou, his cousin Kyouko Fujibayashi, his older brother, his older sister, and even his own father as people with magic abilities clearly inferior to his own.

Kyouko Fujibayashi—who he adored like his own sister—was supposedly searching for a cure for his ailment, but no progress had been made to date. As things stood, Minoru wasn't allowed to participate in any important discussions that may affect the future of the Kudou family, and he wasn't even taken seriously by his older siblings, who possessed only mediocre magic abilities.

Before he knew it, the despair of being excluded from important family matters began to eat away at him.

Before asking for his opinion at all, the head of the Juumonji family proposed that Minoru's older brother by seven years attend the meeting instead of Minoru himself.

So he wondered why all his brothers were in this place now. His older brothers were supposed to be at work, and his two older sisters were already married with children. Normally, he would be the only one in the house.

What am I even doing here, then? Minoru thought absentmindedly, before remembering he was eating. He had told a servant he felt well enough to have lunch in the dining room, and when he got there, he found his siblings gathered around.

In front of each of them was an elaborate and vibrant dish. In contrast, Minoru's meal was a bland porridge seasoned with a heaping portion of supplements. Minoru had already finished it, partly because it was such a small serving to begin with. Seeing no need to stay any longer, he stood up to leave.

The scraping noise the chair made as he stood must have drawn his older brother's attention, because he turned to Minoru for the first time.

"Leaving already?" he said.

"How are you feeling?" Minoru's second-eldest sister asked. It was also the first time she had spoken to Minoru all day.

"I'm still a little feverish, so I think I'll rest a while longer," Minoru replied, still standing. This was his way of saying he wanted to leave the room as soon as possible.

"That's too bad," his older brother said. "I was thinking of taking you with me to Tokyo if you were feeling better."

Clearly, he didn't sense how Minoru felt. Minoru had no choice but to stay.

His brother continued. "You know the Yotsuba heiress, right? Once you get your health back, you should rekindle old friendships."

"Yes, that would be nice." With that, Minoru curtly bowed his head, then left the dining room.

His older brother's intentions were obvious. He wanted to get the Yotsuba on the Kudou family's side to regain the power they once had. To this end, he thought Minoru would be useful.

It was a sad attempt, to be sure. But an expected sense of nostalgia swelled inside Minoru. He had met the Yotsuba siblings—now engaged—about half a year ago. There were days when they were each off doing separate activities or when Minoru was sick in bed, so he could only claim to have been together with them for two days at the most. But the memory of those two days shone brightly in Minoru's mind.

He remembered guiding the group through Nara and fighting together against the foreign magician Gongjin Zhou at the foot of Mount Kasuga. Then they walked around Kyoto in search of Gongjin.

During those two days, Minoru was able to be the magician he had always aspired to be. After that, he confronted Gongjin himself and prevented him from escaping, but that wasn't too hard. Gongjin turned out to be a small fry and a piece of cake for Minoru to handle.

He felt embarrassed about ultimately collapsing from his illness and having Minami nurse him back to health at the hotel, but it was a good memory overall. Minoru honestly envied Tatsuya and Miyuki for having friends like Minami.

My brother's expectations aside, wouldn't it be amazing to reunite with Tatsuya, Miyuki, and Minami in Tokyo? Minoru mused. Despite himself, he was beginning to think it would.

Masaki learned about his invitation when he came home from school. The first thing he did was visit his father's sleeping quarters.

"I'm coming in," he announced.

Having fallen into a state of unexplained weakness after a battle, Gouki Ichijou, the head of the Ichijou family, was recuperating at home. He hadn't gone to a hospital because there was no way to treat him there. He had no external injuries, no abnormalities in his bones or internal organs. But that wasn't the only reason he was at home.

"It's good to see you, Masaki," Gouki replied.

Gouki's battle scars prevented him from walking around freely. But he was at least conscious. He spent more time asleep than usual, but he was completely lucid while awake. And it was his wish to recuperate at home.

"Are you sure you should be sitting up, Dad?"

Gouki had pushed a button to make his electric bed rise into a seated position.

"Yes, my arms and legs feel a lot stronger now." Gouki signaled to the servant at his bedside. The servant quickly used a remote control to turn the page of the electronic document his employer was reading.

Gouki had been using his waking hours to command the magicians who served the Ichijou family. Normally, he would have left them to their own devices, but there were signs of an impending invasion threatening the Tohoku and Hokuriku regions. In preparation for this, he decided to issue instructions from his bed.

Masaki overheard the ship that had caused his father's injuries come up in conversation with his servant. He couldn't help but pry. "I thought the New Soviet Union ship disappeared, Dad."

"That ship was of unknown origin," Gouki corrected unnecessarily. "It was never confirmed to be a Soviet ship."

"This is a private conversation, so who cares what I call it? Besides, do you seriously believe it's anything *but* a New Soviet Union ship?"

Gouki paused before replying carefully to his son's first question. "The ship of *unknown origin* is certainly missing. Some believe it may have scuttled itself."

"They're trying to cover their tracks," Masaki mused. "Then when you said you wanted to search for them, you meant pulling up wreckage from the bottom of the ocean?"

"Perhaps," Gouki replied. His answers had been somewhat cryptic since Masaki entered the room. It wasn't so much that he was hiding something, but Masaki got the impression that his father was avoiding definitive statements.

It's almost as if he's worried someone's listening, Masaki thought. That's when he realized his own mistake. He hadn't asked about the suspicious ship out of curiosity, but there was something he should have said first.

"I see," he said, curtly ending his conversation with his father. Then he turned to the third party in the room, bowing respectfully. "Thanks for stopping by to see my father again, Tsukuba."

"Of course. It's such a relief the master of the house is gradually regaining his strength. I guess I wasn't useless after all," Yuuka Tsukuba joked playfully. She was the other reason Gouki decided not to be hospitalized.

When Gouki was brought to the hospital on the day he fell ill, his family was overwhelmed with anxiety. They didn't know the reason for his paralysis, let alone if there was a cure. His daughters, Akane and Ruri, were emotionally unstable, to the point where they sometimes wailed uncontrollably. His wife, Midori, put up a strong front, but it was obvious to bystanders that she was just doing this for her daughters' benefit. Masaki, too, maintained his outward composure, but he had a hard time suppressing the turmoil he felt inside.

To everyone's surprise, it was the Yotsuba family who reached out first. The Ichijou family was alarmed that the Yotsuba knew of Gouki's condition so quickly. But without any other solution in sight, they couldn't help but cling to the hope of a specialist the Yotsuba promised to send.

This specialist was none other than the young woman standing in front of Masaki at this moment—Yuuka Tsukuba. She was a graduate student at the Magic University and had no certification whatsoever in the field of medicine. Magic-calculation regions weren't currently considered an area that required medical treatment. But Yuuka's goal to restore Gouki back to health from his debilitated state clearly involved some kind of treatment.

The decision to allow an unqualified person to treat a patient at the hospital would have caused a myriad of problems. It was much easier for everyone if Gouki received this kind of treatment from the comfort of his home.

"Is my dad…getting better?" Masaki ventured.

Just a couple of days ago, Gouki hadn't even been able to move his head. Even speaking had been a struggle. The day before, he still hadn't been able to sit up in bed. All things considered, the fact he was sitting up now—even if it wasn't on his own—was a huge improvement.

Then again, Masaki had heard of cases where patients started to look better even when their symptoms were getting worse. He couldn't trust his eyes alone.

"He is. There is still much I need to explore in terms of treatment, so I can't say when he will be completely cured. But I can assure you his condition is steadily improving." Then she added with a sweet smile, "Don't worry. He will recover."

"Yes, there's no need to worry, Masaki," Gouki commented. "I can't be laying around forever. I'll regain my strength in no time."

Both Yuuka's and Gouki's promises to recuperate helped calm Masaki's nerves.

"Well, I'd better be going, then," Yuuka said. "I'll stop by again tomorrow."

"I'll see you to the door," Masaki offered.

"That's all right. I appreciate the offer, but I can see myself out." Yuuka bowed briefly to Gouki, then left the room. Gouki's servant followed to see her out.

Now that it was only the two of them, Masaki dropped the polite smile pasted on his face. He turned to his father. "Tell me the truth, Dad."

"About what?" Gouki leaned back on his pillow and looked up at the ceiling. It was clearly still hard for him to sit up. Masaki quickly pressed the switch to lay the bed back into a reclining position.

As the bed whirred downward, Masaki asked, "Do you trust her?"

"She is clearly curing my illness. There's no guarantee of recovery without some sort of treatment. At this point, trusting her is all I can do."

"I guess so…"

Deep down, Masaki wasn't entirely convinced about entrusting his father to a magician who had an introduction from the Yotsuba family. Although everyone called it treatment, what Gouki was ultimately undergoing was a form of mind-altering magic. Even if he were to recover safely from his current paralysis, there was no telling what kind of repercussions the treatment might cause in the future.

"Masaki. Being suspicious of them isn't going to solve anything."

"I know," Masaki said. And he did. Just as his father said, this was a risk they had to take.

Then he added, "As long as we don't have a better solution, we have no choice but to trust what we have." So far, no one else had the slightest clue how to help Gouki recover.

"Exactly," Gouki replied. Then, changing the subject to prevent his son from sinking into a bottomless pit of doubt, he said, "Anyway, Masaki…"

"Yes, Dad?"

"See that envelope over there? It's for you. Go on and open it," Gouki instructed, knowing it wasn't a private letter.

"O…kay." Perplexed by his father's orders and without a good reason to decline, Masaki picked up the letter from the side table.

He glanced at the sender's address on the back of the envelope and immediately grimaced. "It's from Juumonji."

He picked up a nearby letter opener and carefully sliced the flap open. Knowing who the sender was, he wanted to avoid any possibility of damage to the letter that could make it difficult to parse. He was intently reading the contents when he suddenly froze.

Noticing this, Gouki twisted his head on his pillow, turning only his face toward his son, and asked, "What does it say?"

"It's an invitation."

"To what?" Gouki pressed.

"A meeting of young magicians under the age of thirty from the Twenty-Eight Families. To discuss how to deal with anti-magicians. It's going to be held next Sunday at the International Magic Association's east branch building in Yokohama."

"Next Sunday? That's sudden." Gouki's immediate reaction resonated with what Masaki was thinking. But Gouki was quicker to come up with a reason for it—though just a guess—due to a difference in experience.

"It sounds like Juumonji doesn't want anyone to get in the way of his plans."

Masaki looked perplexed. "Who would get in the way?"

Someone like Kichijouji might have understood Gouki's speculation right away. But Masaki wasn't up to speed on topics that involved scheming.

"The National Defense Force," Gouki explained. "Or local law enforcement."

"Are you saying the government would dare interfere with one of the Ten Master Clans?" Masaki asked in shock.

"I'm just saying there's a possibility," Gouki said calmly. He wasn't trying to push his son in one direction or the other. He believed in letting his children come to their own conclusions.

"So..." he continued, intentionally posing a question rather than an order, "what will you do?"

Masaki was intelligent enough to know what his father meant. "I'll attend the meeting. I'm worried about possible trespassers, but I don't want to be left out of something like this."

"Good," Gouki said approvingly.

Masaki had not been worried about his father saying no. But it was still a relief to hear the endorsement directly. Before long, another worry bubbled up.

He hesitated. "I should respond to the invitation, shouldn't I?"

"Of course you should," Gouki replied.

Unfortunately, Masaki didn't have much experience corresponding with the other members of the Ten Master Clans. He asked, at a loss: "What should I write?"

Gouki immediately sighed at his son.

It was the night of April 9.

When Katsuto came home from school, the housekeeper informed him that a guest was waiting. When asked how long the guest had been waiting, the housekeeper said for about half an hour. Katsuto hurried to the parlor without changing his clothes. Even though this guest had come without an appointment, she clearly wasn't someone Katsuto could treat with disrespect.

"Sorry to keep you waiting," Katsuto apologized as soon as he entered the parlor.

His guest was a young woman in a suit. She stood up from her chair and bowed politely.

"Well, I'm sorry to have stopped by while you were out," she replied.

"Not at all," Katsuto replied. "If you had given me a call, I would've gotten here sooner."

Sensing the criticism in his voice, the young woman seemed apologetic. Katsuto motioned her to return to her chair, and they both took a seat.

"It's been too long," the woman said. "A belated congratulations on being named the Juumonji family's heir."

"Thanks," Katsuto said. "I was expecting to see you at the Master Clans Council in February."

"Oh, I'm sorry. I thought you knew I leave all the Tooyama affairs to my younger brother. Our family policy is to focus on military service, you see."

Katsuto's guest was a member of the Tooyama family, which was one of the Eighteen Support Clans. Her name was Tsukasa Tooyama. The Tooyama last name used the characters for *ten* and *mountain*, but in the military, she spelled it with the characters for *far* and *mountain*.

This was clearly a way to hide her connections to the Ten Master Clans, but her superiors at least were aware of who she was. Under a secret agreement between the Tooyama family and a powerful person who was practically in charge of the military's entire intelligence department, Tsukasa engaged in extrajudicial intelligence missions while concealing her true identity.

"Then are you here on National Defense Force business?" Katsuto asked.

"Actually, no." There wasn't an ounce of emotion behind Tsukasa

Tooyama's smile. Her negative response wasn't even accompanied by any noticeable gesture.

"Then why are you here?" Katsuto probed.

Tsukasa didn't seem to mind his need to get to the point. She was twenty-four this year, four years older than Katsuto.

Age gap aside, most people usually found it difficult to maintain such composure in front of Katsuto. Tsukasa's poise was proof she had been raised in an environment befitting a ten-numbered family.

"I've come to speak to you about the invitation you sent. Or rather, to apologize. The Tooyama family's situation being what it is, I won't be able to attend your meeting."

"I see," Katsuto said. "I'm sorry to hear that, but it can't be helped."

The "situation" Tsukasa mentioned had to do with the Tooyama family's connection to the National Defense Force.

The Tooyama clan was created at Magician Development Institute Ten as the last line of defense for protecting the capital from attack. Unlike the Juumonji clan, which was developed to intercept missiles and disrupt mechanized units, the Tooyama clan was designed to defend important facilities and escort VIPs in the case that the front line had been breached.

In other words, Tooyama magicians protected critical state functions rather than the people. Their relationship with the National Defense Force's center was the strongest among the Twenty-Eight Families. When push came to shove, they were committed to helping those in power escape. It was their life's mission. So it was safe to say the Tooyama family was deeply connected to the darker side of the National Defense Force, cloaked in shadow.

The Ten Master Clans were created to ensure magicians were not used as disposable pawns by the state. In short, it was an organization designed to respond to the Japanese people's concerns. While they were active participants at the core of the Ten Master Clans system, the Tooyama family never became one of the ten clans. To this day, they weren't even allowed to assert magicians' interests to the state.

The Juumonji family, which was created at the same Institute Ten, was the only member of the Ten Master Clans who knew about this. It was possible other clans were aware, but they feigned ignorance. This made the Juumonji the only ones the Tooyama could talk to openly.

"What do you want me to tell everyone?" Katsuto asked. He and Tsukasa both knew the Tooyama's position within the Twenty-Eight Families could worsen if their absence at the meeting was called into question.

"That's precisely what I came to talk to you about," Tsukasa said. "With all your knowledge, you must know what I should do."

Even though the Tooyama family had the National Defense Force on their side, it would still be a huge disadvantage to be ostracized by all the other magicians created at the same institute. Tsukasa needed a good excuse to avoid this at all costs. Yet, despite the troubling situation she was in, she looked strangely calm.

"I'm not quick-witted enough to help you." The lack of enthusiasm in Katsuto's voice made him sound earnest.

Tsukasa was unfazed by his somewhat curt response. "There must be other families who said they can't attend the meeting," she said.

This was Katsuto's first attempt at calling a meeting of the Twenty-Eight Families since assuming his position as head of the Juumonji family and the Ten Master Clans. Psychologically, it was difficult to refuse the invitation. While most of the families knew there probably wouldn't be any consequences for failing to attend the meeting, most were worried about missing out on something interesting.

Then again, Katsuto had practically sent out invitations at the last minute. It was reasonable for Tsukasa to believe some had already answered that they wouldn't be able to attend.

"I've only received a few answers so far, but…the Tanabata did send a message saying they couldn't come."

"What was their reason?" Tsukasa immediately asked.

Katsuto frowned. He didn't appreciate her wanting to know the contents of his mail. It wasn't exactly polite.

Before he could answer, Tsukasa came up with her own answer. "Is it because the family's heir is attending the National Defense Academy?"

Katsuto reluctantly nodded. "That's right."

"If that's the case, the heirs to the Gotou and Hassaku, who go to the same academy, won't be able to attend, either."

"Tsukasa. Could you say that with a little less enthusiasm?" Katsuto's reply passively admitted she was right.

"What a relief." Tsukasa grinned. "There are several other families not attending the meeting for the same reason as us."

"...Great," Katsuto responded sarcastically, a discouraged look on his face.

He didn't appreciate Tsukasa declining his invitation to the meeting with a smile, but knowing the backstage connections between the Tooyama and the National Defense Force, he couldn't exactly force Tsukasa to come, either.

At this point, Katsuto was getting tired of dealing with his insolent guest. This was different from the discomfort he often had when talking with Mayumi. Mayumi could be a bully sometimes but never in a malicious way. She was essentially a good person.

Tsukasa, on the other hand, lacked both good and ill will. Doing something for the sake of making someone else happy was the last thing she would ever do. She, of course, could feel joy, anger, sorrow, and pleasure herself, but other people's feelings simply didn't rate.

To make matters more complicated, as long as it didn't interfere with her mission, she never did anything that violated the rules or her morals. She wasn't a robot without feelings, nor a foreigner with different values. Katsuto could communicate with her fairly smoothly, and yet there always seemed to be something off, causing small amounts of fatigue to pile up at an alarming rate when he talked to her.

But thankfully, her business was done here. All that was left was to say goodbye. At least, that's what Katsuto thought. This was just wishful thinking on his part.

"By the way—" Tsukasa began again. "What about the Yotsuba heiress and her fiancé? Miyuki and Tatsuya Shiba?"

Katsuto responded grudgingly, "I haven't received a response from them yet, but I'm sure they'll come to the meeting."

"So you know them?"

"From First High, yes."

A sociable smile spread across Tsukasa's lips, and she grabbed Katsuto with her eyes, which held not a welcoming spark but an all-consuming abyss.

"What are they like?" she prompted.

"I can't really say." Katsuto shrugged. "We weren't that close."

"You can just tell me what you do know," Tsukasa urged. "You must at least know them well enough to get a secretive family like them to join your meeting."

So this is what she's after, Katsuto thought. He finally understood Tsukasa's true motives for stopping by this evening.

If he had taken a moment to think about it, he should've known she wouldn't go out of her way to visit him just to announce her absence from his meeting—no matter how badly she wanted an excuse to do so. She was a member of an organization constantly engaged in clandestine business. She was also someone with an important role. If she needed a messenger, there were several people in the Tooyama family who could fill that position.

Katsuto finally realized Tsukasa had come to him under the guise of an apology to obtain information about the Yotsuba magicians. He could have easily brushed her off. He had neither the obligation nor the duty to answer every single one of Tsukasa's questions. But he ended up answering just because he thought there was no reason to be silent.

"The Yotsuba heiress's fiancé is a fiercely loyal person," Katsuto said.

"Fiercely loyal? Not devotedly loyal?" Such confusion was reasonable. But her tone suggested she knew what Katsuto meant.

"In other words, once he makes a pact, he will never be the one to break it. But he's quick to turn on someone who has betrayed him first. That's the kind of person I believe Tatsuya Shiba to be."

"I see..." Tsukasa mulled over Katsuto's words before asking another question. "Do you think the same would apply if the government— or perhaps, the National Defense Force—was the one to betray him?"

"An act of self-interest against the state would never amount to anything worthwhile."

"You mean Tatsuya isn't afraid to antagonize the military and government?" Tsukasa was clearly trying to lead the conversation into dangerous territory, but Katsuto wasn't having it.

He answered calmly but firmly. "Tatsuya isn't foolish enough to make an enemy of the state."

"But his loyalty can't be completely infallible," Tsukasa argued.

"I've just told you my opinion of him," Katsuto spat back. "Even if he isn't loyal to all individuals, I believe he is loyal to a fault to this country."

"Isn't a dramatic, self-righteous patriot as harmful as a dogmatic pacifist?" Tsukasa pressed.

"Neither patriots nor pacifists are evil. Infighting is never good unless it's to prevent something worse." Katsuto stared sharply into Tsukasa's gentle eyes.

"Goodness. The Tooyama family would never try to stir up trouble with the Yotsuba family."

Katsuto frowned. But Tsukasa innocently sipped her tea, which by now had completely cooled.

[4]

USNA Roswell suburb, April 10, 4:00 PM (local time). April 11, 7:00 AM (JST). Lina finally returned to the base after a weeklong mission. She had been dispatched to rescue a federal security force—more specifically, the Wiz Guard, a group of relatively low-level magicians who failed to become Stars—who had been tasked with quelling a riot in former Mexico only to find themselves surrounded and in deep trouble.

It wasn't an easy task to pull out armed troops in such hostile conditions without harming the rioters while also preventing the outbreak of more fighting. But Lina gallantly led the second, fourth, and fifth Stars' units on the morning of April 2 to bring the rioting to an end, though there were several occassions this required the use of force—against the Wiz Guard, specifically. They then escorted the Wiz Guard back to their headquarters in Houston before finally returning to Roswell.

In the end, Lina and her colleagues were tasked with putting the insurrection down without the use of violence. Lina bitterly assumed the General Staff must have intended to do this from the very beginning, and that may have been the case.

But Lina found herself useless at times like these, where negotiation skills were a must. In effect, it was the fourth unit, made up mainly of female officers, that did most of the work defusing the situation. Lina just gave the Wiz Guard and the National Guard the evil eye.

It didn't help that Vega, the fourth unit's leader, wasn't on good terms with Lina. In fact, Lina felt a one-sided bitterness toward Vega because she was always trying to act like the big sister of the group.

All in all, this had been an exhausting mission for Lina, so it was a relief when she finally found the time to take note of her surroundings after reporting a successful mission to the base commander.

That's strange, she thought. *Everyone is running around like we're about to mobilize.*

She was technically the commander of this Stars unit, even if it was partially for show. And whether or not she was a member, if a dispatch order had been issued, she should have been informed.

Instead of going back to her own room, where she had left her luggage still unpacked, Lina swerved over to Silvia's room. Canopus was probably the best person to ask about the entire unit, but Silvia was more approachable.

Thankfully, Silvia was in her room. Lina knocked, and Silvia graciously welcomed her in. Once inside, Lina gawked at the sight of a fully packed, civilian-sized suitcase.

"Silvie… Are you going on some sort of pleasure cruise?"

Silvia gave Lina a proud, childish grin, as if she had just been praised. "Nope. I've been dispatched on a planet-class undercover mission."

Planet-class missions were led by logistic support-type magicians. Silvia was one of these types who specialized in gathering and communicating information. The fact that the mission was planet class meant that there was no immediate plan to use direct force.

"I haven't heard anything about this," Lina complained.

"That's because it isn't technically a Stars mission," Silvia explained. "Only individual magicians from the intelligence department were recruited for it."

"That sounds reckless," Lina mumbled. But she knew if the order had gone out already, it was pointless to complain about it. The intelligence department was not particularly inclined to listen to logic.

"So where are you being dispatched and what do they expect you to do?" Lina asked.

Silvia was reluctant to answer at first. This mission was supposed to be a secret. But when Lina showed no sign of taking back her question, Silvia had no choice but to convince herself that this was an order from her superior.

"We've been dispatched to Japan to resume our operation to secure the strategic-class magician who can cast Great Bomb."

Lina cringed like she had a sour taste in her mouth. "You're resuming *that* operation?"

Lina had been deployed to Japan from December 2095 to March 2096. Her original mission was to secure the strategic-class magician nicknamed the Great Bomber, who had caused the Scorching Halloween. If this wasn't possible, she at least had to neutralize his strategic-class magic, known as Great Bomb. Lina later found out in the second half of the mission that the mission was disguised as a way to dispose of a magician who had become a monster and deserted the army. When the deserter was dealt with, Lina was ordered to return home.

Around the time of her return, the personnel who had infiltrated the Magic University, magic high schools other than First High, and magic-related companies were also called back. The original mission to secure the strategic-class magician then came to a natural end. But the Pentagon never forgot the threat of Japan's secret strategic-class magician.

The Defense Intelligence Agency (DIA) was now taking the lead in preparing a task force to secure a search network in Japan and resume what they had started. The fact that strategic-class magic had been used again in open warfare must have had a significant impact on the timing of the decision to go ahead with intelligence operations targeting allied countries.

Everyone had witnessed the actual use of the strategic-class magic spell Synchroliner Fusion in South America. There was no guarantee that Great Bomb wouldn't now be used in the Pacific. Since the threat was more real, it was only natural that it became a priority to dispatch assets to the area.

"But why you?" Lina asked. While she saw the need for the operation, she wasn't quite convinced about the specifics of how it was being carried out.

"Well, I was sent to Japan before," Silvia reasoned aloud. "They probably chose me because they think I'm familiar with the situation."

"But the last time you were in Japan, you spent most of your time searching for parasites," Lina pointed out. "You even came back before the parasite case was resolved. You're no different than someone going to Japan for the first time, especially when it comes to the Great Bomber case."

Everything Lina was saying was close to how Silvia actually felt. Silvia listened to her superior's overly frank speech with a wry smile.

"Besides," Lina continued, "I'm sorry to say this, but I don't think you're strong enough to fight Japanese magicians in battle."

Silvia's smile suddenly froze.

"Japanese magicians have extremely high fighting skills, and most are star class! It was only after I came back to the USNA that I found out Miyuki and Tatsuya were part of the Yotsuba family, so I might have just witnessed the cream of the crop. But still."

"They're really that strong?" Silvia asked.

Silvia had heard a lot about Japanese magicians from Lina's complaints about her stay in Japan. But now that Lina was seriously concerned, anxiety reared its ugly head.

"Every time Tatsuya and Miyuki come to mind, I think about how the notoriety the Yotsuba have gained isn't just for show," Lina said. "Miyuki's magic is on par with mine. And I'm a Sirius. What's more, Tatsuya is much stronger than me in a one-on-one fight."

"It's that bad, huh?" Silvia said stiffly, in a daze.

"Silvie, do you have the list of members being deployed with you?"

"Just one that hasn't gone public."

Still in shock, Silvia opened her folding tablet and pulled up the document Lina asked for. The names of about fifty people were displayed in six columns across the screen.

Lina took one look at the list and frowned. Once she read through all fifty names, her grave look transformed into one of sheer terror.

"I knew there weren't going to be any star-class members on this list, but I can't believe there aren't any constellation-class members, either. Is Intelligence trying to get all its people killed?"

Stars members were grouped into five classes—star first class, star second class, constellation class, planet class, and satellite class. Of these classes, the star first, star second, and constellation classes were considered standard fighters.

That didn't mean those in the planet and satellite classes were totally helpless in combat. In fact, some members of the satellite class—who were primarily sent on noncombat missions—were stronger than the constellation class and on par with the star second class as a whole. But there was still a logic within the class divisions. Planet-class magicians were by and large less powerful than magicians in the first and second units of the Stars, collectively referred to as star-class magicians, as well as constellation-class magicians. And satellite-class magicians generally didn't stand a chance against constellation-class magicians in a one-on-one fight.

The only reason Lina could come up with for sending planet-class magicians on a mere intelligence-gathering mission was to throw away their lives.

Realizing that Lina wasn't joking, Silvia was speechless. She had a feeling she was being naive in thinking the mission was going to be easy, being in an allied country. But now all she was filled with was sudden dread.

"This is an official order, so you can't back out of it now, but..." Lina paused before continuing. "Please be careful, Silvie. Don't push yourself too hard. I'll try to convince the brass to at least send some planet-class people with you."

"...Okay," Silvia replied.

"Intelligence may try to lure the Great Bomber out by using a satellite or Stardust unit to conduct sabotage operations in Japan. If this happens, you may be ordered to provide logistical support, but please don't do as they say. Satellite and Stardust units don't stand a chance at defeating magicians from Japan's Ten Master Clans."

Before Silvia could even nod, Lina continued in a harsher tone: "If they try to recruit you again, use my name to decline the order."

Lina wasn't sure how much weight her name had ever since she got back from Japan. But as long as she was still being hailed as the best magician in the USNA—even under a false name—she should be able to protect her most trusted confidant. At least, she hoped so.

Friday, April 12. Evening. Three days had passed since the National Magic University First Affiliated High School began its recruitment week. A wild party was being thrown on First High's campus this year, but no major incidents had occurred yet. Tatsuya and Miyuki were keeping a close eye on things.

This was nothing new. The two of them had joined forces to crack down on solicitors violating school rules the previous year. In Tatsuya's first year at First High, he even caught several violators, even though he didn't have the authority to do so at the time.

This year, it helped that both Miyuki's and Tatsuya's titles were different. They weren't only the student council president and secretary, respectfully. They were now the heiress to the Yotsuba family and the son of the current Yotsuba head. Both for the students who were already involved in their family businesses and those who were just easygoing high school students, the Yotsuba name wasn't one that could easily be shrugged off. The Yotsuba family was an object of awe for those who lived in the world of magicians.

But the First High students' nervousness had nothing to do with Tatsuya, Miyuki, and Minami. The three of them were busy studying and training as normal high school students in the Department of Magic Sciences over the past few days.

Their peace and quiet was broken by a phone call that came while they were relaxing after dinner.

"Sorry for the way I'm dressed," Tatsuya apologized over the video call with a polite bow.

"I don't mind." Maya smiled at him on the screen. *"Is Miyuki out?"*

"I had her go get Minami," Tatsuya lied. He actually had her get changed as soon as he saw that the Yotsuba family was calling. Maya probably knew this but didn't take the subject any further.

"I see," she said. *"Then I'll just talk to you. I called to speak with you anyway."*

"Thank you for calling." Tatsuya bowed at the camera again.

He may have a new status within the Yotsuba family now, but that was all thanks to Maya. In the same way, she could easily change her mind and rip away that status in an instant. Tatsuya could never be too careful about the ground he stood on.

"Just to confirm," Maya began, *"your meeting is Sunday morning, yes?"*

"That's right."

Just as Tatsuya answered, Miyuki came back into the living room. She wore the same lace blouse as before but had changed out of her pale flared miniskirt into a dark-colored maxiskirt.

"I'm sorry to keep you waiting, Aunt Maya," she said.

"It's fine. I'm the one who called out of the blue."

"Thank you for understanding." Miyuki bowed politely.

Maya gave her niece a perfunctory glance and continued. *"Anyway, I'd like you to pay me a visit on Sunday afternoon. You still haven't filled me in about Kumejima."*

Tatsuya didn't appreciate Maya's attitude toward Miyuki, but Miyuki understood what this meant.

"All right." Tatsuya immediately agreed, bowing. He had plans to visit the main Yotsuba house in April, anyhow. His aunt's selfishness was no skin off his nose.

The only problem was if the meeting carried on into the afternoon. It wasn't a long journey from Yokohama to the main Yotsuba house, but it still took some time. He also had school the next day. He, Miyuki, and Minami couldn't take the day off all at once.

At the same time, it didn't even cross his mind take a different path than his sister.

"If the meeting goes on for too long, should I just leave early?" Tatsuya asked. Rather than change the date with his aunt, the only thing he could come up with was to leave the meeting early.

"Goodness. Isn't Juumonji the one holding the meeting? Surely you can't just leave halfway through." This was a natural courtesy for Maya to pay toward a fellow member of the Ten Master Clans.

But Tatsuya was more concerned with being forced to deal with the troubles a meeting that dragged on could cause. "I think staying at a meeting past its planned end time would be more of an inconvenience," he said.

"I'm sure the eldest Saegusa son is on the same page." Maya smiled at her nephew, understanding the worry in his voice. *"He might even be thinking of giving you and Miyuki a chair at the front table,"* she continued in a tone suggesting she knew the Saegusa family's plans. *"Then again, I'm sure he won't try anything like that with Juumonji around. There's no need to worry about the meeting going overtime."*

"All right," Tatsuya replied, nodding.

Sunday's meeting was supposed to be a gathering of young people, but it wouldn't be driven by the thoughts of young people alone. At least, that's what Tatsuya believed.

"I will see you on Sunday, then," Maya said.

Tatsuya bowed once again. Just as he was about to hang up, Maya spoke.

"But before you leave—" She clearly wasn't finished with the phone call. *"There might be a job for you to do."*

The way she said this made Tatsuya uncomfortable.

"You sound unsure," he said.

"That's because the request doesn't come from me," Maya explained.

Tatsuya gave her a quizzical look. "You mean the National Defense Force might come to me with a mission. But what does that have to do with you?"

The National Defense Force was the only organization other than the Yotsuba family that gave him work. Four Leaves Technology (FLT) jobs were under Tatsuya's purview, and it wasn't possible for anyone to interfere with these.

So why is Maya even mentioning the National Defense Force job? Tatsuya thought. *Maybe she doesn't want me to take it.*

But Maya replied, *"We share the common cause of preventing foreign militaries from encroaching on Japanese soil."*

Tatsuya suddenly realized he had been very naive.

"Is the situation in Hokkaido that bad?" he asked.

"It isn't," Maya replied. *"In fact, I'm rather curious as to why the New Soviet Union military is acting so confident."*

Miyuki and Minami didn't understand what Maya was getting at.

But Tatsuya immediately connected the dots with a shiver. "Do you think they might cast Tuman Bomba?"

Miyuki and Minami suddenly went pale.

"Yes," Maya immediately answered. *"To be completely honest, I believe the magic that injured the senior Ichijou was also Tuman Bomba, though on a smaller scale."*

"You suspect Tuman Bomba is a spell that produces large amounts of oxyhydrogen gas and ignites it all at once?"

"I would say it is more like a bomb fueled by oxyhydrogen gas. I couldn't tell you how it works exactly, of course."

Tatsuya thought about what would need to happen for a spell like that to work. But he was stumped at the very first step of how to get enough hydrogen and oxygen to produce a powerful enough blast.

Would the magician have to confine the elements while creating them, or generate them all in an instant? Tatsuya wondered.

Maya interrupted his thoughts: *"If Tuman Bomba was cast off the Sado coast, it would be strange—unnatural, even—to hesitate to cast it again at the Soya Strait."*

"So you want me to counter it?" Tatsuya asked. "Material Burst can't be used in close-proximity combat. If Tuman Bomba really is a type of magic that burns oxyhydrogen gas, it wouldn't be difficult to adjust its power. Material Burst, on the other hand, converts mass into energy, limiting how much I can narrow down my conversion target."

It was rare for Tatsuya to display weakness like this. For a split second, a sadistic smile seemed to play on Maya's lips.

"Don't worry about that," she said. *"I'm sure the National Defense Force won't ask you to use Material Burst near the Japanese coast. All they are probably expecting you to do is to stop enemy ships via long-range sniping. Oh, and nullify the enemies' magic."*

Maya's last comment made Tatsuya realize why she had been encouraging him to support the National Defense Force.

He asked her forthright: "Are you trying to get me to analyze Tuman Bomba?"

"Oh, I don't believe you can analyze it all in one go. Picking up some clues about it would be more than enough. Any details you discover would be appreciated."

"I'll do my best."

Tatsuya's answer put a grin on Maya's face.

"I look forward to seeing you on Sunday."

"I'll see you then." Tatsuya bowed his head and hung up the call.

He had been standing while talking to his aunt, but now he collapsed rather loudly onto the couch.

"Tatsuya… Thank you for taking such a difficult call." Miyuki knelt in front of him and looked up into his eyes. Tatsuya smiled at her, straightened, and tousled her hair before leaning back into the couch again.

"Things have gotten pretty hectic all of a sudden," he said.

"They really have. Do you want me to go to Juumonji's meeting in your place?" Miyuki offered.

"No, that's okay." Tatsuya placed his hand over his sister's. Not thinking about what she was doing, Miyuki hastily withdrew her hand.

"Oh, I'm…sorry." She shyly lowered her eyes.

"…No, that was my bad. I shouldn't have done that."

Tatsuya must have not been aware of his own actions, either. In a state of slight shock, he stared at the hand that had touched Miyuki. The expression on her brother's face made her panic even more than before.

"I-it's not that I don't want you to touch me!" she quickly explained. "In fact, having you hold my hand is more than I could ever ask for. It was just so unexpected, and—"

Seeing her in such a panic helped Tatsuya regain his senses.

"Relax, Miyuki."

"All right. But wait, I—"

"It's okay."

"Right." Miyuki looked up into her brother's eyes. After confirming he wasn't upset, she nodded. Then she cautiously extended her hand and placed it on his knee. Tatsuya placed his own hand over hers again. This time, she didn't budge.

"It's so strange," she said. "I wonder why I panicked like that."

"Are you okay now?" Tatsuya asked.

"Yes… I mean, no."

Tatsuya didn't press for an explanation about what she meant. Eventually, Miyuki's charming lips parted, and she said, "My heart is reeling right now. It's beating so fast, I can barely breathe."

Despite this inner turmoil, her expression was steady. She continued. "I can never stay calm when you touch me. But for some reason,

I'm not losing control of myself this time. My heart is still racing, but it feels rhythmic, like the rise and fall of large waves. Even the pain in my lungs feels almost relaxing."

Miyuki gently leaned her cheek onto Tatsuya's fingers. "My heart is reeling more now than when you were simply my brother," she confessed. "And yet…it feels so right. It's almost as if this is the way things are supposed to be."

Tatsuya, who had been smiling at Miyuki as she spoke, suddenly sensed a disturbance in the air and looked up. He was just in time to see Minami fleeing into the kitchen, her ears red beneath her hair.

An ominous prophecy or an auspicious prophecy. If asked which had a higher probability of coming true, most people would answer the former. Unfortunately, the ominous prophecy that Maya told Tatsuya also came true.

Saturday, April 13. An urgent message from the school appeared on Tatsuya's terminal during a classroom lesson. Following the message's instructions, he turned off the lesson being streamed on his terminal and left the classroom. His classmates looked up for a moment but quickly turned their attention back to their own terminals.

Tatsuya headed for the reception room. Sanada, dressed in a suit, was waiting for him there. Tatsuya decided to bow rather than salute, then sat in front of the major. Sanada glanced at the staff in the area. Albeit reluctantly, they left the room.

Sanada used his magic to envelop the reception room in a soundproof field. After confirming the field was stable, Tatsuya was the first to speak. "Major Sanada, I thought you had been dispatched to Hokkaido."

"I returned rather suddenly. We need your help." Although Sanada was expressionless as always, there was a hint of panic in his voice, and he was less direct than usual.

"All right. I'll ask the base for details." Tatsuya knew there was no time for asking questions now. The room they were in may be sound-proof, but he couldn't talk about a mission on school grounds.

Instead, he simply asked, "Are you stationed at Kasumigaura?"

"Yes. Can you leave right away?" Sanada sounded impatient.

"Sure," Tatsuya replied. Since he was in the student council, he didn't have to leave his CAD in the office. And unlike some other students, he didn't need to carry any additional personal belongings with him other than his information terminal.

"Then let's go now," Sanada rushed him.

"All right. I'll just tell the school I'm leaving first. Please wait here," Tatsuya said calmly, as if talking to a small child. He left the room.

Tatsuya flew to Kasumigaura by helicopter from the Tachikawa air base. An hour after leaving school, he found himself in the control room of the 101st Brigade's headquarters.

This room, like the observation room at Fort Tsushima, was equipped with facilities that processed three-dimensional information from satellites and UAVs in the stratosphere to create ground-like views. Tatsuya sat on a chair with Third Eye—a specialized CAD in the form of a rifle—in his hands. He wore a pair of goggles and a MOVAL helmet, both of which were connected to Third Eye. Since the seal was still intact, he couldn't use Material Burst. But he was ready at any time to begin sniping at an ultra-long range.

Third Eye was a CAD system designed to operate Material Burst. But that wasn't the only way it could be used.

Its original function was as a super-remote precision tool used to magnify regular and magical sight. Naturally, this was useless if a magician didn't know how to use it properly. Third Eye could perform its prescribed functions only when processing information obtained from satellite and stratospheric cameras, in much the same way the brain obtained information from the eyes.

Tatsuya was one of the few magicians who could put it to good use. Using Third Eye, he could cast Mist Dispersion and Program Dispersion in a location hundreds of kilometers away.

"Special Lieutenant Ooguro."

Tatsuya stood up.

"No changes to the mission."

Kazama wasn't giving Tatsuya his orders this time. Instead, it was the brigadier general, Major General Hiromi Saeki—nicknamed the Silver Fox, for her silvery-white hair.

A real-time image of the Soya Strait, internationally known as the La Perouse Strait, appeared on the screen via a stratospheric camera.

"The first goal is to nullify the enemy's magic. If that proves impossible, we will attempt to obstruct the path of the invading vessels. Sinking them is to be avoided if possible."

"Understood."

After Saeki's final instruction, Sanada approached Tatsuya. "Are you ready, Special Lieutenant?"

"Yes, my preparations are complete," Tatsuya answered solemnly. "I'm already monitoring the enemy's magic."

"Good," Sanada returned. "Be seated."

Tatsuya did as he was told. Saeki didn't want her soldiers to stand around and wait for nothing. All she demanded from them was flawless execution of their orders.

The screen showed numerous small boats moving south from Sakhalin. At first glance, they appeared to be fishing boats, but the various sensors on the stratospheric cameras indicated that most of them were disguised combat vessels. The real fishing boats that were mixed in were most likely there to better sell the ruse or simply to act as decoys.

Hitting a target without accidentally sinking the others was the job Tatsuya had been brought there to do. For magic, physical distance wasn't a problem. Magic could be cast from a distance of thousands, or tens of thousands, of kilometers away, as long as the target's information could be accessed.

In other words, a magician could perceive only the direction from which another magician cast their magic and whether they were accessing the information of nearby phenomena. Even if they could sense magic being cast, they couldn't tell where it would land on a map. If the magic was being cast relatively close by, it wasn't too difficult to match its informational position with its relative physical coordinates. But if an ordinary magician were a few hundred meters away, it quickly became an impossible feat to confirm where the magic was originally cast.

Mechanical sensors, on the other hand, depended on physical distance to derive more accurate results. Long-range sensors were used to pinpoint the location of a magician who unleashed magic over a larger-than-average area. However, when the range of a particular spell was on a scale of tens of kilometers, it became difficult to match it with the magician who cast it. With the current technology, it was only possible to deduce that when a spell was activated in one place, a magician in another place used the same type of magic. But this could only be inferred; it was difficult to confirm with anything approaching certainty.

When the distance between the magician and the magic activation point exceeded several hundred kilometers, it became virtually impossible to even estimate where the magic originated. This was partially why Tatsuya favored ultra-long-range magic.

He stared at the screen from his seat. Whether or not Tatsuya was standing, Third Eye was linked to the information equipment in the room, so his goggles displayed multiple sets of numerical data not visible on the large screen.

Eventually, the value indicating the amplitude of psionic waves began to fluctuate unnaturally, rising and falling irregularly over a short period of time.

Tatsuya stood up and readied his Third Eye. No one was surprised by his sudden movements. The console where each officer sat showed the same information visible through Tatsuya's goggles.

"Confirming active psionic waves!" The operator's voice echoed across the room.

The camera panned, centering the location of rising psionic waves on the screen. This was a good place—right in the path of the Japanese naval vessels.

Tatsuya pointed his Elemental Sight toward the coordinates with the assistance of Third Eye and began to write a small-scale magic program.

Not only was the scope of the event modification narrow, but the amount of information the expected magic formula affected was also considerably limited. In a matter of seconds, Tatsuya analyzed the magic as one that broke water into hydrogen and oxygen to ignite them. The resulting effect wouldn't be more than the force of a small land mine.

Tatsuya pulled his CAD's trigger. Based on the information he analyzed using his own magic-calculation region, he was ready to cast the magic program Program Dispersion at the enemy's magic program.

But he stopped midway.

He noticed an unknown element in the enemy's magic program. As things were, it was possible to destroy the magic module that would split water and ignite the resulting hydrogen gas. But it was a module he had never seen before that grabbed his attention.

Two elements were added to this module. The first element—delayed activation—was not difficult to decipher, even though it was arranged somewhat differently than usual.

It was the second element that made Tatsuya pause.

Magic program copies? he thought. *...No, they're not just copies. Rather than duplicating the exact same magic program, they're automatically constructing new magic programs while changing the projection coordinates and points of activation.*

Magic programs were constructed inside the magic-calculation region. This was common practice in modern magic but did not apply to all magic. For example, old magic using spellbooks constructed the final magic program on the spellbook itself. Old magic in general built magic programs on the few magical mediums available, such as altars, books, and wands.

But what Tatsuya was seeing now was completely different.

This magic program had the ability to construct other magic programs built into it.

It was similar to loop casting. But whereas loop casting gave magic programs the ability to assemble activation sequences within the magic-calculation region, this module differed from the original magic program in that it could automatically populate new variables.

In the moment Tatsuya was lost in thought wondering what this could be, the enemy's magic program multiplied all at once, covering the surface of the sea.

So this is why it has delayed activation! he realized.

The magic program adjusted the slight time lag for each of its copies, and all the programs were activated simultaneously to generate and ignite oxyhydrogen gas at once.

Is this Tuman Bomba?!

Tatsuya couldn't wait to be certain if this was the strategic-class spell. There was no time to lose.

He erased the magic program for Program Dispersion and switched over to Mist Dispersion. Tuman Bomba's event modification separated water into hydrogen and oxygen. The combustion of oxyhydrogen gas was caused by the combination of hydrogen and oxygen—a water synthesis. The enemy's magic program didn't burn hydrogen with heat energy, but did it by chemically fusing hydrogen and oxygen. In other words, it used magic to both synthesize and separate water.

Magic that forces opposite event modifications creates a conflict that cancels itself out! Tatsuya realized.

"The enemy's magic has been neutralized," Sanada announced.

Without turning toward Sanada, Tatsuya stared at the enemy ship. He had cast the spell just in time, but there was no guarantee it would work next time.

Tatsuya's magic wouldn't be enough, especially if the range of the enemy's magic activation were to expand any farther. But if the magic program wasn't nullified before the enemy finished copying it, it may grow to an unmanageable size. If that wasn't enough, the magic program that was the source of the copies was itself capable of continuous copying.

This is some problematic magic, Tatsuya thought.

He couldn't come up with a surefire response on the spot, so he decided to seal the enemy's movements. His Mist Dispersion disintegrated the screws of the enemy vessels one after another.

The ships at the front of their formation were now dead in the water, causing a traffic jam. Once he confirmed a third of the enemy ships had come to a standstill, Tatsuya finally lowered his hand with a death grip on Third Eye.

Vladivostok, Far Eastern headquarters of the New Soviet Union's Science Academy. In the corner of a windowless building loomed a throne-like chair positioned in front of a three-meter-high case. Seated in the chair was the New Soviet Union's publicly known strategic-class magician Igor Andreivich Bezobrazov.

He slowly removed his helmet, which obscured the top part of his head down to his nose. Then he stood up, shaking out his hair.

"Was that dispersion magic?" he muttered to himself, looking around.

This research tower had no windows because all its contents were highly classified. For example, the case behind Bezobrazov was a magic-calculation region auxiliary supercomputer that a magician could sit inside and operate. It was a device that assisted in the activation of large-scale magic and was noticeably different from a simple CAD system. By calculating all elements on a case-by-case basis and providing the optimum activation sequence, a magician could perform magic without much conscious effort; a feat that was impossible to perform alone.

When someone looked out into the room, all they would see was a wall. But Bezobrazov's gaze seemed to pierce through the thick walls to the northeastern sky.

To the south, the faltering invasion forces should have started withdrawing. If Bezobrazov had continued to provide support, an opportunity to turn the tables would still be in the cards. But this operation wasn't a serious attempt to invade Japan. After recently concluding a major conflict with the Great Asian Alliance, Japan couldn't afford to mount their own offensive. At least, that's what Bezobrazov believed when he started this operation.

Well, I'm probably not wrong, he thought.

It was not yet confirmed, but as far as he could see, there was no momentum for Japan to pursue Sakhalin. If there was anything Bezobrazov had miscalculated, it was the magician who nullified his magic.

Who could they be? Could it be the mass- and energy-conversion strategic-class magician who destroyed the Great Asian Alliance's fleet? He mused. He wasn't too far from the truth.

[5]

Sunday, April 14. This was the day of the meeting Katsuto organized for the young heirs of the Ten Master Clans. But Tatsuya went to Yakumo's temple to practice as per usual; he wasn't about to let the meeting change his daily routine.

That wasn't to say this day was the same as any other. The previous day's possible confrontation with the strategic-class magician Bezobrazov had left Tatsuya feeling on edge. He was worried about not being able to use Program Dispersion to nullify what was probably Tuman Bomba. While he interrupted the strategic-magic spell, it was clearly difficult to completely nullify it—even if he really tried.

This was a first for Tatsuya. He wondered what he had to do to be like Katsuto and Minami and automatically replicate powerful defensive magic while countering a large-scale spell. It was very rare for Tatsuya to be focused on something other than what was in front of him. But these thoughts floated around in his mind.

He, of course, wasn't distracted during his training session with Yakumo. It was only when he returned home that he let his mind wander.

As he took a shower, wiping away his sweat, most of his head was occupied with how to counter the magic from the day before. He was so focused on this that noises and presences he would normally notice right away went under the radar.

He thought: *Program Dispersion should be able to process a single magic program no matter how large it is. If the magic programs' descriptions are exactly the same, even thousands of programs can be processed as one.*

But yesterday's magic was a collection of countless magic programs with slight differences. And it wasn't only the coordinates and locations that were different. There was even a shift in the activation timings, meaning they can't be processed as the same information.

A type of magic set off as a chain reaction via automatic replication can't be anything but trouble. I'll call it "Chain Cast" for now. Once Chain Cast is completed, there's nothing I can do about it with my current abilities.

The most effective method to get rid of it would be to destroy the initial magic program before its deployment is complete. But that's easier said than done. I'm sure the spell caster has thought of how to counter something like that.

I remember each magic program on its own wasn't very powerful. Although they had a wide range of attack, the explosion's epicenter didn't produce particularly high heat or pressure. As my aunt said, it's not much different from a fuel bomb.

I bet high-power barrier magic would counter the spell. The problem is I can't use barrier magic well enough to begin with.

Should I program barrier magic into Relic? No, Relic's analytical abilities are getting better, but they're not at the stage where I can rely on them in real combat.

Then should I have Pixie learn barrier magic? No. It's not realistic to think we can keep Minami by our side all the time.

Maybe because Tatsuya was so deep in thought, he was caught by surprise when the door to the changing room opened. He may have not noticed anyone's presence until then, but he did hear the door open. He paused in the middle of wiping his hair and saw Minami standing wide-eyed outside the room.

Tatsuya quickly recovered. Even though he had just finished showering, he had wrapped a towel around himself to hide the most important parts of his lower body, an unconscious habit that had been drilled into him as a custom of etiquette. The only part of his body that was naked was his upper half.

"Minami." Tatsuya tried not to make eye contact, speaking to her in as level a voice as possible. But there was no reply. It was impossible Minami didn't see him. Her face was boiling red.

He spoke a bit firmer this time: "Minami, close the door."

"......"

Minami just stared, dragging out the silence. Then, after a few seconds, she yelped: "S-s-sorry to disturb you!"

She slammed the door with a bang, and Tatsuya heard a loud crash as she tripped and fell in the hall. Feeling bad for surprising her, Tatsuya quickly finished getting dressed.

In the dining room, breakfast was ready on the table. And Minami knelt pathetically on the floor. Tatsuya glanced at Miyuki, who was already seated, and she shook her head. *I didn't do anything!* she seemed to say with her eyes. Clearly, Minami's behavior wasn't a result of one of Miyuki's bursts of anger.

Tatsuya opened his mouth first. "Minami, uh… Don't worry about earlier."

"But that's impossible!" She reeled. "I can't believe I looked upon your body with Miyuki under the same roof! I'm a failure as a maid!"

"What is that supposed to mean?" Miyuki murmured to herself. But Minami didn't hear.

"Please!" the short-haired girl cried. "Please punish me!"

"Hey, it's my fault for not locking the door," Tatsuya reasoned. "Don't be so hard on yourself."

"But it's one hundred percent *my* fault for not noticing you were in the bath!" Minami fought back. "Take me to the stocks for being the world's worst maid!"

"Take you to the stocks?" Tatsuya looked to Miyuki for help. Minami was clearly taking things too far.

"Minami has been hooked on European love stories lately,"

Miyuki offered with an awkward smile. While this explained that peculiar choice of words, it didn't exactly help navigate the situation.

I have no choice, Tatsuya thought. He didn't want to get angry at Minami, but if things dragged on any longer, it would get in the way of his plans.

"Listen, Minami. You know how I have an important meeting today."

"Yes!" she squeaked, her forehead plastered to the floor.

"I'll be stopping by the main Yotsuba mansion afterward, and I'll need you to accompany Miyuki there to meet up with me."

"Of course."

"Long story short, I'm very busy today and don't have time to punish you. Do you understand?"

"Yes."

"Good. Now get up, have breakfast, and get on with what you have to do. No one is going to 'take you to the stocks' if you can't do your job."

"Understood."

Minami dejectedly took her place at the breakfast table. Tatsuya was filled with guilt, although he didn't want to admit it.

The unexpected early-morning drama not only sapped Tatsuya's stamina, it also convinced him to put the chain-casting countermeasure on hold. With a new outlook in hand, he headed for the Kanto branch of the Magic Association in Yokohama.

At the entrance to the Yokohama Bay Hills Tower, where the branch building was located, Tatsuya happened to see a group of three familiar sisters.

They noticed him right away and called out.

"Hello, Tatsuya! Long time no see." Mayumi, dressed in a brightly colored suit, waved in a rough way unbecoming of her formal attire.

The tight suit accentuated her petite but curved figure, sadly making her seem older than she was.

"Hi, Mayumi. Are you attending the meeting, too?" Tatsuya replied.

He was under the impression that Tomokazu would be the representative for the Saegusa family. But then again, there wasn't a limit to the number of attendees for this meeting. Five to ten more people than planned might be a lot, but two or three was within the bounds of common sense.

"Nope," Mayumi replied. "We're just here to help at the reception desk."

Apparently, Tatsuya was mistaken. At Mayumi's side, Kasumi and Izumi were also dressed a little more maturely than usual to help receive and guide guests.

"Mind if I ask why? I thought the Juumonji family was in charge of today's meeting," Tatsuya proded lightly, only half expecting to get a straight answer.

But Mayumi was quick to reveal what was really going on. "My older brother was the one who proposed this meeting to Juumonji in the first place. It's only fair we should help."

Tatsuya was surprised. "Are you sure you can tell me that?"

"It's fine," Mayumi replied flippantly. "Our father didn't stop us from coming here."

If Mayumi went out in the open with her sisters and acted like the organizer of this meeting, there was a risk that the meeting's backstory would be exposed to various kinds of scrutiny. Her logic seemed to be that she didn't care if people found out.

"That sounds like a pretty rash conclusion," Tatsuya retorted.

Tatsuya vaguely knew about the feud between Mayumi and the Saegusa family head, Kouichi. But he felt it was unlike Mayumi to do something like this. Her feelings toward her father aside, she usually prioritized the interests of the Saegusa family.

Then a sudden thought came to Tatsuya. "Wait, do you feel bad for using Juumonji to make this meeting happen?"

A look of shock came over Kasumi's and Izumi's faces.

"O-of course not! Our helping out has nothing to do with that!"

Tatsuya's—or more so, her sisters' wide-eyed stares made Mayumi's tongue tangle.

Everyone's surprise caught even Tatsuya off guard, and he fell silent. "......"

"Wh-why are you looking at me like that?" Mayumi stammered. "There's nothing going on between me and Juumonji!"

"I never said there was," Tatsuya defended. "I just—"

"You just what?" Mayumi challenged. "I said what I said, okay!"

She doesn't have to get so upset, Tatsuya thought. But he decided not to push the topic any further.

Instead, he said, "Everyone's staring."

This seemed to strike a chord, because Mayumi immediately fell silent and froze.

Then he said, "I'll be going now. Don't worry; I know the way."

He then proceeded to the elevator hallway and headed toward the meeting floor to get out of Mayumi's way.

The meeting was set to start at 9:00 AM. There were still twenty minutes left until then. A large group of magicians had already gathered in front of the conference hall where the meeting would take place. The doors were open, but most participants were standing around chatting and gathering information outside.

Just then, Tatsuya spotted a familiar school uniform.

"Shippou."

"Oh! Hello, Shiba."

It was Takuma Shippou, standing outside the hall in his First High uniform and looking a bit out of place. Shippou was a year younger than Tatsuya, and—although he would never admit it—he seemed to be shying away from the older magicians he had never met before. So when Tatsuya approached him, he looked relieved.

"Aren't you going inside?" Tatsuya asked directly. He didn't bother asking whether Takuma would be participating in the meeting. Even without checking the school records, it was clear he was an only child. Magicians were encouraged to marry early and have many children, but they weren't forced to have any set number. They weren't treated like livestock. If a couple had fertility issues, they didn't have to get treatment just to produce a second child.

Since Takuma was an only child, Tatsuya knew he would be attending this meeting to represent his family. Takuma wasn't surprised to see Tatsuya, either. But this surprise was most likely due to a lack of awareness of what was going on around him.

"Well, it seems we *can* go in..." Takuma began tentatively. "But we don't have assigned seats?"

This sounded almost like a question. As if he were asking Tatsuya where he should sit.

"Do you want to sit together?" Tatsuya offered.

"Yes, please!" Takuma smiled.

People like Tomitsuka would probably think Takuma was acting childishly sincere. But Tatsuya didn't feel any particular way about Takuma's behavior. The younger boy was just his junior at school. They both walked into the conference hall together.

Inside, long tables were set up in the shape of a square, with a large hollow space in the middle. There were six seats on each side of the square and five at the back of the room, meaning there were twenty-three participants in total. Tatsuya took a chair on the right-hand side of the square, not paying attention to whether he was in an upper or lower row. He chose this seat because he recognized someone there.

Tatsuya greeted the familiar face sporting Third High's crimson uniform. "Hi, Ichijou. Long time no see."

"It's only been a month," Masaki retorted indignantly. He didn't mean to act annoyed; he just didn't know how else to respond. Then he asked, "Are you alone?"

"One person per family is enough," Tatsuya replied with a serious expression.

Masaki had been expecting Miyuki to come along, but he must have also realized Tatsuya wouldn't bring her to a place like this; he showed no surprise at all.

"By the way, Ichijou…" Tatsuya turned his whole body toward Masaki and lowered his voice to a whisper not even Takuma could hear. "How is your dad doing?"

Masaki scowled involuntarily but knew Tatsuya was trying to be discrete.

"He's a lot better," he replied. "Thanks for all your help."

Masaki's gratitude was aimed toward the Shiba family for sending Yuuka.

Tatsuya realized this immediately and replied, "Not at all. That's what friends are for. Besides, all we did was introduce you to an acquaintance of ours. Nothing worth a grand gesture."

He made sure to keep the ties between Yuuka and the Yotsuba family a secret.

"Right." Masaki must have thought saying anything more could come off as rude, so he kept his response brief and said no more. Tatsuya also turned back to the table.

This gave Takuma the signal the two were finished exchanging pleasantries. He stood up and walked over to Masaki.

"Hello, Ichijou. My name is Takuma Shippou. I'm sorry I didn't get the chance to talk to you when you came to First High last month. I hope we can talk more today."

"I'm Masaki Ichijou. And same here." Knowing he was older than Takuma, Masaki bowed briefly from his seat.

If this had been a year ago, this kind of behavior would have probably made Takuma angry. But now, he simply shrugged it off and moved on.

"I see you're wearing your uniform, too," he said, feeling some sense of camaraderie.

"I'm a high school student. This is the only formalwear I have,"

Masaki replied, as if it were obvious. A wry smile twisted Tatsuya's mouth.

It was five minutes before the scheduled meeting time, and the conference room seats were almost completely filled. A few people were still talking in the hall, so it was probably safe to assume that most of the expected guests had already arrived.

But there was one person who was not yet among them. Three minutes later, this person finally appeared, attracting the whole room's attention.

She was tall for a woman. Under her short chestnut-colored hair, her face wasn't quite masculine but not overly feminine, either. Her figure, on the other hand—wrapped in a whitish pantsuit—was decidedly feminine. At twenty-nine years old, she was probably the oldest person at the meeting.

"Tatsuya Shiba. Or should I call you Tatsuya Yotsuba?"

"Tatsuya Shiba is fine," he replied. "I believe this is the first time we've spoken in-person. It's good to finally meet you, Mutsuzuka."

"The pleasure is all mine. Allow me to formally introduce myself. I'm Atsuko Mutsuzuka."

For some reason, the head of the Mutsuzuka family, Atsuko Mutsuzuka, spoke to Tatsuya as soon as she entered the room.

It was quite well-known among the Twenty-Eight Families that Atsuko Mutsuzuka practically worshipped Maya Yotsuba. She probably walked up to Tatsuya to speak to him in the first place because he was Maya Yotsuba's son. Technically, he was just her nephew, but even if he had been announced as such, the connection to Maya probably would have still convinced Atsuko to choose Tatsuya as her first conversation partner of the morning.

"It's been so long, Mutsuzuka." Masaki stood up. As someone who had direct contact with the Ten Master Clans since birth, he was well acquainted with the woman who sported chestnut hair.

"Masaki! Yes, it has. How is—?" Atsuko paused.

"My father is much better," Masaki replied quickly.

"Oh. That's good to hear."

Takuma—standing up along with Masaki—greeted Atsuko for the first time.

It was only in February that the Shippou family joined the Ten Master Clans. The Shippou head, Takumi Shippou, never interacted much with members other than those who had the numbers seven and three in their names. So Takuma had little acquaintance with any of the Twenty-Eight Families living outside the Kanto region.

Atsuko gave Takuma a casual reply, then moved to a seat on the opposite side of the square. She, Katsuto, and Tomokazu were the only ones who seemed to have assigned seats.

It was exactly 9:00 AM when Katsuto and Tomokazu appeared together at the back of the conference room. By this time, all seats were occupied.

After greeting the room, Katsuto took a seat at the center of the farthest side in the assembly.

"Thank you all for taking time out of your busy schedules to join us today," he said. "Instead of spending time exchanging pleasantries, I'd like to jump right into the issue at hand."

There were no objections from the crowd. More than half the people gathered in the hall were over the age of twenty. The only ones still in their teens were Katsuto, Tatsuya, Masaki, and Takuma. It seemed silly to go around the room introducing themselves like schoolchildren.

Katsuto began: "I've gathered you here today to hear your opinions on the ever-increasing anti-magician movements and what we should do about them. This month, troubling incidents are occurring not only in Japan but throughout several countries all over the world. While they haven't been announced at the national level, there have been rumors of several worldwide revolts and insurrections. So what are we going to do about this? I'd like to hear everyone's frank opinions."

Masaki raised his hand. "I'm Masaki Ichijou."

He waited for Katsuto's silent approval before continuing to speak.

"Before I state my opinion, I'd like to confirm the goals of this meeting. I understand the importance of addressing the issue of anti-magic groups, but why the thirty years and under rule? Why exclude many of the heads of families?"

About half the participants nodded in agreement.

Katsuto shifted his gaze from Masaki to Tomokazu. This gesture alone told those at the table that it was the Saegusa family, not the Juumonji family, who had truly planned this meeting.

This didn't come as a surprise to most.

Tomokazu looked up, unafraid to meet twenty sets of apprehensive eyes. Katsuto and Tatsuya were the only ones not spearing him with a piercing gaze.

Tomokazu spoke up. "I'm Tomokazu Saegusa. This meeting actually came about after consulting with Juumonji about how to handle the anti-magic movements. So I think I should answer Ichijou's question."

He gazed around the room, but no one cut in. It seemed everyone was prepared to hear what Tomokazu wanted to say.

He continued. "Measures to counter the radicalization of anti-magic movements were discussed at the Master Clans Council after the anti-magic terrorist attack in Hakone. But ultimately, I heard only passive measures, such as strengthening surveillance, were put into practice."

Tomokazu paused for a moment. Two members of the Master Clans Council—Atsuko and Katsuto—were present at this meeting.

"That's correct," Atsuko said, speaking out of turn.

Tomokazu thanked her with his eyes and continued speaking. "However, there is a limit to how long we can keep silent and simply monitor the situation. I learned that the hard way while involved in a terrorist search."

"Hold on a second."

Just then, a voice interrupted Tomokazu.

"I'm Soushi Kudou, from the Kudou family. Sorry for interrupting, but what do you mean by a terrorist search? I'm sorry to say I haven't heard of any of the Ten Master Clans being involved in anything like that."

A few voices of agreement rose among the Eighteen Support Clans.

"The police stated the Hakone terrorist attack remains unresolved and it's still being investigated," Soushi continued. "Is this not true? If the Ten Master Clans had some sort of hand in solving things, why weren't we told about it?"

Tatsuya silently listened to Soushi's protest. *So this is how he really feels*, he thought.

The Kudou family had been one of the Ten Master Clans until this past February. But they had been demoted to the Eighteen Support Clans after getting dragged into a feud with the Saegusa family—or rather, into a private fight between Maya Yotsuba and Kouichi Saegusa.

The pride of originally being one of the Ten Master Clans made it harder to accept being kept out of the loop.

I feel bad that Minoru has to be part of a family like this, Tatsuya honestly thought.

Immediately after the meeting began, the first floor of the Yokohama Bay Hills Tower was all abuzz. The appearance of a handsome boy whose beauty seemed almost otherworldly caused men and women alike to forget their manners. The boy frowned at the impertinent stares fixated on him. But even this sullen expression mesmerized the crowds.

"Well, if it isn't Minoru."

Recognizing the voice that suddenly called out to him, Minoru felt the tension in his face give way to relief.

"Mayumi… Kasumi… Izumi."

A wave of abject disappointment washed over the area as three beautiful girls surrounded the handsome boy. The men in the crowd were intimidated by Minoru's perfect beauty, while the women felt they didn't stand a chance against the Saegusa sisters' unique charm.

"Long time no see, Minoru," Izumi said.

"I haven't seen you since the composition contest, so...it's been half a year," Kasumi chimed in.

Though not in-person, Izumi had last seen Minoru during a conference call between their respective student councils in mid-February. But, as she mentioned, Kasumi hadn't seen him since the Thesis Competition in Kyoto, where they had talked briefly backstage.

Minoru, Kasumi, and Izumi were the same age, and—though not often—they had hung out ever since they were kids. Izumi and Kasumi were some of the few friends Minoru had who weren't intimidated by his good looks.

"If you're looking for the meeting, it already started," Mayumi said.

"Oh, my older brother Soushi is the representative for our family," Minoru replied.

"Really? I think you should be there instead," Kasumi blurted out.

Mayumi panicked at her younger sister's thoughtless response. "Hush, Kasumi!"

While Kasumi shouldn't have said what she did, everyone agreed with her. Minoru, unsure what to say, gave the girls a wry smile.

Just then, Izumi cut in with perfect timing. "Mayumi, it looks like everyone who's supposed to be at the meeting is already present, so we don't need to stick around here. Why don't we go somewhere else to talk?"

"Right," Mayumi agreed. "Let's find somewhere to sit."

The group started to move. Minoru knew Mayumi was concerned about his health, which was affected by the slightest thing. He followed her obediently, without the slightest hint of stubbornness.

Meanwhile, Katsuto was responding to Soushi Kudou's comment in the conference room.

"You weren't informed about the Hakone terrorist incident because it ended poorly. You might even call it disgraceful," he said firmly.

"By disgraceful, do you mean you failed to apprehend the terrorist?" Soushi pressed, snickering.

"Whoever caused the terrorist incident was definitely killed," Katsuto responded.

"Then what's the problem?"

"The problem is the perpetrators' bodies were never found."

Masaki gritted his teeth, while Tatsuya listened casually, as if the conversation didn't concern him.

Katsuto continued. "A USNA military unit sank the ship carrying the terrorists."

"USNA military intervention?" Soushi asked in apparent surprise.

"The attack hit the terrorist ship so hard, the terrorists' bodies didn't retain their human form," Katsuto explained. He never checked the body of the Hakone terrorist leader, Gu Jie, himself. But there was no need to explicitly say that here.

Instead, he said, "Without a body, we can't say for sure that the terrorist leader was killed. A lack of physical evidence also makes it impossible to declare the case fully resolved."

"...Now I understand why the police are still investigating." Soushi managed to pull himself together, and he continued. "But the general public is one thing. Did this really have to be kept from us, too?"

Soushi's voice was much weaker now, having lost much of the eloquence from before.

"We actually didn't mean to keep it a secret," Tomokazu interjected at the perfect time. "I'll admit our failure to tell you was an oversight on our part, but why don't we put the past aside and talk about the future?"

This shut down any opportunity for Soushi to object. If Tomokazu showered him with any more specific attention, it might be perceived as interrupting the answer to Masaki's earlier question. A feeling of exasperation began to rise in some parts of the room.

"Very well. Just make sure you keep us informed of important incidents like this in the future," Soushi mumbled like a sore loser.

"We'll do our best," Tomokazu replied casually.

Soushi clenched his fists in frustration. Tomokazu either didn't notice this or ignored it and continued with the meeting.

"Although not limited to terrorists, the cooperation of the local populace is essential in seeking out the dangerous elements lurking in society. However, our search didn't obtain the cooperation of nearby residents."

This was the first thing Tomokazu said that sparked Tatsuya's interest.

He and Masaki had been the ones physically pursuing Gu Jie on their own from the beginning. Tomokazu—or rather, the Saegusa family—seemed to have tried to gather information from residents via short interviews.

Using the police for this type of investigation would have been a much easier route. But for some reason, the Saegusa family decided to blunder around and try their hand at what approximated as police work.

Maybe the Saegusa are more fractured than they appear, Tatsuya thought, going off on a tangent completely unrelated to the meeting.

"Not everyone is hostile toward magicians. In fact, there are some who understand us, and even more who at least act as if they care."

Someone in the room spoke up. "Really? ...Sorry, I'm Hirofumi Itsuwa, from the Itsuwa family."

Hirofumi was Mayumi's former fiancé, so Tomokazu knew him. His introduction was meant for the people in the room who he had never met before in person.

"What do you mean?" Tomokazu asked. It was the first time this topic was being brought up among the Ten Master Clans.

"I think everyone who understands us is actually afraid deep down," Hirofumi replied.

"Afraid of being subject to violence by the anti-magic movement?" Tomokazu clarified.

"That's right. I don't think anti-magic groups make up the majority of this country's citizens. But their activities are radical and conspicuous. So much so, in fact, that I feel like I'll be the target of violence if I say or do anything that empathizes with magicians."

This sounded true enough. No one voiced any objections.

"I believe anti-magic groups are a noisy minority," Tomokazu argued. "The silent majority understand magicians, or are at least sympathetic to our kind. Ultimately, however, we failed to achieve our goal of apprehending the Hakone terrorists because we lacked the population's support."

Just as Tomokazu was jumping to a hasty conclusion, the kid brother of the head of the Yatsushiro family suddenly tugged on the reins: "Excuse me. Takara Yatsushiro here. Even if we had the people's support earlier, that doesn't necessarily mean we would have caught the terrorist leader."

"Yes, that's true. However, it's possible that the people's support could have sped up the process of pinpointing the terrorist's whereabouts. We might have even avoided losing track of the leader's body."

"That all sounds very hypothetical," Takara retorted.

"I prefer to call it in the realm of possibility," Tomokazu corrected.

Takara bowed and backed down. It wasn't that he felt defeated. He simply thought any further discussion would lead to nothing more than a pointless argument.

Afraid he would seem as if he was getting carried away, Tomokazu toned down his own rhetoric slightly. "This is just my personal impression, but I feel that people who empathize with magicians are in a situation where they can't speak up for fear of those who are hostile to us. But my personal impressions are just one perspective on the issue," he continued. "I would like to ask you all to consider this: Maybe we receive so much hostility and a complete lack of support because we only answer the anti-magic movement with passive responses."

"I'm sorry to interrupt, but it sounds a bit extreme to say there are absolutely no voices speaking in our favor," Atsuko Mutsuzuka expressed. No one complained about her not introducing herself.

Atsuko was the head of the Mutsuzuka family. Everyone in the conference room was familiar with the names and faces of all the heads of the Ten Master Clans.

Atsuko continued. "In fact, there are even some politicians willing to defend us. For instance, I believe the Saegusa family is very close with Senator Kouzuke."

"You're right. I went too far," Tomokazu quickly admitted. "All I meant to say is people like that are few and far between. It's undeniable that there are opposing groups that put pressure against us."

"Of course. But what does that have to do with limiting this meeting to people thirty and under?" Atsuko brought the discussion back full circle.

As if expecting the conversation to go in this direction, Tomokazu didn't look surprised.

He explained, "The opinions of the head of each family are directly related to action. Therefore, discussions among family heads have to be done with caution. Wouldn't you agree?"

"I suppose so," Atsuko conceded.

"Well, I thought if we—the younger generation—exchanged our opinions freely with one another, we could come up with some worthwhile ideas."

Katsuto suddenly spoke up again, seeing a perfect spot to contribute. "This meeting isn't meant to reach any concrete solutions or conclusions. I may be the head of the Juumonji, but I alone can't make decisions for my entire family. Even if we reach some semblance of agreement here, it might prove fruitless when the time comes to put thought into action. That said, I still think there's meaning in exchanging opinions here."

"In other words, this meeting is meant to provide a space to discuss how to fight against anti-magicism at the conceptual level?" Takara asked, intentionally blowing things out of proportion.

"Well, it's not meant to be anything that grand," Katsuto answered seriously, shaking his head. "But if we reach an agreement on something by the end of this, we can put it on the agenda for the next meeting of the Master Clans Council. Or something like that."

Takara seemed satisfied with Katsuto's response. Masaki, Hirofumi, Soushi, and Atsuko also didn't object. Tatsuya, on the other hand, felt something was off.

Katsuto said this wasn't a space to reach conclusions, and yet he was expecting the group to reach some sort of "agreement."

This strange inconsistency made Tatsuya decide to keep a close eye on things for the rest of the meeting.

Mayumi led Minoru to the Magic Association's tearoom. The Saegusa sisters agreed that if they—especially Minoru—went into a normal restaurant, it would cause a huge scene.

No one complained. Compared to most coffee shops and restaurants, the food available in the tearoom was inferior in both flavor and variety. But when it came to the question of what they were willing to put up with—subpar food or rude stares—the answer was obvious.

The staff tried to serve the group tea, but Mayumi chose her own tea leaves and utensils and brewed the tea herself. This was an obstruction of business, but this branch knew of Mayumi's love of tea and were accustomed to her selfishness. In fact, Mayumi had long been on friendly terms with this branch's tearoom staff.

She placed a teacup in front of Minoru. "Here you go."

"Thank you," he replied with a grateful bow. Even this ordinary gesture looked like a work of art when Minoru did it.

The waitress who followed with some tea scones Mayumi had bought froze next to the table, mesmerized. Kasumi smiled awkwardly, having no choice but to wrench the basket of scones and small plates from her stiff grip.

Izumi spoke first. "Now that I think about it, it's rare to see you around these parts, Minoru."

"I guess you could say I'm here to keep Soushi company," Minoru said.

"Did he ask you to help him with something?" Izumi asked.

"Not exactly. I think he's just counting his chickens before they've hatched." He clearly sounded annoyed, so Izumi gave him the space to share more.

"What do you mean?" she urged.

"Long story short, my brother wants me to visit Tatsuya and Miyuki and deepen our friendship. He was really disappointed when I told him we didn't know each other well enough for them to invite me over."

"Wow. Your brother never changes," Kasumi said, wide-eyed.

Mayumi yelled at her little sister again. "Kasumi!"

"It's fine," Minoru reassured her, smiling. "I think my older siblings are pretty naive, too."

"In other words, they're trying to get you to deepen your family's ties with the Yotsuba family," Izumi summarized, avoiding the topic of Minoru's siblings' personalities.

"That's right." He gave Izumi a grateful look for her tact. It seemed he wasn't in the mood to personally bad-mouth his family.

"Making friends with Tatsuya and Miyuki isn't a bad idea to raise the Kudou family's rapport with the Ten Master Clans," Mayumi began.

Izumi didn't blush and fall silent at this point because she was used to staring at Miyuki for hours. "But it's really too bad!"

Minoru was startled by Izumi's sudden loudness. He glanced at Mayumi for a translation, but she just returned a wry smile.

"You see, only Shiba is at today's meeting," Izumi explained.

"By Shiba, she means Miyuki's brother—I mean, fiancé," Kasumi added, with some confusion.

Izumi didn't seem to care that she was interrupting the conversation. She might not have even been listening.

"Apparently, the lovely Miyuki is going to be leaving her house this afternoon," she said with exaggerated reverence. "And here I was excited about visiting her without Tatsuya around! I wouldn't even be here if she were free right now."

She looked to be on the verge of crying tears of frustration.

"I told you to go visit her this morning," Kasumi said.

"How can you say that, Kasumi?" Izumi exclaimed dramatically. "She's probably busy getting ready for her outing. I can't get in her way!"

"Right, of course."

Minoru turned away from Izumi's excitement and saw Mayumi looking like she was getting a headache from her little sister's antics.

"What's—?" he began. He was trying to ask what was wrong with Izumi, but Mayumi interrupted him.

"Don't worry about her. She's just having a spasm," she said, sadly used to this behavior.

"O...kay," Minoru said.

"Hey, Minoru," Mayumi began.

"Yes?"

"Would you like to come to our house instead? We may not have as much status as the Yotsuba family, but you could tell your siblings you rekindled old bonds with the Saegusa. I'm sure that would satisfy them."

Mayumi's invitation was exciting. It would definitely allow him to spend more of his day without worry about unwanted gazes.

"Are you sure?" Minoru questioned.

"Of course I'm sure. Let's go."

"What? Right now?" the younger boy's eyes widened.

"Yes. As Izumi said earlier, our work is done here. Come on, you two. We're leaving." Mayumi called Izumi back to earth and stood up from her chair.

As Tomokazu hoped, the meeting moved into brainstorming some concrete plans.

The Mitsuya family's heir, Motoharu Mitsuya, was speaking.

"Let me get this straight, Saegusa. You're saying we need to proactively win over the masses in a popularity contest?"

"I'm not sure if I would call it a popularity contest, but essentially, yes." Tomokazu Saegusa responded with a smile that was reminiscent of the smile of his father, Kouichi.

"What? Do you want us to be on television? Unfortunately, I'm not particularly good at singing or dancing," Atsuko joked, causing the room to burst into laughter. The young girls in the room found it especially funny.

"I'm sure you would be extremely popular if you sang on TV." Tomokazu added to the joke, holding back a laugh. But he was careful not to derail the conversation too much.

He immediately continued. "I believe we need to do more to show how we're benefiting society, and in a much clearer way."

"The International Magic Association could create a public relations division," suggested a representative from one of the Eighteen Support Clans, Ichinokura. So far, the opinions of the participants were leaning entirely in Tomokazu's direction.

"That could work," Tomokazu said. "But I don't want to just focus on advertising. We should also stream actual footage of us actively working in the field."

At this point, he didn't have to push too hard for everyone else to agree with him.

"Hmm…" one participant said. "It might not be possible to stream that footage on local channels, but I might be able to pull some strings and put it on satellite TV."

"Isn't appearance important if we want to intentionally increase our media exposure?" another participant posed. "Someone who represents us on visual media should probably be good-looking."

The conversation began to take on a somewhat shallow and frivolous direction since the family elders weren't around.

Maybe this is what the Saegusa family was planning from the very beginning, Tatsuya thought. But he kept his mouth shut.

"But if someone needs to be deployed to a violent incident or major disaster, they need to be competent. Not just good-looking," yet another attendee pointed out.

"Who among us is both good-looking and competent? Hey, what about your younger sister, Saegusa? She would be a perfect fit."

Both Masaki and Katsuto raised their brows in surprise.

"You mean Mayumi?" Tomokazu asked. "I mean, she's a fairly competent magician, but I don't know about her looks."

Tatsuya stoically closed his eyes and listened closely as Tomokazu spoke humbly about his sister's appearance.

"What are you talking about?" the participant said. "She's the epitome of a fairy princess. I think she'd do great on TV."

Tomokazu refused to back down. "She would be thrilled to hear that. But if we put our own greedy preferences aside and think objectively, I'm sure we can come up with many other magicians who are better than my sister in both looks and magic."

"You speak pretty harshly about your own family. Let's see. Who has better looks than Mayumi?"

A quiet voice in one corner of the room suddenly gasped. "What about the heiress to the Yotsuba family? She's the perfect princess to represent us."

Half of this suggestion, embellished with an old-fashioned phrase, was probably meant as a joke. But the other half was dead serious.

Tomokazu's eyes lit up, as if he had been waiting for this moment. He was on the verge of making an important statement to decide the outcome of the meeting.

But Tatsuya—who had kept quiet the whole time—spoke first. "Juumonji."

"What is it?" Katsuto asked quickly.

"I thought you said we weren't here to make any decisions." Even though this was his first time speaking, Tatsuya didn't announce his own name. He didn't think it was necessary. He was speaking not to the representatives of the Twenty-Eight Families gathered in this conference room; only to Katsuto, the host of the conference.

"Yes, that's what I said," Katsuto confirmed.

"Then I take it that means no matter what is decided, the Yotsuba family isn't bound to obey. Is that correct?" Tatsuya's words were polite, but he was essentially picking a fight. On the other hand, it wasn't an accusation. It wasn't Katsuto but the other members who were trying to subvert the rules.

"Yes, that's fine," Katsuto said.

"But, Yotsuba—" With a disappointed look on his face, Hirofumi Itsuwa hesitantly called out to Tatsuya.

But Tatsuya made himself completely unapproachable. "Sorry. I don't think I introduced myself. My name is Tatsuya Shiba."

Atsuko Mutsuzuka and Takara Yatsushiro gave him amused looks. Masaki gave him an exasperated but empathetic glance. When Mayumi was mentioned, Masaki had worried about the possibility of the conversation switching to Miyuki. Katsuto now shot Tatsuya a look tinged with reproach. But it wasn't out of anger for ruining the peaceful agreement. He was silently urging Tatsuya to fill the chilly silence.

Tatsuya began, "I have no problem with proactively finding a way to contribute to society and making a good name for ourselves. That's a great idea."

Knowing he had disturbed the peace, he had no choice but to comply with Katsuto's request and speak.

"But many magicians already serve as police and firefighters. The National Defense Force also has many magicians serving in the military. I don't think it's a good idea for us to butt in on their work and claim all the achievements for ourselves."

Unfortunately, this just made the air in the conference room grow even chillier. No one refuted Tatsuya's statement. But no one openly approved of it, either.

A lot of hostility was directed at him for ruining the previously jovial atmosphere. But he refused to say anything more.

Unaware a blizzard was brewing at the Yokohama Bay Hills Tower conference room where her brother was, Shiina visited Institute Three for some independent training.

Magician Development Institute Three—or Institute Three, for short—was one of five of the ten magician development institutes still operating under their original name. It was also the most active of the five remaining institutes still in operation.

Its research theme was to help magicians improve multicasting skills and master the limits of the number of spells that can be activated at the same time. This was a useful technique even for magicians who weren't a part of the Ten Master Clans. For military magicians in particular, multicasting was considered an important technique to raise the combat potential of individual soldiers to the level of the Chiba family's white guards. Many military magicians came to Institute Three for this reason. Of these magicians, some were military researchers, but most were active combat magicians.

Since Shiina had been training in this environment since childhood, her fighting abilities were quite high, despite her gentle appearance. As her father, Gen Mitsuya, often told people, if it weren't for the unexplained handicap in her ears, she would be the best combat magician in the Mitsuya family. But the handicap also helped Gen worry less about the possibility of Shiina pursuing a career as a combat magician.

Shiina also had many opportunities to get to know military personnel who frequented Institute Three. She was particularly close with a fellow member of the Twenty-Eight Families.

"Tsukasa!"

"Hello, Shiina. Are you training again today?"

Sergeant Tsukasa Tooyama was a member of the National Defense Force's intelligence department. Although she went around calling herself Tooyama, with different characters, Shiina realized early on that her real name was spelled with the characters *ten* and *mountain*.

"I don't see Saburou with you." Tsukasa's unexpected comment made Shiina pout.

"He went to the Chiba family's dojo," the younger girl said.

"The Chiba family?" Tsukasa said with mild surprise.

"Yes. He might want to join them."

Since Shiina seemed completely serious, Tsukasa held back her laughter and met the younger girl's gaze. "Considering Saburou's personality, the Chiba family's swordsmanship techniques might do him good. You should think of it as warrior training, not an initiation into a club."

"How are those two things different?" Shiina puzzled.

"Oh, I guess they're not really." Tsukasa winked, flashing a mischievous smile. Shiina smiled, too.

"By the way, Shiina," Tsukasa continued. "How is magic high school? Not too stressful, I hope."

"It's a lot better than I thought it would be," Shiina said. "But I'm sure things will get more stressful as the school year goes on."

"Isn't the Yotsuba family's heiress the student council president?"

"Yes, but she's fine. I was nervous to be around her at first, since she's so pretty, but she's not as scary as I thought she would be."

"I see. Then would you mind helping me with a little something?" Now that she had warmed up the situation, Tsukasa tried to slip in a favor.

"You want me to help you? With intelligence department work?"

"Yes, but it's not as difficult as it seems. I'm looking for someone to play hostage in a training exercise to rescue a VIP."

"And that's part of an intelligence agent's job?"

"The department I'm in is tasked with counterintelligence. I'm also in charge of recovering kidnapped VIPs to prevent information leaks."

"Would I really be able to help you?" Shiina seemed hesitant, but she was also excited. In fact, she was the type who let her curiosity get the better of her; Tsukasa could tell.

"You don't have to worry about that," Tsukasa reassured the younger girl. "And we wouldn't keep you for more than half a day."

"Well, let me think about it," Shiina said.

"Of course. I can give you more details once you've made up your mind."

"What? You can't tell me right now?"

"Sorry, those are the rules."

Shiina was on the verge of giving in to her curiosity. At this rate, she would definitely agree to Tsukasa's proposal. Tsukasa knew of a certain young man who wouldn't be able to ignore the fact that a fellow First High and student council member was being held captive.

Shiina will be the perfect bait to put him to the test. She furthered her schemes with a kind smile on her face.

Edward Clark, a scholar affiliated with the USNA's National Security Agency, specialized in large-scale information systems. More specifically, he was the designer of Echelon III, the latest version of the communications-interception system operated by the NSA.

It would be false to say Edward Clark designed Echelon III on his own. But no one disputed that he was central to the overhaul of the Echelon system. That said, the details of Echelon III's design were classified, so the number of people who knew about Clark's achievements was extremely limited.

Under normal circumstances, Clark was supposed to be working on further improvements to the intelligence-interception system in his private office at the NSA's California field office. But he was currently being kept in captivity to make sure information about Echelon III remained classified.

Clark understood the reasoning well. And surprisingly, it didn't make him bitter. Instead, he actively accepted the situation. He possessed important information that the director of the NSA, the secretary of defense, the secretary of state, or even the president wouldn't know. In fact, Clark had built a system under everyone's noses that provided him with unfettered access to all the information in the world.

He shared his secrets with a very small number of people among his peers who he deemed worthy. These peers were not limited to Americans, but he had no intention of betraying the USNA. In fact, Edward Clark was a fervent patriot. But his loyalty was first and foremost to the nation, not the government.

He was convinced that information controlled the world. He was also convinced that his country and its loyal allies were the only ones qualified to use that information to take over the world. And on this day, he continued to gather, select, and analyze the information necessary to lead the world in a direction he believed it should go.

"Hmm… It's ten AM local time in Japan," Clark murmured to himself.

Most of the staff at the bureau had already gone home for the day. But Clark showed no sign of leaving his desk.

He mumbled again. "Well, well. He's isolated himself. How dim-witted can these Japanese be?"

The conference room discussion in Yokohama, which was supposed to be impossible to listen in on, was being simultaneously interpreted on his terminal, thanks to the power of the backdoor system built into Echelon III.

"I shouldn't speak too soon, but this could be a great opportunity for my fellow patriots. If all goes well, we may be able to eliminate the greatest threat to our nation."

Clark fell deep into thought. His terminal displayed a log of Tatsuya's remarks in the conference room at Yokohama Bay Hills Tower that led to his falling out with the other attendees.

(To be continued)

AFTERWORD

You have just finished reading Volume 21, *Upheaval Prologue Arc I.* Did you enjoy it? *The Irregular at Magic High School* protagonists are finally seniors. I had originally planned to limit this Upheaval Prologue arc to one volume, but well…there ended up being much more information than expected. In the end, I split it into two volumes.

One thing that led to this miscalculation was the fact that I didn't initially expect to go so in-depth into the current state of the world. My original plan for the series only touched upon the Synchroliner Fusion episode in this volume and then covered the situation in Mexico, Ukraine, and Germany in the next volume. Then I decided to pursue the South Sea Riots arc and realized I needed to put this first for the other episodes to have any sense of cohesion. Of course, as a result, the New Soviet Union's magic made a much earlier appearance than planned. But well…this added an extra dimension to the structure of the series, so I feel it all worked out in the end.

Then again, that alone isn't enough to increase the series by an entire book. My biggest miscalculation lies with the two new freshmen students. I didn't expect them to expand so much and take on lives of their own. In fact, I had planned to keep their stories simple, but they ended up the new protagonists of this sequel series.

The spotlight doesn't often fall on characters two generations younger than the main characters in a school story. But who can say whether this series really qualifies as a school story? I'm sure Shiina and Saburou will continue to make their naive appearances in the next arc, too.

This series is currently in the process of revealing many new things. In this volume, two strategic-class magicians appeared, part of the reason why strategic-class magicians other than the Thirteen Apostles haven't been made public was explained, and the identity of the developer of the you-know-what system was exposed. In that same vein, I'd like to reveal a few details here that I haven't gone into thus far.

First of all, the title of this entire series—*The Irregular at Magic High School*—was originally meant to be the title for only the Enrollment arc. This may be familiar to some of you. In fact, we planned to change the title after the Nine School Competition arc. But we ultimately decided to unify the entire series under the same title for the rather petty reason that changing the title might lose some of our readership.

Another thing. *The Irregular at Magic High School* title isn't just referring to the story's male protagonist—or I should say, it's not *only* referring to Tatsuya. Nor is it *primarily* referring to him.

The "irregular" character in the Enrollment arc is Sayaka Mibu. Then it's Chiaki Hirakawa in the Yokohama Disturbance arc. In the Visitor arc, Lina is extremely competent, but her quirky personality makes her "irregular." And in the Double Seven arc, Takuma Shippou is "irregular," since he has a strong inferiority complex despite being the freshman valedictorian. In this way, this series tries to discuss the contrast between the key "irregular" figure in each arc with Tatsuya, who is named an "irregular" by those around him.

Whether this was actually successful is a different story. In fact, the logic falls apart in the Steeplechase arc. But such is life.

The next volume will be the end of the prologue to the Upheaval Prologue arc. My editor thought it was funny there's two parts, even though it's a prologue. But I promise you it will definitely end in the next volume.

I hope we'll meet again in Volume 22, *Upheaval Prologue Arc II*.

Tsutomu Sato